THE CAGE

A GRIPPING PSYCHOLOGICAL THRILLER PACKED WITH TWISTS

A.G. TWIST

Welcome to A.G. Twist's second masterpiece....

ALSO BY A.G. TWIST

The Cage

The Hospital

The Stalker

PROLOGUE

Dear Maddie,

It's been a long time, and I haven't heard from you. Are you going to make me regret not killing you? Because I let you live for a reason.

Forgive me if the letter is bloodstained. My latest cocoon failed to transform, so I killed her.

Do you think I'm asking too much of these girls?

Only you transformed, Maddie. That's why I set you free.

Did I ever tell you that I'm your #1 fan?

But you're also a bad girl. You can fool everyone with that police badge—but not me. I know you better than you know yourself.

Is that why you don't answer my letters? You fear that I'd see who you really are?

But we've got work to do, Maddie. My masterpiece isn't complete. I need you to be part of it. That's why I'll send this letter to the NYPD commissioner.

You have to answer now. There is nowhere to hide.

My next victim will die if she doesn't transform into a butterfly. Her blood will be on your hands.

Oh, I wish you could see how I've changed. My methods are

sharper now. I no longer cage girls, Maddie. I'm not the collector who locked up cocoons like wealthy psychopaths did in the past. I'm setting them free.

All of them.

I've caught a new cocoon now. She is beautiful. She has a chance to transcend. But I'm no god—I only do God's work.

If she doesn't transform in forty-eight hours, she will die.

AND IT WILL BE YOUR FAULT!

Unless you solve the clues I left for you.

Follow the night, Maddie. It always leads back to me.

—**XO**
The Collector

ONE

The NYPD's Special Victims Division isn't what I expected. Instead of the cramped, busy offices in the main branch, I'm led to a basement that feels more like a bomb shelter. The walls are mostly bare. The air is thick and damp. And a steady drip sounds from a rusty sink in the corner.

"Hey, Maddie, I'm talking to you," Commissioner Sara Johnson calls, pulling me back to reality.

I snap back to reality. It happens more often than I'd like. I spend most days in my head, staring through the bars of my mental cage.

"I was asking if you really want to go after this killer," the Commissioner continues.

Johnson looks totally out of place in here. Her charcoal pantsuit clashes with the crumbling walls and rusty pipes. She must have come straight from a mayor's meeting. It's not her position that makes me uneasy—it's how her blue eyes notice every twitch and breath I take.

"I've waited six years for this," I say, my voice steady. The weight in my chest feels heavy. "He asked for me in his letter. I'm ready to put him behind bars."

"Don't be so sure of yourself, Maddie," Commissioner Johnson says. She never calls me detective, and I doubt she ever will. "The girl is already dead."

"That's your fault," I say, hands behind my back. "You should have assigned me to the case when you received the letter."

"Well, well. There's a fighter in you after all," she says, her voice full of smug amusement. Her eyes are unreadable. They're soft like waves, but deadly like the undertow. He asked for you just to toy with your weakness. And you took the bait.

The word hits me like ice water. "What do you mean by that?"

"Can't you see the game he's playing? You're his only living victim. Yet, you can't remember what happened or why he spared you. Six years later, you're still his perfect victim. You're stuck in the past, and he haunts your thoughts." Johnson leans forward, hands pressing against the desk. "He didn't send this letter to ask for your help. He sent it to use you while he keeps killing. He'll leave misleading clues for you to chase, risking this department's integrity. You're his biggest joke, and he likes retelling it."

Her words cut deep, bringing back dark memories I can't shake. The sound of a dripping faucet sharpens in my ears. It's not the one in this room, but the one from when I was caged in a basement.

"Hey!" Johnson snaps her fingers at me. "Come back to reality!"

I snap back again. That faucet really sent me back in time.

Johnson grabs a rusty padlock and key from the desk. She swings it my way, ensuring I catch it to show I'm paying attention. "Lock the door behind you and follow me outside."

"Where are we going?"

"To the crime scene," Johnson scoffs. "Let's see if you have the stomach to revisit your nightmares."

I follow her up the stairs. Her athletic grace surprises me. She moves like someone decades younger than her late forties. Perhaps once I've proven myself, she'll become a mentor. I've been craving that guidance since my parents passed away.

Outside, the New York winter slices through my red leather jacket. Each gust sends shivers racing down to my very bones.

I lock the metal double door with trembling fingers. Cold seeps into my soul. The rusty, corrugated steel doors slope down into the ground. They remind me of storm shelter entrances.

Johnson stands next to a worn Toyota Camry in the narrow, dim alley.

"Get in the back," she says, pointing to the rear door. "And tell me more about the Collector on the way."

TWO

I'm in the back of the Camry, watching Commissioner Johnson take the front seat. The driver looks about my age, wearing a black leather jacket like mine. His thick mustache stands out on his face. His eyes scan the street like a hawk. They are sharp and watchful, even in silence.

"Maddie, this is Officer Rush," Johnson says with a lazy wave. "He'll be your driver and backup—within reason, of course."

Rush nods quickly and then looks away. He's either as socially awkward as I am or avoiding the crazy victim girl, just like everyone else.

"So tell me why he calls himself the Collector," Johnson says, staring out at New York's packed streets. "I heard you, unlike everyone else, call him the Comedian."

"He never called himself the Collector—though it would fit him," I explain. "To us, he was the Comedian."

"Then why did he sign his letter as 'XO, the Collector'?"

"I'm not sure. But I have a feeling he wants to appeal to the masses this time. If the press calls him the Collector because he collects cocoons to turn them into butterflies, then he'll go with it."

"And the XO? Hugs and kisses? Really? I find that a bit too intimate. Don't you think?"

I stare back at her, realizing she doesn't know what it really means. "X for X-ed—or 'exist'—and O is for 'out.'"

"Oh." Johnson looks like the twisted realization just hit her—like a pebble to the face.

"I'm his only butterfly. He let me go. He X-ed me out. But he also sends me love and kisses."

"Wicked man," Johnson mutters. "Still, the Comedian is a rather tame name, don't you think?"

"Not if you see him wearing the mask." I shrug. It's exposition time. And it hurts every time I revisit the past. "It comes from Greek theater," I say, my voice catching briefly. His golden mask shines under the fluorescent lights. The scalpel in his hand reflects a yellow glow. He always circles my cage, staying in the middle for some reason. "The Greeks had two masks—Thalia smiled for comedy, Melpomene cried for tragedy. They showed life's two sides, but he twisted it. He was happy, and we—the girls—were miserable."

"Why do you think he picked the Comedian mask, not the tragic one?" Johnson asks, turning to face me.

"A statement, maybe. He was joyful. We, in his eyes, were in pain," I say, my throat tightening.

"Because in his eyes you were cocoons, right?" Johnson seems well-informed. She only thinks that because of my selective memory issues after the accident, I'm the one who isn't.

"Only the girls who transformed into butterflies were destined for happiness."

"You don't look happy to me," she says. Her dismissive tone is what hurts the most.

"No, I don't," I admit. Why would I hide my misery when it's the pale color of my face every day?

"What was the process of transforming girls into cocoons, Maddie?" Johnson is back in interrogation mode. I'm not a detective now. I'm a suspect.

"You know that I don't remember that," I challenge back. I'm sad, but not stupid.

"Did the Comedian ever explain it? Did he elaborate on the mask's meaning?"

"I said don't remember," I say, blinking to escape her stare. My memories blur before my eyes. His shoes click closer, the other girls shake, and his mask presses against the bars.

"Come on, girl. You must remember something," her eyes lock onto mine, piercing. "Even I remember some of the bad men in my life."

I lean back, the intensity conjuring his mask again. "I said I don't know."

Johnson sighs, frustrated, and turns to Rush. "Can you believe this girl?"

Rush is still tense. He shrugs, not knowing what to say. Like everyone else, he can't look the commissioner in the eye. I know she has an impressive track record, catching killers and climbing ranks like it's a sport. I just didn't know she was the kind of person who could make a psychopath feel like they disappointed her.

We drive through New York's chaos in silence—though no one ever escapes the noise here.

Johnson's phone rings. She picks up immediately. "Not now, Sam. I'm working," she snaps, hanging up.

I'm guessing it's her husband, Sam and Sara. I picture him cooking at home, taking care of the kids, and listening to her about how stressful her day was.

Officer Rush arrives at the crime scene. It's in Bushwick, Brooklyn. A yellow police tape flutters like a warning flag. I used to love yellow. But then the Comedian's golden mask changed it into a color of my nightmares.

I close my eyes, breathe deeply before I leave the car. Johnson is right. I'm not sure I'm willing to see another basement or cage again—let alone a dead girl. I catch Rush watching me in the rearview mirror when I open them. His eyes dart away quickly.

Do I look this crazy to everyone? Or is he asking himself the same question: why was I spared?

Johnson steps out. The officers quickly straighten up at the crime scene.

"Officers," she says, not breaking pace. "Don't let Officer Rush near a razor—that mustache might be our prime suspect."

One officer laughs. The other is hesitant. You see, Johnson is always testing, even when she is joking. You can never really tell.

I follow her past the yellow tape. We walk into an abandoned construction site. Past a few buildings, we arrive at the one where the Comedian killed his last victim. I stand before the basement entrance. Darkness glows from down there with memories I can't shake.

"Are you okay, kiddo?" Johnson's voice is distant, but surprisingly sincere.

"Does it matter?" I hate that my face exposes my fears.

"Not really. But HR says I should ask."

I chuckle—surprised that I do. "You really don't like me, do you?"

"I like detectives with daddy issues who enjoy being yelled at," she says, pointing to the basement. "Now get down... to business."

THREE

The cage looks just like I remember.

It's shiny red steel, with a yellow light bulb hanging above. The floor rests on four concrete blocks. A small opening in the floor is where he'd kick in our food. Surprisingly, it was healthy—vegetables and lamb, perfectly cooked.

I swallow the bile rising in my throat and scan the basement. It's a mix of bare walls, cracked concrete below, and one boarded-up window. Everything down here is in decay—except for that damn cage.

Slowly, memories of the Comedian resurface. He called us cocoons. Beautiful cocoons. I remember his low and eerie voice through the voice changer behind his mask.

Forcing myself to look at that cage again, I notice new things.

This cage looks more like the work of an artist than a villain. Custom-built with care, it shows a strong investment of time and money. It has unique qualities, but its secrets elude me, like sand slipping through my fingers.

My red leather jacket feels cold and tight against my skin. Its color, matching the cage, seems like an odd choice. I wonder if I've ever truly left the cage.

"Was the victim still in the cage when you found her, Commissioner?" I ask.

I dislike calling the girl he killed a victim—she deserves a name. But names make it too real, and I'm not fully ready yet to face reality.

"She was," Johnson says, her Upper East Side accent slipping through. I never noticed that before. "She had been dead for a week. The building, after being empty for years, had new owners who planned on renovating it."

"So he didn't kill her because you didn't send me the letters right away?" I'm thinking out loud. "But because his underground bunker was about to be exposed?"

"Interesting point. But what makes you say that?"

"There's only one cage in the basement. There were five when he kidnapped me," I say. "Mine was the only one in the middle. The other four were in each corner of the basement."

"I didn't know that."

"The point is, that one cage looks like just the beginning of what he called a 'masterpiece.'"

"Masterpiece?" Johnson scoffs. "You're starting to sound like him."

"To catch him, I may have to be him," I murmur, almost unaware she is in the room with me. It's more of a realization than a statement. One that scares me more than escaping in the first place.

"I like that attitude," Johnson says. "But what if his old setup of several girls is a thing of the past? He told you he has evolved in the letter, after all."

"You're right about that," I say. "However this means he is now looking for another basement somewhere else."

"You're saying he's not going to stop?"

"Not until he finds his new butterfly and sets her free like me?"

"But you still don't remember why you were his butterfly, right?"

I don't answer her. We've been there a thousand times. I don't know. I don't remember. My therapist says it could be my selective memory protecting me from a dark memory.

"You should look for similar abandoned basements. He is building a new cage somewhere."

"Don't worry, it's covered. We've got eyes on all abandoned buildings in Brooklyn—his spot, like with your case."

Thinking of my case only shakes me to the core. I pull my jacket tighter as the cold slips through the seams. It feels like a red shroud I can't shake off. Water drips from a nearby faucet, each drop echoing like a ghost from my past.

Years ago, the Comedian released me in Brooklyn. I don't remember the exact building. The drugs he gave me stole my clarity, leaving only memory fragments behind.

Johnson snaps her fingers. I must have dozed off again. "Do you want to get off the case?"

"I don't want to get off the case!" I clench my fist. "If he wants me to find him, I will find him."

"In that case, let's do things my way," she raises both hands in the air and rolls her eyes, as if I'm a lunatic. "Did you know the Comedian killed her by drilling a hole in her head?"

"He did?" I hadn't had a chance to read the report yet.

"Forensics suggest he took his time. She died a slow death."

The image hits me—his mask, the drill's screech, her screams.

"My question is," Johnson continues. "Did you ever see him kill any of the girls that way?"

"Only once. Otherwise, he never killed anyone in front of us."

"What happened that one time?"

"There was that girl—her name was Kelly—who blocked the cage's lock with her tooth. She broke it off to jam it in."

Even Johnson winces at the detail. I thought she was tougher than that.

"Kelly ran out but couldn't escape the basement."

"The door was locked?"

"No, it was open. The Comedian hit her with a hammer on the back of her head."

"I can't believe you remember Kelly's details so vividly—but none of your own."

"I'm not here to remember," I say. Playing that game with her isn't helping. I've been interrogated so many times. I know the drill. My mind has blocked it out. And no one will ever believe me. I decide to get things going by stepping closer to the cage. "I'm here to find the clues he talked about in the letter."

"Which you have done nothing about so far."

She isn't wrong. I may as well be the worst detective at the moment. Shrouded by my fears, I haven't investigated a single corner of the cage. "Let's start with the victim's name."

"What?" Johnson grimaces again.

"She has a name, right? I will read the report when I go back to the headquarters. Right now I need to know about her."

Her name is Ivy Williams. She was nineteen and a sophomore at Columbia University. She studied psychology, not medicine like you. She was kidnapped while leaving the campus wellness facility late at night.

"Same as me," I say. "I was hit on the head after a late night of studying."

"Good to know. Where is this going? You're wasting my time here."

"I'm trying my best."

"Trying your best is what victims do to escape. I need you to do your job," Johnson pulls out her flashlight and shines it in my face. "I want you to tell me what Ivy Williams felt when he drilled that hole into her."

"I don't know her. I wasn't there." I shield my eyes with my hands.

"You said that to catch him, you have to become him. Show me."

"I'm not sure how to do that," I say, knowing what she is implying.

"But I do." She reaches for the cage's barred door and says. "Get inside."

CHAPTER 4

Once I step inside, the past presses against me—Ivy Williams lingers in the cage's shadow. My therapist says my mind conjures these scenes to process trauma—I see her lying on the floor beside me.

Johnson's distant voice cuts through the silence. "What do you see, kiddo? I know it's painful, but you need to remember anything that'll help catch him."

"Ivy sees the Comedian enter," I say, gripping the bars. "Wearing the mask."

"And?"

"She's not worried he'll kill her—just scared of what he'll do."

"Sexually, you mean?"

"No. Not sexually. He had this unsettling gentleness sometimes —as if he genuinely wanted to be your friend. Your protector."

"So he never hurt you or the girls?"

"He did—using strange tools." In my mind's eye, Ivy's eyes reflect his image as he nears the cage. "A scalpel... other things. I can't pin it down."

"Or you don't want to pin them down," Johnson says, louder now, never letting up on my so-called selective memory. "He drugged you?"

I'm not sure whether I'm talking about Ivy, the other girls, or myself now. "We never saw it, but the girls thought it was in the food," I snap. "We slept too long and woke with wounds, like he'd experimented on us. I remember feeling dizzy—barely able to walk when he let me go."

"How did he let you go, kiddo? Did he say something?"

"No. He wasn't there. That was the worst part." My shoulders ache, but I stay standing. "I woke up, cage open, basement door too. He wanted me out—or he'd have stopped me. Like the girl with the hammer—the one who tried to fight back."

"Why do you think he didn't let Ivy go then?"

"I don't know," I say, fighting tears.

"Why you?"

"I don't know!" My hands grasp nothing, Ivy's absence a void I can't fill.

"This isn't enough," Johnson says, shining the light in my face. "He wrote you a letter—he must've left a clue."

"Maybe all the clues are in the letter? That's what he said, right?"

"But you read it and couldn't interpret anything out of it," Johnson says, frustration coloring her voice. "He's playing you, like I said."

She pulls the light back, then turns it off.

Darkness swallows me. I scramble for my phone—dropped when I stepped in. The faucet's drip grows loud, his footsteps louder. I can't breathe.

"Where's my phone?" I claw the floor, Ivy's presence moving with me, silent but searching too.

"You're afraid of the dark?" Johnson's voice sharpens.

"Please turn it on," I beg.

"No." Her voice closer, growling from outside the cage. "Be the light, kiddo. Look into the darkness—tell me what I need to know."

I can't speak. Ivy—or whatever hallucination I have of here—pats my shoulder.Her skull still bears those drill holes. My chest tightens.

"Tell me!" Johnson snaps. "Find it!"

"Of all the girls, why did he let you go?" she growls.

Suddenly, my eyes adjust. A faint strip of light seeps through the barred window, revealing what darkness had hidden. Not the cage, not Johnson, not Ivy—she's gone.

I find my phone, grip it tight, and sweep its beam across the basement's vast space behind Johnson.

"My eyes, kiddo," she shields them with her hand.

But I don't care. It's what I see that matters now. There's something in the middle of the basement. Something I should've seen the moment I walked in.

"You saw something, right?" Johnson says, catching up. "What is it?"

"There's an empty space in the middle of the floor."

I step forward, voice steady despite trembling hands. "My cage was always in the middle of the room. He had a thing for middles—centered my cage, laid out his tools around it, always circling me in silence. If Ivy was the start of a new masterpiece, this cage would be centered."

I point at the long marks on the floor, drag lines stretching from the middle to Ivy's cage, now pushed against the wall.

Johnson follows, alert now. "That's the clue he left you."

"Turn on your flashlight and look!" I'm sweating despite the cold.

She does, her beam tracing the drag marks to writing carved in a circle, etched on the concrete floor.

"He was working on it," Johnson says, pulling her gun. Shock edges her voice. "Why break the pattern?"

I step back, pointing at the floor's center. "This."

Johnson stares at the words carved into concrete:

If you don't know who you are, you can be whoever you wish to be... G.H.

"That's his clue," I say, my old scars itching under the jacket. "Left for me to chase."

CHAPTER 5

I'm back in the Special Victims Division basement, reading Ivy's report.

Johnson steps outside to the alley. Her silence on the ride back was heavy. But I'm focused on cracking the Comedian's message.

I edge the door open, catching her mid-call.

"I don't like this, Sam," she says. "Please stop calling. I need time."

I pull back. Her private life's none of my business.

"Commissioner?" I call from the flight of steps.

"What?" Her fingers drum the wall impatiently.

"Sorry, but I need the Wi-Fi password."

Even after locking me in that cage, she still has my respect. Her hunch paid off. I found the clue.

"Cuckoo1812," she snaps.

"Weird password," I mutter.

She whips around, eyes flashing.

"It belongs to the building above us."

"Is it safe to use a civilian's Wi-Fi?"

"Not civilians. It's an asylum."

The absurdity makes me almost laugh. "Our office is under an asylum?"

"This isn't our office. It's yours. I'm just helping," she says, annoyed. "We call it The Yellow."

The Yellow? His golden mask flashes in my mind. Maybe it's a coincidence. Maybe not. I log into the Ashwood Asylum's network. Such a cliché name, but the password works.

I search the quote he carved: *If you don't know who you are, you can be whoever you wish to be... G.H.*

Nothing online matches. No books, no movies. Google suggests Alice in Wonderland, but it's not there. The quote only sounds similar to nonsensical phrases from the famous children's book.

I search the NYPD's database. Another bust. Nothing.

Defeated, I sink into the chair, thinking of coffee. But I have a feeling it would taste like mold down here.

"Found anything?" Johnson's back. Sudden and stealthy. I didn't even notice her entrance.

"Nothing," I say, showing her the screen. "I can't find this quote anywhere. Seems like the Comedian made it up."

"Strange," she says. "I'd swear it's from Alice in Wonderland."

"It sounds like it, but Google says it isn't."

"It does sound like the quote 'I can't go back to yesterday because I was someone else then.'" Johns says. "The more I get older, I like it more."

I beg to differ. In my case, I have to go back to yesterday, so I know what the hell happened then.

"Did you look up who G.H. is?" She says, her hands poised to type.

"Can't find an author with these initials who wrote this quote."

"Did you check our database?" Johnson shoves me aside, taking the chair.

"Yes," I point to the open tab.

"Not this one."

She types an encrypted address in the browser. "Use this for old unsolved cases."

She types the password: *yellowjackets,* then elaborates: "Back in the day, straitjackets used to be yellow. That's why we call the place The Yellow."

"Referring to the asylum above us?"

She nods nonchalantly, as if it's not the weirdest thing I've heard all week.

Johnson searches the quote in the secret database. A result pops up immediately. It links the quote to a psychology professor in Columbia university: Gabriel Homer.

"That explains the initials. G.H.," I say, reading the screen.

"I know him," Johnson sighs, pulling a mint cigarette from her bag and lighting it. "Homer's a disgraced shrink. He worked with us years ago. I never liked him. Too slick. This quote is from some a book that Columbia banned from publishing."

"Banned?" I frown.

His theories are complete bullshit. Talking about how the mind and memories work," Johnson says. "No wonder that two of his past patients were convicted serial killers.

"I see." I say. "Are you suggesting the Comedian could be infatuated with Professor Homer's theories?"

"Worse. He could have been his patient at some point."

I squint. This can't be so easy. If he ever met the professor, it means he saw the Comedian's face—let alone knowing who he really is.

"Don't get your hopes up, Maddie," Johnson says, picking up her coat. "Go see Homer—just don't let see inside your head."

CHAPTER 6

The Camry growls through Manhattan's chokehold, glass towers leering down like they're in on the joke. Rush hunches over the wheel like he's holding back a detonation. His mustache twitches—wild, not groomed—and his knuckles bleach white, tapping a frantic beat that drills into my skull. No rookie jitters here. He's a live wire, strung tight by this case.

"Professor Homer resides in the Empire Psychiatry Institute," Rush says, voice tight. "Fancy name for another asylum. Rich people and their euphemisms."

I catch his eyes in the rearview—dark, darting, pinning me before he yanks the mirror away. He knows something. Maybe everything. His fingers pound harder, a rhythm I swear I've heard through bars.

"They say he's charming and manipulative," Rush says, surprisingly defensive. "But I've heard he's really good at his job. Contrary to what everyone believes, he may actually be a good man."

"How so?" I say, looking Homer up on my phone. A charming, good-looking man in his early forties—Rush is right about that one.

"People criticize him for releasing so many of his patients," Rush continues, a hint of admiration in his voice. "But a couple of relatives say he genuinely believes in them. Most doctors just write prescriptions and collect checks. Homer actually listens."

"I see." My mind reels with possibilities. I don't think the Comedian's insane, but if he crossed Homer, wouldn't he twist that into excuses for his murders? "How come he's still working, then, if his methods are so controversial?"

"Rumor has it he knows big secrets about big people in the Big Apple." Rush's jaw clenches. His words spill out fast. "This city's a sewer—nothing's clean. You're in deep, Brooks."

"I grew up in this city too," I cut in. "Trust me, I know. I've swallowed enough of its garbage to qualify as a landfill."

Rush shoots me a look—not quite disbelief or disgust. More like he's worried I'll misjudge Homer before meeting him.

He slams on the horn at a stalled cab. Eyes blazing, he isn't putting on a show. He's coming apart. It reminds me of the Comedian—gentle with a tray, feral when I refused to swallow.

The Institute looms.

The building is a Gothic slab clawing through the skyline, with iron gates jagged as teeth. Red brick bleeds into the gray, paths snaking like veins. I'm not sure why, but cold sweat glues my jacket to my skin. I'm marinating in my own fear. Again.

"Detective Brooks, here for Professor Homer," Rush says sharply at the gate mic. Cameras glide, slick as that golden mask tilting in the dark. My stomach lurches.

"Homer lives here, by the way," Rush mutters, voice tight. "Chose this over Columbia's residence. He says he wants to watch his patients 24/7." He shakes his head with what looks like respect. "Everyone thinks the shrink's got screws loose, but I've seen how he helps people. The man's just dedicated—puts his patients before himself."

I don't answer, more focused on the clue. Could it be that easy—that I'll figure out the Comedian was Homer's patient? It'd mean I'd know what he looks like, where he lives, how he thinks.

I really don't think so. Coming here feels more like walking into a trap I haven't figured out yet. When things seem easy in this city, that's just the moment someone's slipping a knife between your ribs.

CHAPTER 7

The Empire Psychiatry Institute towers over me like a fortress of secrets. Its Gothic sprawl makes me feel small—but free. Only someone who's felt steel bars on their skin knows the thrill of walking away.

A posh nurse guides me through endless corridors. Her shoes squeak against bleached linoleum. The hallway reeks of industrial disinfectant, failing to mask the sour tang of despair. Muffled screams leak from behind locked doors. She doesn't ask why I'm here. Doesn't praise Homer. She just brags about his luxurious cell, which is clean and spacious as an apartment."

Prison with a view," I mutter. She doesn't laugh.

His cell surprises me. No cold institutional bars. Just staged elegance that belongs in *Architectural Digest* for the criminally sophisticated. Artwork lines the walls. Expensive furniture placed with precision. A gilded cage sketch catches my eye—intricate, unsettling. Of course, a man who locks himself up would hang that. Subtlety isn't required for a psych degree.

"Professor Homer?" I step in, voice steady despite my hammering heart. "I'm Detective Brooks."

He rises from an antique desk. Tall. Sharp-featured. He's in his forties and full of life. My therapist says I'm drawn to that age. His hazel eyes calculate like mine. Too good-looking for this job—and I know that's judgmental. But dangerous men usually come gift-wrapped. The kind of handsome that makes you forget he knows exactly how to break you.

"Please, call me Gabriel," he says. He gestures to a leather chair, pipe in hand. His smile is practiced. Professional, not warm. It's the smile of a shark who mastered etiquette class.

I sit. My nerves hum like live wires. "Fancy pipe you got there," I say, trying to sound casual.

He reminds me of my last almost-boyfriend. Forties. Lively. My therapist says I'm drawn to that age because I miss my parents. Both gone at forty. Maybe that's why I admire Johnson's energy too. Or maybe I just have the emotional development of a traumatized teenager. Potato, po-tah-to.

"Thank you," Homer says. He glances at the pipe with a playful eyebrow. "Can't play the sophisticated psychologist without it, right?"

"Can't play detective without a badge," I counter. I reach for mine, then pat empty pockets. I must have left it somewhere. Then again, neither prop makes us who we pretend to be.

He sits on the couch's far end. Fit and poised like he's posing for his author photo.

I mirror his eyebrow raise, pointing like a gun. Why do I feel so comfortable doing this? "You have the right to remain silent. Anything you say about your past can and will be used against you in the court of emotional baggage!"

Silence hangs heavy. My cheeks burn. I'm awkward, aren't I? Our eyes lock. Rush's warning echoes: Charming, but dangerous. The two adjectives that precede every terrible decision I've made about men.

"I'm the one who got away," I blurt. I twirl my hair. "I say things..."

"It explains why the Comedian let you go," Homer says, straight-faced. A cheeky smirk flickers at his mouth's corner. "Most killers prefer a captive audience."

We both smile briefly. I look down. Haven't bantered like this in years. Especially not about my near-death experience.

There's nothing like trauma to keep your social calendar clear.

"Yeah, I talk too much. I just say what I wanna say..." I trail off, almost sad. I've never spoken so casually about the Comedian before. Life moves on, I guess. Even when the past wanted to wear you like a costume.

"I'm a psychologist, not a serial killer," Homer says. His tone turns clinical. Cold. "My job is to listen. Speak your mind."

I straighten. Match his seriousness. "The Commissioner briefed you?"

"She did." He takes a drag from his pipe. Smoke curls like question marks between us. "However, I'm sorry to disappoint you. The Comedian was never my patient."

I lean forward, as if pressuring him to tell the truth.

"I keep detailed records of every consultation since I started, and I'd flag homicidal tendencies if present. Never met him. I'm sure."

If he's not lying, the Comedian wouldn't be here. My hope deflates faster than a dollar store balloon. This was my shot. My chance to nail him. It's dissolving like Homer's pipe smoke.

I pull crime scene photos from my bag. Slap them onto the table hard enough to make him flinch. At last, a real reaction.

"Then explain why he carved your quote into the basement floor. Right next to the cage where he kept his latest victim."

CHAPTER 8

Homer puts on a pair of expensive glasses and leans forward to look at the picture. His eyes narrow as he studies the images. He reads the quote: *If you don't know who you are, you can be anyone you want to be.*

"Is this from my book?"

"Your banned book, you mean," I fact-check him. "Looks like it."

"Banned is one way to put it." He smiles faintly. "It's called *The Sky Below and the Earth Above*, by the way. I can't see why it would attract a killer, unless he is really sophisticated."

"What do you mean?" He lifts his eyes to meet mine.

"A killer whose work transcends the act itself—at least in his mind."

I like this Professor Homer. Manipulative or not, this is the kind of mind I want to work with. The Comedian's elaborate stagecraft with his victims shows he thinks he's creating something meaningful. Art through atrocity.

I ask, "Do you see something in his acts that might give him away?"

"I don't know anything about the case, Detective Brooks."

"Fair enough." I like his honesty. "Why do they say these things about him?"

"So tell me, how did he get your unpublished book?"

"I use a highly controversial method for treating mental illness." He adjusts his glasses. "In short, I don't believe in mental illness that requires hospitalization unless proven without a doubt. Think of it like the rule you have in the police force—"

"Innocent until proven guilty," I complete his sentence.

Whatever this is—this feeling while speaking to him—it's not normal. It's that familiar tug in my chest, the one that's gotten me into trouble with men who are too smart, too charming, and too dangerous. My dating history reads like a psychological case study of terrible choices.

He's definitely bad news but maybe I can fix him syndrome, now in its exciting new academic flavor. My therapist would have a whole new notepad.

"Why does your quote sound like something from *Alice in Wonderland*? I know it's a strange question, but it does sound so familiar, yet it shouldn't be."

"I designed it to sound like a quote from *Alice in Wonderland*."

"Why?" I squint.

"I wanted to mess with the academics' minds. Memory isn't reliable. If you think a quote is from your favorite childhood book, it's because your mind wants it to be."

I let that sink in. I can see how clever Homer is, but I can't tell if it's science or manipulation. Like recognizing the difference between a cage and a room with no doors. "So how does this affect the Comedian?"

"In many ways. He might have made it up himself, heard it somewhere, or thought—"

"—he read it in *Alice in Wonderland*." I finish his sentence. Our instant connection worries me. Maybe we're just two people who understand each other. Or maybe we both think like criminals.

"I'm interested in this idea of unreliable memories, Professor."

"I thought you might be," he nods slightly. "Like I said, call me Gabriel."

Using his first name is a no-go for me. Not if I'm planning to open up to him. Names create a kind of closeness I can't afford.

Homer takes off his glasses and sets down his pipe. "Are you sure about that?"

I give him a painful smirk and shake my head.

"It's okay," he says. His voice stays neutral, neither warm nor cold. The voice of someone who's heard worse confessions than mine.

"Maybe he didn't find the quote in *Alice in Wonderland* after all."

"Why?" I tilt my head at his confidence.

"If his message is for me—which is why you're here—then he must have read my book."

I watch him stand and pick up his black trench coat. "There's only one way to find out."

I nod. "You have to see it yourself at the crime scene."

CHAPTER 9

Homer ignores Rush entirely. He doesn't even acknowledge Officer Rush's presence, let alone the mustache. He just asks for the case file and reads it without looking at me. I sit quietly. I know he's not supposed to see it, but I'll break rules if it helps catch the killer.

To catch him, I may have to become him.

I didn't notice earlier that Homer uses a cane. One he doesn't need. Like his pipe, it's part of his distinguished psychologist costume. It feels like playing dress-up for adults with doctoral degrees. It sounds childish, but isn't that how the world works? People judge the package before they check the contents.

I've seen it before. It's a red flag when someone puts this much effort into perception. I file it away in the mental folder labeled "Reasons Not To Trust Gabriel Homer." The folder's getting thick.

That reminds me of the Comedian. If he isn't a patient of Homer's, who is he really? Could he look completely normal in everyday life? A face that wouldn't turn heads. The thought makes my skin crawl. I might have passed him on the street. Stood behind him in line for coffee. Never knowing there was a monster behind the mask of ordinary. I don't know why I've never thought about this before.

"Nothing here about the killer. He's more of a caricature of a killer—whoever wrote this report watched too many movies." Homer looks genuinely offended by the report. "You sure this is the report Johnson keeps?"

"Yes. Besides, why would she keep anything from me? She may be intolerable, but she wants to solve the case."

Homer doesn't comment. His silence speaks volumes—like he knows something I don't. It's the kind of silence that makes my stomach tighten

"I need to know more about the killer to profile him."

Homer turns a page.

"But it's you who is the real puzzle in this report."

"Me?"

"Everyone forgets things. Selective memory is a real condition after trauma. But you've forgotten almost everything. This isn't a defense mechanism to avoid past trauma. It's borderline denial, which isn't good for anyone trying to live their life and interact with society."

I grab the file from him. My hand moves before my brain gives permission. As if it belonged to someone else. I hate when my body makes decisions without consulting me first. But I'm also sick of people doubting me all these years. I should be hunting the killer. Not defending my sanity.

"I'm sorry, Detective." Homer's tone doesn't change—just his words. "I didn't mean to be harsh, but you have issues."

"Issues?" I thought I liked this man. What changed?

"For instance, your file says you failed every hand-to-hand combat test?" His eyes size me up as if he doesn't buy it.

I know what he's talking about. It's a glaring no-no in my file. "It's not like I can't fight. I'm strong. I know the tactics. I'm actually very enduring." I hate talking about this side of me. "I just vowed to never hit a fellow officer."

Great. First I'm psychologically damaged, now I'm physically incompetent. Maybe my next evaluation will tell me I'm also terrible at karaoke and making toast.

"After the kidnapping, I fought a guy in a bar. He was bothering me." I shrug. "I hurt him badly. Gave him a concussion."

Rush's eyes go wide in the mirror. His intensity cranks up another notch. Great. Now both men think I'm unstable.

"Makes sense." Homer's skepticism softens into understanding. "You were fresh from a terrible thing that happened to you, so you saw the killer in that bar guy."

"After that, I blocked it out. Decided not to hurt anyone, especially friends, and only during training tests."

"It's a questionable decision, but I assume it won't cause setbacks in the field?" he says, looking out his window. "I'm only worried about your safety."

"Don't worry, Professor, I'll protect you if the killer pops up in the basement," I tease him. But then the building shows up in the distance, and my heart races again. My toes begin to curl inside my shoes like they're trying to cling to something. My body remembering what my mind wants to forget.

Once Officer Rush parks, Homer looks back at me and blocks my door with his cane.

"I'll help you catch him, Detective," his voice turns cold. "If you promise one thing."

"I'm listening."

"That you will always tell me everything about that night in the cage. You promise me that you haven't left anything out." He leans close. "It's okay if you're keeping a secret from Johnson—but you have to tell me, or I will walk away."

I nod. I promise. Like I have a choice. Sure, I'll pick between emotional striptease and total failure. It's either spill my guts to the mysterious doctor or go back to square one in this investigation. Some choice I've got here.

And though I hate when people get this close—hate it like I hate small spaces and golden masks—Homer, in spite of his mysterious personality, is different for some reason. I feel like I'm used to his proximity, if that makes any sense.

His eyes scan over intimate details of my life, my trauma. It feels invasive, like he's peeling back my skin just to study what's underneath. I resist the urge to cross my arms over my chest.

He moves his cane back. I get out and breathe in cold air. I need a moment before walking with him to the building.

"Take off your jacket," he says as we enter.

"Excuse me?"

"It's red," he says, taking off his trench coat while biting his pipe between his teeth. "Like the color of the cages, according to the file I just read."

"I'm good." My stubborn, solitary mind speaks up.

"You're not. It's showing. You feel like suffocating in it the closer we get to the basement. I'm pretty sure your heart rate is around ninety at the moment."

Is he that good, or am I too much of an open book? A case study with legs. I take off the jacket, wondering how long I can keep up this act. Because no one can know what really happened that night—at least, according to my memories.

CHAPTER 10

It's almost sunset when we climb down the stairs to the basement.

The staircase swallows us in darkness. My phone light catches the walls, and something feels different. My eyes adjust faster now. Like my body remembers this place better than my mind does.

Homer leaves his cane at the door. Just drops it there, like he's shedding a disguise. Down here in the dark, I guess he doesn't need to pretend. Living in an asylum probably makes this feel like home.

He stops halfway down, light pointed up. "These stairs. There are two landings, each too long. This was a two-level basement once." His beam traces the ceiling. "Look at these edges. Someone broke through here. Knocked out the floor above."

My light follows his. "I thought two-level basements weren't common in New York."

"Older buildings have them. They were mostly used as wine cellars." His eyes cut through the dark. Sharp. Clinical. Like I'm one of his patients now.

"The basement where he kept me..." My voice trails off. "I don't remember if it was like this."

"Had to be." Homer moves down the stairs. His steps are smooth and silent. Like Johnson, but deadlier somehow. "They needed height so they could be installed from above."

"It's true, the cages are slightly oversized. I wonder why, since we spent most of our time near the floor."

"I assume the lightbulbs on top had to be out of reach so none of his victims would break them to create darkness. Just a guess."

"That's a solid theory. I wonder why I never thought of something like that."

"Definitely not alone, which means you might be looking for more than one killer."

"I never thought of that," I say, then point to the middle of the basement. "Anyway, here's your quote if you want to inspect it."

Homer kneels and touches the carved letters.

"You've mentioned he held a scalpel in the report," Homer says. "You think he used it to carve the quote?"

"Good point," I nod, wondering why this detail matters. Am I missing important clues because I'm too focused on the end goal? "Should we look for a scalpel?"

"Or whatever tool made these marks."

"I'll look into it."

I watch him walk past me, distracted by that ceiling again, then enter the cage. The light catches his white shirt—my jacket was too small for him to wear—it makes him glow like he's on stage.

Homer's image underneath the light bulb in the cage conjures a revelation in my mind. Suddenly I get why the Comedian liked dark basements and installed those light bulbs. We were all in the spotlight down here. His own twisted Broadway show. He was the master director—or actor—putting on his golden mask. A thought to file away for later.

For now, I need to know more about Homer.

"How do you think he obtained your book?"

"I give away free copies to whoever is interested. It could be leaked online."

"Or he could have befriended one of those you gave the books to."

"Possible. But that'd be a list of over two hundred people, some of them people I only met once, maybe at a conference, and never even got their names."

"One of them could be him."

"Again, possible," he says. "I'll send you a copy. Maybe it helps."

"I'd appreciate that. What was the title again? The Sky Below and—"

Homer tenses all of a sudden.

I watch him beam the light back at the center of the room and get out of the cage. When I attempt to question him, he raises a forefinger in my face and shushes me. He kneels down again, touching the carved quote, then from his position shines the light upward to the ceiling. "You said the cage belongs in the middle, right?"

"Yes."

"Look," he points upward, right over the spot where the cage should've been. "This is the only spot in the basement where the ceiling is boarded up from above."

"How do you know that?" I squint, tiptoeing.

"We know this is a double basement where someone broke through sections of the floor to make it higher probably for the cages to fit with the large theatrical light bulb above and all," Homer explains. "But this part in the middle has a hole between the basement and the ground floor."

I finally see what he's pointing at.

The far ceiling is boarded with wooden planks from above. There certainly is a hole leading upwards. "You're right, but what do you think this is, professor?"

"A surveillance hole, if you ask me. Watching your caged prey from where they can't see you—classic voyeurism 101."

"I think you're wrong about voyeurism as I've never seen him treat us in a sexual way. But I think you are right about him watching us from above." Now something clicks in my head. I'm not sure if it's a memory or just my interpretation. "He drugged us and always demanded we sleep. Maybe he watched us from above."

Homer looks back at me. "Call for backup. You need help to investigate the ground floor upstairs."

I nod, impressed by his detective work. But before I pick up my phone I have to ask. "What made you check out the middle again?"

"When you asked me about my book," Homer says. "It's called The Sky Below and the Earth Above."

I gasp. "He wanted me to look at the ceiling, but only you could have figured it out."

"The quote from the book isn't supposed to lead to me," Homer says. "It leads to the book's title, which hints at the ground floor, 'The Earth Above.'"

CHAPTER 11

I leave the basement first, watching Homer follow me up. Wearing Homer's coat, I tuck my hands into the pockets for warmth. I can't lie, it makes me feel ecstatic. I'm one step closer to catching the Comedian.

"Sure you don't want to call Johnson before checking the ground floor?" Homer bites his lip against the cold. Without his pipe and coat, he looks different. Normal. Like someone I could trust, though I know I shouldn't.

"It's my case, not hers," I say, almost tiptoeing with pride. "I mean, you solved the puzzle, but I decide what happens next."

"If you say so, Detective." His lips barely curve, but it's definitely a smile. Subtle, but real.

"Follow me." I walk ahead, searching for the entrance to the room above the basement.

"Didn't know detective work was this exciting," Homer muses behind me.

"Shut up," I say playfully, waving a hand at him. Then I catch myself. Snatch my hand back. Walk faster.

Stop acting like a teenager with a crush. You're a detective, for God's sake.

"Someone sealed off every doorway with bricks." His fingers trace the wall's surface. There's a mark on his finger—the kind a wedding ring leaves behind. I've never noticed it before. "The cement's barely dry. Couldn't have been more than a few days ago."

A chill runs down to my toes. After days of studying me inside that cage, maybe he knows my thoughts better than anyone.

"The Comedian is laughing at us." My voice echoes in the abandoned hallway. Is he watching me right now?

Homer senses my distress and reaches out his hand, palm up. He doesn't speak, but his eyes are tender. As much as I need it, I wonder if I'm just another patient to him. Which I probably am.

I nod in appreciation but don't take his hand. I shrug off his coat and hand it back, leaving him standing there, confused.

Back outside, the night air stings my face. "You'll need it tomorrow."

"I'm good," I say, gripping my jacket and letting the cold bite through my pride.

"It'll bring you luck," he says, folding it over my shoulder.

"Thanks." Our fingers touch. I pull away too fast, though. "For everything today."

"Don't thank me yet." He turns to leave, then hesitates. "I might not make it tomorrow. Other commitments." I don't like how carefully he avoids eye contact.

Something in his voice twists my stomach. "But you'll want to know what we find."

"I'll call Johnson," I say as he steps away. "She'll keep me informed."

I watch him vanish into darkness. The urge to call after him, ask for his number, sticks in my throat. Stupid. Stupid to feel this pull. Stupid to think he'd want more involvement than necessary.

Maybe he's avoiding me. Or maybe he's afraid of Johnson. Neither option sits right.

"Ready to go?" Rush materializes beside me, keys in hand. I've never seen him upright before—perfectly my height, wearing casual white sneakers. Fake Nikes, I can spot them. I have a pair of fake Jordans myself.

"You know my apartment's address?"

"Don't have to, Detective. You're sleeping in the Yellow tonight. Commissioner's orders."

"You're joking," I scoff, and dial her number. She picks up immediately.

"Talk to me, kiddo." Her voice is heavy with sleep.

"I can't sleep in that shithole—" I catch myself. "That basement."

"You don't have a choice. Until you catch the Comedian, you do as I say. I have reasons. I want you focused. I want you suffering until you remember everything—and away from the public eye, of course."

Did she just say she wants me to suffer?

"I thought you'd be calling to brag about some progress you made in the case."

"I made real progress!" I fire back, keeping Homer out of it. She needs to know I'm good at what I do. I tell her about the holes in the ground floor.

"Huh. I didn't expect you to go this far," Johnson says. "Don't do anything until I tell you tomorrow. I want to be there when we break into these blocked walls."

She hangs up.

CHAPTER 12

Back in the Yellow, I open the Bilco door and descend into the basement. The metal stairs creak under my weight. Nothing like the soundtrack of impending collapse to welcome you home.

I kick off my shoes and drop into the nearest chair with my take-away. Rush bought it for me without me asking, so I guess he has his merits. Or he's fattening me up for sacrifice to whatever bureaucratic god the department worships.

The food sits half-eaten. Greasy takeout from some dive—fitting, when you're eating solo in a basement after a brutal day, just to crash and slog through another day in hell the next morning.

I pull out my phone, trying to reread the Comedian's letter, but reading his words this late would only spook me, maybe even depress me. And I'm already sleeping in a basement that makes most horror movie sets look like the Ritz-Carlton.

I've done good today, and I have a thread to follow. His letter can wait—not because it isn't important, but because I'm scared to read it. That, and the possibility that he could be messing with my mind, like Johnson suggested. As if my mind needs any more messing with. It's already like a junk drawer filled with trauma, half-memories, and takeout menus from restaurants that no longer exist.

I put the phone down and my eyes dart around the place as I take my final sip of fizzy drink. I sip my diet soda—because clearly, watching my figure is the priority when I might be murdered in my sleep.

I wish I had time to discover what this place really is. How many cases were investigated here? What's its history? Or is it just a place Johnson made up to keep me away from the public and under her eyes? If it's the latter, she could've at least sprung for a mini-fridge and some artwork that isn't water damage shaped like continents.

The way the basement is constructed suggests it has been used as an operations center many times before. It has about four rooms, only one with a proper locking door—the one with the bed where I will sleep, I suppose. The others probably housed officers who didn't kiss up to their superiors enough.

The rooms are full of lockers filled with files and a couple of desks with ancient computers that, surprisingly enough, still work. Each file, each computer, could be holding pieces of a puzzle I'm desperate to solve—or just decades of police memes and solitaire high scores.

I'm exhausted. Need to rest before tomorrow's wall break at the crime scene. Nothing says "good night's sleep" like knowing you'll be sledgehammering through suspicious walls tomorrow.

Lord, how I miss my dog, Stray.

Stray's not just any dog. I found him lost in New York six years ago, right around the time I escaped from the Comedian. He's a mixed-breed mutt with no personality at all—I laugh at this, and worry for him. His only distinctive trait is that he loves me to death. That makes one of us in this cruel world.

Sometimes I wonder if he saved me as much as I saved him. I was shattered glass, and somehow this furry idiot who eats socks helped me put the pieces back together.

Most people don't believe me when I say he loves broccoli—

apparently, that's impossible for a dog. But Stray eats whatever I give him, as long as it's from my hands. I once accidentally dropped an aspirin, and he ate it before I could stop him. I panicked and called the vet, who told me to watch for symptoms. The only symptom was that I stayed up all night while Stray snored like a chainsaw with allergies.

His favorite is actually steak, when I can afford it. Another story of survival. Another testament to making do with what you've got. And when you can't afford steak, there's always the neighbor's unattended barbecue.

Rush has my apartment keys for tonight. Usually, Mrs. Gonzalez next door checks on Stray—she's got a spare key and a soft spot for him—but I've been gone too long, and I want to spoil him with a fat, juicy steak. I told Rush to take it over, show him my photo so he'd eat, then bring him back tomorrow. If Rush screws this up, I'll turn his cheap knockoff shoes into a felony-level art project.

I'm so tired.

Before settling in, I file a short report to Johnson about everything that happened today. Paperwork: the bureaucratic straitjacket that turns people into zombies. I'd rather be catching criminals than feeding bureaucratic monsters. Death by paper cut—the real danger in law enforcement nobody warns you about.

Gabriel Homer haunts my thoughts again. Mental visitations from a psychiatrist—just what I need. I already pay one to pretend to listen to me once a week.

I dig through the database, my fingers moving faster with each frustrated click. Nothing. No records. No mentions. No trace of his supposed police work. Johnson's story feels like smoke. I wonder if she was telling the truth. Maybe Homer is just a figment of my imagination, and I've spent the day following an imaginary friend around a crime scene. Wouldn't be the strangest thing that's happened to me.

I'm tempted to look up his personal life online, but my drooping eyelids save me from my stupidity. I know I have a weakness for some men when they're present, but I'm quite capable of forgetting about them when they're gone—same brain glitch, different guy.

I head to bed.

The bedroom is decent enough—for a maid. Or a prisoner serving life for petty crimes. Lock and key. A bed. A commode. Bare minimum.

But no complaints. I've slept in worse places—if you can call cages places.

A strange sense of pride settles over me while I'm in bed. Six years of chasing the Comedian, and I'm finally making progress. I think I'd have made my parents proud—even if I never met them. I spent my teenage years bouncing between boarding schools and adoptive parents who couldn't handle me.

Suddenly, I hear sounds.

I sit up.

Is that someone pushing the basement door open?

I jump out of bed, pick up my gun, and check the door. It's closed. But I glimpse the lower part of someone's shadow running away from the basement window. I think I glimpse a long black coat covering all the way down to the ground, but full of shades. I could be mistaken.

By the time I go to open it, the shadow is gone. But when I open the window and stick my head out, I find no one. Only the Camry is still outside, locked and empty.

Perfect ending to a perfect day. The only thing missing is a hockey mask and ominous violin music.

CHAPTER 13

I wake up to sunlight slicing through a hole in the ceiling. It's just one more broken piece of New York's forgotten infrastructure. Holes everywhere in this city—not even counting the ones in my memory.

Get a grip, Maddie. You're doing good. And you didn't need a pat on the shoulder to get this far.

But I slept too well last night, and with a day of wall-breaking ahead, I'm not letting this bother me. My chance to prove myself gleams brighter than any structural mystery.

The prehistoric coffee machine in the so-called kitchen is a piece of junk. Surprisingly, it makes good coffee. There's no sugar, though, and I love sugar.

I sip my coffee as my watch ticks closer to Rush's arrival. Whether it was him or not yesterday, I'm starting to fully realize that I can't trust anyone. It could be as dumb as him being a weirdo stalker, or as serious as something truly rotten going on all around me.

You're the fishy one, Maddie. You and your secret. That's why you keep low and don't question the obvious. Homer, Johnson, Rush —there's something bigger going on here.

"Shit!" I snap again. I slam the cup against the sink, shattering it.

It's a heavy moment when you realize you've been talking to yourself. Heavier when it's because you have no one to talk to.

I wash my bloody hands in the sink. It's just a scratch.

I usually avoid looking at myself in the morning. I'm too insecure about my looks, even though I know I'm good-looking.

"Shit!" I snap again. "Rush has my keys. What if he's a stalker and hurts Stray?"

A few minutes later, I'm in the Camry again, tearing up at a picture of Stray licking my photo on Rush's phone after eating his steak. His tongue sticks to the screen.

I guess I was wrong about Rush. My talent for misjudging people remains undefeated. I should have it professionally certified. Maybe frame it next to my detective badge—World Champion at Jumping to Conclusions.

"I'm sorry I couldn't bring him," Rush says. He actually meets my eyes today. "The Johnson said no."

"So you tell her about everything?"

"I have to. It's my job." He finally looks at me as he hands back the keys, then starts the engine. "But don't worry. I left out the part where you called her 'The Dick' six times yesterday."

I snort, surprised by his attempt at humor. "Seven times, actually. You missed the one under my breath."

Rush actually smiles. It transforms his face completely.

"Tell me, officer," I seize the moment. "That Camry in the alley last night—yours?"

"Police property." Rush turns onto the next street. "Budget cuts. Can't expense gas without official business. Even the Camry's radio is busted—budget cuts hit harder than Johnson's ego."

"I see. But you didn't leave right after dropping me off, did you?"

"Last night?" He blinks at the road. "Exhausted. Left immediately. Subway home. Why?"

"Someone tried getting into the basement."

"Happens." He shrugs. "Place looks like homeless heaven. Should've warned you."

"Great. So I'm living in the hottest homeless destination in Brooklyn. Five-star accommodations with premium floor sleeping and vintage cobwebs."

"Don't forget the luxury dripping pipes providing ambient white noise." Rush laughs unexpectedly. "The Yellow Special Victims Division—where the real victim is interior design."

We both burst out laughing.

"So what changed?" I ask. "Yesterday you were wound tighter than my therapist's schedule. Today you're... different."

Rush shifts uncomfortably. "Your reputation in the department was rather..."

"Ah." I roll my eyes. "They told you I'm crazy. The girl the killer let go, who spent six years in a job she hates just to catch him."

Rush nods, face flushing red.

"What changed your mind, then?" I click my fingers. "Let me guess—Stray's infinite charm? It made you think of me like an actual human?"

"Stray's an obnoxious little charm ball, I'll admit," Rush laughs. "But mostly how you handled the case yesterday."

"Meaning?"

"Working a case this personal, with Johnson being an ass and forcing you to sleep in that basement? Most would crack."

"Is she always this tough on new detectives?"

"She tests everyone to breaking," Rush sighs. "Thinks pressure makes diamonds. Not everyone survives the crush."

"And I thought I was special, huh?"

"Special enough she risked putting you on this case. I don't think she expected you'd find something so fast. Truth is, I think she wanted you to quit. Without that letter from the Comedian, she'd have handed this to someone senior."

"So her plan was to watch me fail, then replace me?"

"It also explains why you're working in the Yellow—which almost no one in the department even knows exists." Rush gives me a look I can't read.

"What?"

"You didn't hear this morning's news?"

"What news?" My stomach drops before he even answers.

"Johnson ordered the wall taken down already."

"You're kidding." I grab my phone, furiously searching her name and the case.

"She claimed the discovery as her own and took all the credit. Press conference and everything." Rush gulps. "She does this constantly."

"Does what?" The first search result shows her talking to reporters.

The headline: Commissioner Johnson Cracks the Comedian's Case With New Clues for the First Time in Six Years.

"Being a dick," Rush answers.

CHAPTER 14

Johnson's team has already torn through the wall by the time I arrive.

Brick dust coats everything, turning the room into some kind of twisted winter wonderland. She is still giving orders and accepting congratulations from fellow officers. The news crews are all over the building, and none of them even know who I am.

But I know who I am. I'm going to catch him—and from now on, Johnson's out of the loop. You could call it professional development —or just petty revenge. Either way, she's now on my list of people who don't deserve updates.

I kneel down before the room's opening. My fingers trace the fresh scrapes left from the wall demolition. Forensics 101: always check what others miss. Or in this case, what Johnson deliberately trampled over in her rush to the cameras.

"Well?" Johnson materializes behind me, clipboard in hand. Ready to take credit for whatever we find. "Any brilliant insights, Detective?"

I ignore her tone. It isn't just condescending—it's entitled, like she believes she earned the credit without lifting a finger. I focus on the marks instead. "Did anyone enter the room yet?"

"No. I was waiting for you. It's your case, after all."

"You don't say." Funny how it becomes *my* case after the press conference is over.

Johnson ignores me and glances over her shoulder, probably making sure the news people can't hear us talking. "Come with me."

I follow her into the room, horrified by the complete disregard for protocol. No yellow tape, no forensics team, no evidence markers anywhere.

"The room is all yours now," she says, dropping her press-conference smile now that we're alone. "Turns out your Comedian is just a peeping Tom."

"A peeping Tom?" The words burn in my throat. "Ivy Williams is dead. They're all dead. How can you say that?"

"The maniac dug a hole in the floor, looking down on whoever he kidnapped and locked up in a cage, kiddo. There are no two ways about it."

"Then why did he kill the girls?"

"You're well aware that I was one of those girls, right? He never did anything like that to me or the others."

"You said he drugged you. Maybe he did it while you slept. Besides, you don't really remember what happened, kiddo, so no, I'm not well aware you're one of his girls. Who knows what really happened back then?"

It takes so much effort not to burst out and scream at her. I keep reminding myself that she can take me off the case any second and replace me.

I take a deep breath and straighten up. "It's my opinion that he is not working alone, Commissioner."

"What?" She's the one about to burst now, clearly offended by my conclusion—like I've just accused her favorite child of shoplifting.

I explain the whole theory about the walls and even show her the original blueprint I downloaded yesterday on my phone. It confirmed Homer's theory. Until months ago, this was a two-floor basement.

"Did Professor Homer feed you all that crap?" is her reply, as if she never listened to what I said. She gets closer and speaks directly into my face. "He is a man who lets insane people who need to be institutionalized go. And I still think the Comedian may have been his patient. So don't give in to his ideas."

"Commissioner," I dare to meet her eyes, not letting her make this about Homer. "Whether I'm right or wrong, the Comedian has probably found a new basement and killed more girls besides Ivy."

"We've checked, kiddo. No kidnappings reported in the past week. Satisfied?"

"Do you know how many people don't report Missing persons right away? Do you know how many have personal reasons to not report their next of kin? And don't let me get into officers who file a report in a drawer and forget to send it out right away."

Johnson's irritation with me is much worse than last time. She keeps close but raises a finger in my face.

"Look, kiddo. I'm the boss here. I say what is and what isn't. If you cause me problems, I will disqualify you. Given your mental health record, that's an easy take. I'm giving you an opportunity you've been waiting for a long time. The only thing I will accept is indisputable facts. Do you understand?"

"I understand."

"Good," she says. "Now don't you dare talk to the press when you leave. You report to me—and by the way, your phone is vibrating."

I look but don't pick up, watching her walk away.

"You should pick up, kiddo," she waves a dismissive hand at me. "It's probably your Mr. Charming Psychiatrist calling to fill your head with more nonsense."

CHAPTER 15

Homer's number flashes on my phone. I hesitate, then swipe to answer.

"Have you looked around the room yet?" His voice is calm and clinical—the kind that belongs in therapy sessions, not crime scenes.

The truth is, I barely got a chance. Johnson's argument consumed every minute, like a black hole sucking up time and patience.

"Not really," I admit, scanning the space now. Empty chairs scattered like abandoned props. Walls scraped raw. No ceiling lighting. Just emptiness and dust. "You actually called right after I finished with Johnson." I keep my voice neutral, but his timing seems too perfect—like he's been tracking me.

"I saw you on TV go into the building," Homer says. "I knew you'd definitely head to the room, but thought I'd give you five minutes before calling."

I wonder why he always has an answer for everything. Trusting Johnson is like trusting a shark with a nosebleed.

"Walk me through what you see." Not a question. He instructs me.

"Two chairs. Dust-covered, like almost everything here. Could be old dust, or from breaking through the walls, which look scraped and bare like the basement." I'm starting to wonder who's the detective here. Maybe I should send him my badge and call it a day.

"Was the room untouched before you arrived?"

"Johnson claims no one's been in here before me." Even I can hear the doubt in my voice.

"I wouldn't trust Johnson if she told me water was wet," Homer mutters. "Are the boards still covering the hole in the ceiling?"

"No." Just realized what it means. Johnson lied. They've been inside before I arrived. Add it to her growing list of deceptions. "You think Johnson tampered with evidence?"

"If so, it's too late. It also means that whoever's footprints you come across in the rubble and dust mean nothing now."

"Let's focus on the hole, then," I move closer, carefully. My feet find clean paths through the debris in case there are more holes covered—or if there are any other types of prints that would help in the future. "I can see the cage from where I stand, but it's quite awkward."

"How so?"

"Nothing stops me from falling. I wonder how the Comedian enjoyed his peeps from such strange angles. Not exactly ideal seating for long-term surveillance."

"But you can see through the cage, had there been a victim inside?"

"If you look from an angle, yes. It's actually quite visible, just from an uncomfortable position."

"It explains why the light bulb is placed above the cages. He had no means to stare perpendicularly, as the huge light bulbs would have blocked his view. The light was only to make the subject in the cage visible from an angle."

"It's called Power Dynamics, Vertical Hierarchy, or even Panopticism," Homer explains in his terms, but it needs no explanation. Watching someone helpless from above—of course it made him feel in control. "The desire to observe from above is deeply rooted in psychological concepts of power and—"

"I get it, professor," I cut him off. Psychology 101: Men Who Think They Can Control Everything. Should be a bestseller. "So the cages are really like a Broadway show to him, a theater, and he is the director who wears the mask. Why?"

"I wish I knew. And I have to apologize, too."

"Why?"

"I called him a caricature of a killer when I read the report. He is far from it."

"I accept your apology." It might be a weird thing to say, but I hardly meet people who apologize for finally realizing what kind of psychopath we're dealing with. Most people just avoid the subject altogether. Like acknowledging evil might summon it.

"But is this all? Why did his clue lead us to break into this room? I don't see enough evidence to forward the case."

"I'm sorry, detective. I wish there was more," Homer holds onto the silence, as if expecting me to lead this part of the conversation.

My eyes desperately scan the room around me, but I can't seem to see anything that triggers a memory or looks out of place. I worry that Johnson wins; the Comedian is playing games. I'm nothing but bait to help tell his greatest joke of all—the punchline written in someone else's blood.

"Wait!" I snap, looking beneath my feet.

"What did you find, Detective?" Homer sounds alive again.

"Prints in the dust under my feet."

"Not footprints, right?" He stresses the syllables slowly, being unusually skeptical this time.

"Marks in the dust." I kneel down, making sure I'm far enough from the hole's edge. No need to add *detective falls to her death* to Johnson's press conference highlights.

"I don't know what that means."

"I need you to stop talking for a second," I say as I tilt my head at the marks in the dust. Then I raise my head and stretch my neck to look around the hole. Sure enough, there are three more marks.

"Tripods," I say. It comes out as a whisper of revelation.

"Explain the strange angles," Homer's syllables are slow and tense.

"Wait," I walk around the hole. "From the prints, I see four tripods covering all angles of the cage."

Even Homer sounds like he's about to gasp. "He didn't need a straight POV of the cages downstairs because..."

"...he wasn't just watching," I realize. "He was recording."

CHAPTER 16

Maddie. Maddie. Maddie.

Click. Click. Click.

Recording.

Capturing.

Collecting.

Every. Single. Moment.

Did I ever tell you how I miss you? I mean really miss you? Of all the girls, I miss you the most—and I'm not used to missing someone I didn't kill.

Remember the freak shows, where the broken and bizarre were caged for wealthy voyeurs? Like scientists watching rats in a maze, I'm simply continuing the grand tradition—observation, performance, control.

My lens is the cage. My stage is their helplessness. And every click of my camera is a ticket sold to witness the most intimate human experiment. I've never sent you the video footage, have I? Unlucky you —missing out on the most intimate human experience in recent history.

I'm getting really impatient. So impatient, I might stop writing you letters you were never meant to read.

Feeling overwhelmed by the case? The exit is right there, kiddo.

Right now, you think you're the one who got away.

You don't want to go down in history as the one who never caught me—because in reality, I am the one who got away.

P.S. *Do you think I should send you these letters and let you in on how my mind works? I prefer not, because I know you're smarter than that. You don't need this much help from me, right?*

CHAPTER 17

"Why would he record us?" I say.

"I can't tell now, but it explains why he drugged you," Homer says. "Are all four tripods angled toward the center cage?"

"Yes."

"Shouldn't forensics confirm it?"

"I can't let Johnson in on this," I glance at her beyond the door. "She cares more about press conferences than evidence. Her team walked right past those tripod marks."

"I don't blame you, though you'll need forensic help eventually."

"I thought you were the unorthodox type."

Homer suppresses a chuckle. "Just don't mention my name when they discipline you."

"Deal," I scan the room again. "So if the Comedian filmed the middle cage, wouldn't he have moved us around?"

"Likely—given that he may have had help."

"But I don't remember changing cages."

"Perfect timing isn't hard when your subjects are unconscious. You just didn't feel it," Homer says.

"That's plausible, I guess."

"If I were you, I'd focus on why he called you Beautiful Cocoons, fed you well, then filmed you. It paints a very different picture now."

"Even though none of us were sexually violated." I appreciate him brainstorming with me.

"I think calling you cocoons suggests he expected the girls to transform into something else inside the cage."

"Something that was so specific he needed to film it."

"While he operated some type of surgeries on the girls."

"Surgeries?" I grimace.

"The scalpel, drilling Ivy's head, filming—it all suggests it. This wasn't strictly murder."

"Are you saying he had medical training?"

"He—or whoever helped him," Homer says, reining in his enthusiasm. "It's a hypothesis, detective. Something to work with until you have proof."

I don't think it's a wild hypothesis, after all. It makes a lot of sense to me. "But he called himself an artist."

"A plastic surgeon would call themselves that too. Again, I'm assuming."

"But it fits," I pull out his letter and read a certain part: "'I no longer just trap women in cages to watch them break. I'm setting them free.'"

"Not just my victims," Homer completes the sentence for me, making me wonder how involved he is in this case. "But all women in the world."

"So the cage as an operating table to transform the girls, after all," I say, almost absently, as my thoughts trail.

"One that was filmed by the cameras on these tripods," Homer says. "Unfortunately, there is no way you can track him or his cameras from those tripods."

"You're wrong, professor," I kneel down and take photos of the tripod prints. "There is a way."

CHAPTER 18

Rush is driving as I sit in the passenger seat.

Earlier, I avoided the officers and snuck out so I wouldn't run into Johnson. I know what I need to do next to find the Comedian—but she can't know what I have in mind from here on out.

Homer, too—I can't trust him for some reason. Mainly my irrational attraction to him. The way his mind works makes me forget every red flag.

"Where are we going?" Rush is anxious again, gripping the wheel and leaning forward. But it's my enthusiasm that makes him that way this time.

"I need your help," I announce.

"But of course. That's my job, after all."

"That's the problem—because I don't want you to tell Johnson about anything that we're about to do now."

Rush's eyelids twitch. "I don't think that'll be possible."

"You saw what she did to me today. You said she does it all the time. I have good evidence that will help catch the Comedian. Her need to tell the press will hinder the case. Please, officer."

"I understand, but..."

"That's what the Comedian counts on, so we have to subvert expectations," I lean closer and whisper in his ear as he drives. "I need a digital forensic expert who won't report to Johnson as well."

"That is a lot to ask."

"Come on, Rush. You must know someone."

"But..."

"What if the Comedian's next victim is your sister, your girl-friend, or your mother?"

Rush swallows hard.

"I know someone who can help."

I'm shocked by how easy that was. "Who?"

"Katarina Volkova."

"I said a digital forensic expert, not the Russian mafia." I laugh out loud.

"She's a first-generation American, and one of the best. And guess who kicked her out of the service?"

I can't help grinning. "The Johnson?"

Rush nods and takes a steep turn already. "The dick herself."

Who knew he and I would bond over our dislike of The Johnson?

CHAPTER 19

The stairs creak beneath me as I walk up to Kat's shoddy apartment.

Rush tells me this area is called Brownsville—a Brooklyn neighborhood where forgotten souls gather, where each building tells a story of outcasts and survivalists.

He makes a big deal of me never having heard of it, but I let it slide.

Twenty-four hours ago, I was a detective with a badge. Now I'm sneaking around with a twitchy officer to meet a Russian hacker. My career trajectory has all the stability of a drunk tightrope walker.

Rush follows behind me, his voice low and precise. "Kat speaks good English, but once her Russian accent emerges, you won't understand a thing."

I can't help but raise an eyebrow. "It can't be that bad, Officer Rush. Don't worry, I'll get along with her."

"It's not the language," Rush continues.

"She came to America as a refugee when her dad got in trouble with the Russian government. When her old memories come back, her accent slips back in. But I have the solution."

"Which is?"

I watch him pull out his phone like he's reading a manual on how to interact with a witness.

"Here are the rules," Rush explains.

"Don't push her until she's tired, don't let her drink, smoking is okay, and don't ask too many questions about why Johnson kicked her out."

I wipe the sweat from my forehead in the middle of winter as we climb.

"Gosh, you make her sound like a Russian robot. Should I bring vodka or WD-40?"

"You're starting to sound like The Johnson, you know that?"

Rush shakes his head.

Coming from him, I feel like the world might end if I upset Kat.

"You're right, I'm sorry," I say as we stand before her door on the third floor.

A cacophony of sounds escapes from nearby apartments—baby cries, cooking sounds, and even the unmistakable rhythms of intimate encounters.

Just what I need—a soundtrack for my second day as a rogue detective. Maybe I should start wearing all black and develop a mysterious backstory.

"How about I get in alone?"

"Why?"

He seems taken aback.

I want to tell him I don't fully trust him, but instead say, "I think your perpetual crazy eyes might upset her enough to slip back into her Russian dialect., and we don't want that."

"Okay," Rush lets out a sigh. He mutters something about parking the Camry and heads off. I guess he's been circling Brownsville this whole time.

"I thought it was the mustache."

CHAPTER 20

Kat's apartment is a shrine to digital chaos. Cigarette smoke hangs thick in the air like a cancerous fog. She's right—it looks more like something you'd use to extract an alien from someone's chest cavity than an investigative tool. Rush warned me she'd kept some confiscated NYPD gear after Johnson booted her—guess he wasn't kidding.

She doesn't waste time on pleasantries.

I like her already.

"What you got?" she asks, exhaling a spiral of smoke directly into my face.

Nothing says "welcome" like second-hand lung cancer.

I show her the photos of the tripod's dust prints. "I wonder if I can trace back the camera used from these tripod marks."

"It's called reverse engineering," Kat says, examining the photos with the intensity of someone looking for a hidden Easter egg in a Marvel movie that will definitely be explained in a three-hour YouTube video.

"So it can be done, yes?"

I try not to sound as desperate as I feel, which is somewhere between "lottery ticket holder" and "drowning person spotting a lifeboat."

"We're living in the digital wonderland, Alice," she says, poking the mind's eye with an ashen forefinger.

She leans even closer. "They are watching everything."

Great. Conspiracy theories. Just what my serial killer investigation needed. Thanks for the Russian tech paranoid, Rush. Maybe next time he can find me a cryptid hunter to track the Comedian's footprints.

"Are they watching us now?" I ask, playing along.

"Oh, not me. They can't."

The smell of nicotine nauseates me as she slowly moves her mouth to my ear like we're at prom and she's about to tell me who has a crush on me.

"Because I'm watching them."

With all the insanity around me, I'm starting to think I made a mistake coming here.

I mean, she's a friend of Rush—what did I expect? A normal person with a normal apartment who doesn't breathe fire with every exhale?

"This needs a professional-grade camera with specialized lighting, precision measurement tools that look more like surgical instruments than investigative tools," she says, poking the photographs with fingers stained yellow from what must be decades of smoking.

"I'm not that savvy with digital forensics. Break it down for idiots like me?"

I glance at her nervously. "Please?" I ask, before I suffocate in this nicotine chamber of horrors.

"It needs a camera you can only find in the NYPD, not here."

"So we can't—"

"I have something better."

A half-empty whiskey bottle sits by her elbow—violating Rush's rule about not drinking—already teetering on the edge. She takes a long drag from the cigarette stuck to her lips, sucking with such force I'm surprised her cheeks don't collapse inward.

"It's called the dark web—a.k.a. the anonymous internet, full of terrible secrets for the ignorant like you."

I watch her enter passwords and prompts at lightning speed. My tech skills peak at remembering my email password, so this might as well be magic.

An image of a complicated device appears in 3D on the screen. She's right—it looks more like something you'd use to extract an alien from someone's chest cavity than an investigative tool.

"Under careful positioning, microscopic details emerge—depth, pressure, the most minute characteristics of the tripods' feet," Kat recites, like she's reading the poetry of surveillance.

I wonder if Johnson kicked her out for hacking, or for boring everyone to death with technical monologues.

I don't understand a thing, but I don't want to upset her by admitting that.

For all I know, "upsetting" her might involve me waking up with my consciousness uploaded to a toaster.

"Careful, Alice," Kat warns, gleefully chain-smoking now. "Technology speaks, but only to those who know how to listen."

"But of course," I say, widening my eyes like Rush does, instead of rolling them all the way back to see my own brain.

"This machine is typically used for shoe-print analysis, but I tweaked it for this specific task. Each comparison, each search is a breadcrumb leading closer to the truth."

"Uh-huh," I nod, not commenting on her use of big words like 'truth' and 'Alice.'

She likes her job, I can tell. Me, I'm just trying not to choke on the smoke that's probably turning my lungs into beef jerky.

"Then we go to Google Lens," Kat says as cigarette ashes drop onto her keyboard.

I wonder if her computer is fireproof or if she just replaces it weekly.

"Every photography forum known to humanity."

In real life, my world narrows to search results, manufacturer databases, comparative analyses. Online searches expand beyond physical evidence, each click potentially bringing me one step closer to the man who locked me in a cage and let me live to tell about it.

"Most people see dust," Kat points at the photo on the computer. "Only the enlightened see a map."

My focus is absolute, praying this works. In tech we trust.

And in Kat's nicotine-fueled brain, apparently.

She looks at me with bloodshot eyes. "Phase one done. We made an accurate print of the tripod's legs from your unprofessional and shitty photographs."

"You did?"

I lean in closer to the screen. She's right—the dust print now looks more like someone's fingerprint in sand than the blurry mess I captured.

"Time to find who bought this," she announces like she's declaring the start of a revolution.

"You can?" I'm impressed despite myself. "How?"

"New tripods often come with protective plastic film on the rubber feet," Kat begins her lecture, Professor Nicotine teaching Stalking 101.

"The machines I used trace details like fingerprints and the residue of the rubber shows."

I'll have to take her word for it. "Did you say new tripods?"

"Yup. This is a Manfrotto tripod," she says, putting on a pair of thick glasses that make her eyes look like they belong to an owl on steroids. "The 055 series."

The Comedian buying recent equipment isn't far-fetched. It's been six years. A new crime scene. A new Broadway show for him. He needs new equipment.

You can't stage a comeback tour with outdated gear, after all.

An idea pops into my head. "Could you take a look at these images, too, Kat?"

She peers from under her glasses at the photos of the cage on my phone. "He keeps his victims here?"

I nod. My five-star accommodations, courtesy of a psychopath with theatrical ambitions.

Her face knots and crumbles, her cigarette crushed between her teeth.

"We'll catch him," she announces with determination. "I've caught worse."

It's the perfect moment to ask her why Johnson fired her, but I focus on the case instead.

"I appreciate your enthusiasm, but I wanted you to look close at the light bulb on top of the cage."

"That's not a light bulb, Alice," she says dismissively, turning back to the screen like I've just mistaken the Mona Lisa for a passport photo.

"It's a ring light for TikToks and YouTube and so on. It's called a Smart Ring or something."

The picture is now complete. Like Homer suggested, the Comedian took girls for some kind of show, there's no doubt about it.

My mind races, wondering if there are videos or pictures of me on some shady website on the internet.

Even with my hyperactive imagination, I can't bring myself to picture how they look. Was I naked? Was someone doing something to me?

I close my eyes, and then my imagination goes even wilder.

"It was you, then, huh?"

I've finally gotten Katarina Volkova's full attention. Better than a goldfish's, but possibly more dangerous.

"The girl who got away, yes," I open my eyes, preferring Kat's crazy gaze over my morbid imagination.

Better the devil with nicotine breath than the one in my head.

Her look doesn't linger. She gives a discreet nod. "Don't tell me about it. I've had my share of nightmares," she says. "But you'll catch him, Alice, don't worry."

"Thank you," I watch her go back to the screen. "Did you say we can track who purchased the tripod?"

"Depends."

"On what?"

"Cash purchase? Check security footage. Credit card? We follow the digital breadcrumbs." She proudly clicks enter and we watch the screen's meter showing that it's scanning the web for recent purchases. "This will take some time."

"Okay," I say, composing myself and making sure I'm breathing. The fact that I'm this close scares me somehow.

I wait with all the patience of a starving dog watching its owner slice steak.

Waiting adds too much weight to everything we want to achieve. Like watching water boil while a psychopath is out there shopping for more cages.

I look back at Kat, and she's drinking cheap whiskey straight from a half-empty bottle. Her hand trembles as she tilts it back, amber liquid sloshing against glass.

No.

Rush's warning echoes in my head like a siren. Don't let her drink. Whatever you do, don't let her drink.

Her eyes begin to glaze over, the precise calculations in them dissolving into something wild and unpredictable.

"Kat." I reach for the bottle, "maybe we should wait for the results before—"

She slams her fist on the keyboard. The search screen flickers dangerously.

"You think I need to be sober to catch monsters?" Her Russian accent thickens with each syllable, her words slurring at the edges. "I catch them better drunk!"

The progress bar on the screen freezes at 98%. So close I could scream.

Kat's eyes roll back slightly as she takes another swig. The bottle slips from her fingers, whiskey splashing across the keyboard.

The screen goes black.

CHAPTER 21

Maddie,

My masterpiece is about to begin, and you're still fumbling in the dark. Pathetic.

Don't you want to know what I'm looking at right now?

A building.

Not just any building.

Does it have a basement? Oh, wouldn't you like to know.

Did you know your cage sisters used to tell me their dreams? Such curious dreams—light bulbs floating in darkness, holes in ceilings, and always, always that watching eye beyond the hole—an eye with pupils that dilated like a camera lens adjusting its focus.

Poor, stupid girls.

Want to know what I told them? They dreamed of a modern god. This god is a digital deity that watches through screens and wires—a judgmental god who punishes sinners and rewards saints for the smallest things—the god that turns nobodies into somebodies overnight.

They didn't believe me, of course. But that's society's little game, *isn't it? I lie. You pretend to believe. We all avoid responsibility. If we pretend not to see evil, we never have to stop it, do we?*

My mind wanders today. That happens when the headache takes a holiday. When my brain isn't being split in two, the thoughts come so clearly.

Wondering why no headache today?

I'm happy, Maddie.

Why?

Listen to you—so many questions—like a child discovering the world is made of "whys."

I'll tell you while I walk toward her—my new Cuckoo—so perfect —my cage practically sings her name.

But you never read my letters anyway, so who cares.

Tick-tock, Maddie—time's not on your side this time.

CHAPTER 22

By the time I pull the bottle from Kat's hands, half the bottle is gone. She gulped it down in one long drink. It burned through her thin, sixty-year-old body, and the burn shows in her face.

I put the bottle away and sit next to her in front of the screen.

"Look," she points at the search results. "Dozens of buyers last month."

I'm not sure if we can narrow it to two weeks. I stay quiet so I don't waste time.

"It's a high-end tripod," She still sounds sober. I guess the alcohol hasn't hit her fully. "So the purchases are fewer than normal—only forty-three in New York—that is, if he didn't use an out-of-state purchase."

Smart move—but not one we have time to chase. If he did it that way, I have no clues for at least forty-eight hours—something tells me I don't have that time frame.

"Look for cash purchases, please."

"I know my job, Alice," she starts fidgeting more, and her excitement is wearing off a little. "Three cash purchases. You know what to look for next?"

She gives me a sharp look. I force a smile. "If you kindly read me the names, I might find a clue."

"It's not the names, Alice," Kat coughs. "Don't make me teach you how to be a good detective."

"I'm sorry?" I really don't know what she's talking about.

"I don't even need to search further. I have the killer's name in front of me."

I stand up, but she does too, blocking my view. "You have to think first."

"Kat," I beg her. "I need that name—now—please."

"You need to know the game, Alice—that's what you need." Her hands sway. The booze is kicking in now.

"What game?" I want to shove her aside and look at the name she found. But what if I upset her and she's wrong? It'll take forever to sober her up.

"The game you're playing," Kat winces. "The game they're playing."

"I don't have time for this, Kat—please show me the name."

"They played the same game with me—and I'm a damn good forensic, Alice," she slips through my hands onto the floor.

"Kat!" I kneel next to her. "I need you awake right now."

Kat is still conscious, but she's not on this planet. I know it well—I've been there too many times—memories come back—half-memories—stained with guilt and injustice—I can't let her doze off.

I kneel down again and slap her on the face. Crazy only begets crazy.

"Stop crying, Kat! I know how it feels," I lean close to her ear.

"You don't know shit," she spits out and hiccups, then stops crying all of a sudden. "You know that killing him won't fix you, right?"

"I've heard that before, Kat," I say. I had, many times in therapy. "Just give me the password—I want to find the Comedian's name and catch him at last."

"You've always been mad, Alice," she smiles wickedly, or sarcastically, I have no idea. "You know what you missed, right? It's not the 'paid in cash' part—it's the fact that of those who paid in cash, someone bought four tripods at once."

She's right—how did I miss that? I watch her hunch over the desk and type in her password—the screen lights up my face.

"Thank you, Kat," I kiss her on the forehead and help lower her back to the floor. God only knows what she has been through, and why Johnson kicked her out of the force. "I'll come back to visit—after I catch him."

"It's not a him, Alice." Her words send chills down my back. "Why do you think they wore a mask?"

"What are you saying, Kat?"

"The killer is a woman."

CHAPTER 23

Yo Maddie! ('Dear' sounds so nineties, right?)

I'm sending you a text this time—no pen, no paper—just digital words in our digital world.

But I won't hit send. You never read these anyway.

She's in my car right now—it was so easy—too easy.

The old ways were dumb. I used to watch them for days, learn their habits, plan every move.

But the internet changed things. Not the happy internet. The dark part. The shadows. Where sick people share secrets.

They'll do anything for money—track anyone—study their lives—report every detail.

I used to wait outside universities at night. Smart girls were always my target—I'd follow them down empty streets—a quick hit or a cloth with drugs—whatever worked.

Six years changed everything—taught me better tricks.

Now I wear the perfect mask. People trust me fast. You wouldn't believe how easy it is, Maddie.

My new girl is nineteen—perfect age—much better than Ivy Williams.

She's sitting next to me, talking like we're friends. She doesn't know we're going the wrong way.

One wrong turn in New York—that's all it takes.

Heaven turns to hell fast here. Dark places hide on every street. No one wants to see the broken or the lost.

People stay blind. Phones. Music. Movies. Anything to ignore the dark.

But I love the cracks. They're beautiful to me. Like cocoons ready to change.

I should go. She thinks I'm texting my boyfriend. Sweet, right?

Little does she know, tonight I'm gonna slay.

CHAPTER 24

My eyes refuse to read the killer's name on the screen.

It can't be a woman.

I don't know why I find it hard to believe, but evidence is evidence.

My breath hitches as I finally squint and read the name: **Poppy Taylor**.

What kind of name is Poppy? Who names their kid that now?

I wonder if it's fake. But the search results show a clear record.

Poppy bought four tripods from a store near Manhattan exactly three weeks ago.

She paid in full with cash. No delivery. No third-party pickup.

She even left a note explaining she was a YouTuber with a history of buying similar equipment.

I can't believe she's a YouTuber. I also don't get why she'd leave a note, though some stores do ask when you pay cash for big purchases.

I search online. No YouTuber named Poppy Taylor shows up.

I search again, wondering if Poppy is a boy's name too. Nothing.

Then I check social media. Still nothing that fits.

Poppy could be a nickname. Maybe she's a Penelope, Paige, Phoebe—anything.

The cashier probably didn't check her ID. Just took her word for it.

She must've had a big car, someone helping her, or maybe just called an Uber.

My mind is spinning with assumptions I don't need.

Am I afraid to arrest her? Or just afraid to see the Comedian's real face?

I exhale and quickly snap a screenshot of Kat's screen for evidence.

Kat is still on the floor behind me, barely awake. Her body is heavy with exhaustion.

I crouch beside her.

"Kat, let me help you to the couch."

Her eyes open, but they don't focus.

"You have to leave. Go get her."

I can't tell if she means Poppy or Johnson. Then a chill runs through me.

Is this my future? Will I end up like Kat—bitter, drunk, and alone with my obsessions?

My heart tightens. I squeeze her hand and thank her again.

"Don't thank me," Kat says with a dry, humorless chuckle.

"Just trust nobody."

It's a long overdue lesson.

I get up fast and rush down the stairs, skipping steps as I go.

Out on the street, I run toward the Camry.

The shadows in Brownsville seem to shift around me.

Guess word spreads fast when a city girl lingers too long.

The car is where Rush left it, but it's locked.

Rush is gone.

A group of men loiters nearby. Tattoos coil down their arms. Pants hang low. Hoods are up.

They look me over from head to toe.

They're not just passing time. They're waiting for something to happen.

I'm in the wrong place.

Where the hell did Rush go?

CHAPTER 25

I avoid the men's gaze and glance left and right, searching for Rush.

All I see is more trouble in my peripheral vision. I have my gun under my jacket, but something tells me not to cause a scene. I need to arrest Poppy before she kills another girl.

I hold a steady, challenging gaze as my fingers tighten around my phone. I start to dial Rush's number, but before I can press the call button, a man steps in front of me. He's tall, broad, and smells like sweat.

"Well, well," he says. "Here for a good time, pretty girl?"

I keep my face unreadable. "Step aside."

"Feisty." He twitches his nose and cheeks. "What brings a cool city girl to the neighborhood? I bet it's drugs, huh?" He nods toward Kat's building. I assume there's some dealer upstairs.

"Those drug dealers get all the pretty city girls, man," another one says.

I could take them down. I know how. But I stay still.

It's not because I'm scared. I just don't want to. Or maybe I can't.

That's my biggest flaw. The one Homer asked about in the

Camry. I've avoided physical fights ever since I gave someone a concussion in that bar six years ago.

I told myself it wouldn't affect my work, but it does. My excuse is weak: I could probably hurt you badly, but I don't want to live with the guilt afterward.

"I said, move aside," I repeat. "I'm a cop."

"No, you're not."

"I have the badge right in my pocket." I could pull it out, but I can't move. My whole body is frozen.

The man leans in close. To avoid touching him, I tilt my head away. All I see now is the Comedian's mask. I can't move. I can't defend myself.

Oh, but you know that's not true, Maddie. That voice again. You know you can't hurt anyone after what you did. It's not just the guy at the bar. Your secrets are eating you alive.

"Let me pull that badge out for you, pretty girl." He reaches for it.

That's when my hands finally react. I grip his wrist hard enough to surprise him and lock eyes with him.

I'm tangled in emotion. If I let my anger out, I might really hurt him.

With the bars of that cage closing in around me, I don't see him anymore. I don't even see the Comedian.

I see the crushed skull of a man who once touched me in a bar.

It wasn't just a concussion. I crushed his head with a heavy barstool. I remember everything now.

"She is stronger than you, ha!" one of them jeers.

That's not good. I see the anger in his eyes. Mine are hard as steel. I silently beg him not to do it. I don't have time for this. I need to arrest the Comedian.

"Maddie!" Rush appears from nowhere. "Are you okay?"

He points his gun at the man and his crew. His stance is off—like he's not sure whether to shoot or break into dance.

Somehow, it works. When Rush gives in to his anxiety, he looks completely unhinged.

"Easy, man!" the guy says, raising his hands. "I was just taking care of your chick until you got back."

"She is my girl, yes!" Rush throws himself into the role. "Right, Maddie?"

I'm not sure why he's suddenly calling me by my first name, but I don't question it. I take a breath and nod. "But of course."

Rush's smile stretches across his face. I don't know if he's thrilled by the girlfriend act or the rush of waving a gun around.

I grab him by the belt and slip my fingers into his pocket. His eyes go wide.

"Don't flatter yourself, Mr. boyfriend. I just need the keys. I'm driving this time."

It's finally time to arrest the Comedian.

CHAPTER 26

I drive like a maniac through the streets, making Rush worry.

He keeps asking to drive, but I'm more worried about the broken GPS. It's just another issue with this old Camry. I don't know why the department keeps me isolated. Maybe they never wanted me to crack this case.

I order Officer Rush to look up Poppy's address: 888 Hamilton Estates, Penthouse A, New York, NY.

"The killer lives in Hamilton Estates?" Rush sounds confused.

"What's strange about that?"

"It's a gated community for the rich."

"You're talking as if people with money don't kill." I grip the wheel tighter, not having driven this recklessly in years.

"Well, there's money," Rush rubs his forefinger and thumb together, "And there's F**k You money."

I know the expression, but I still don't get why he's so rattled. "A killer is a killer, Officer. Stop talking and give me the directions."

"It's not about that, Detective." Rush mutters. He seems more bothered by her address than the fact we're flying through traffic. "First of all, you need an arrest warrant."

"I know that!" I snap. They all know we won't get a warrant. The evidence comes from an ex-forensic specialist working off the books. This isn't by-the-book police work. It's messy and unofficial. Exactly what Johnson warned me against.

"I'm glad you do," Rush says, nodding for me to turn left. "But even if you barge your way in, the guards won't let you through."

"Let them try," I mutter.

I know I'm being reckless. Probably insane. But nothing will stop me from looking the Comedian in the eyes and bringing her to justice. Badge or no badge.

"Maddie," Rush stammers, voice shaky but earnest. He's looking at me, trying to catch my attention. He even dares to call me by my first name. "Did I tell you my first name is Gregory?"

"What the hell are you saying?"

"I'm trying to make you listen to me. Please look at me as if I'm your friend. I know it's inappropriate to call you Maddie, but I'm worried for you."

His sudden, unexpected change of tone has my attention now. I glance at him, risking the road ahead.

"There are important people in this city," he says. "I think you should wait for Johnson. Otherwise, you'll lose your job."

His shift throws me. Is this the real Rush? Was the twitchy, awkward officer just an act? Or is this calm, concerned version the performance?

Maybe Johnson never sent him to help me at all. Maybe his only job was to watch me. Report back. Keep me from getting too close.

I want to question him, but the words die in my throat.

Looking at him now, all I see is an obstacle between me and the Comedian. A voice urging me to let her slip away.

Not this time.

I slam the brakes so hard the seatbelt cuts into my chest. A horn blares behind us—someone nearly hit us. I don't care.

The impact throws me forward, then snaps me back like a rag doll.

"Get out!" I scream at Rush, who suddenly realizes there are more anxious people in the world than just him.

"Maddie, you can't just—" Rush starts, panic rising in his voice. "You're a detective, for God's sake!"

"I'm done playing by the rules. Not when she's out there."

He doesn't even try to argue further. He just fumbles with his seatbelt and tumbles onto the street.

A man from another car pounds on my window, spittle flying as he curses me out for stopping. I don't care. I don't have time for his road rage when there's a killer out there.

I floor it, leaving Rush and the chaos behind in a screech of burning rubber.

Sometimes you have to destroy things to save others.

Like my career, apparently.

CHAPTER 27

With trembling fingers, I pull out my phone and grip the wheel with the other hand. Hamilton Estates is close.

If my phone is ringing, I can't hear it. If the police are chasing me, I can't see them. And if I'm bleeding or hurt, I don't feel it at all.

As I approach Hamilton Estates, my heart races. I don't think I can properly speak to anyone right now. I know I'll face resistance from security, and I don't know what I'm going to do about it.

I look down the street and don't see traffic or asphalt. Instead, I see six years of frustration rolling past me. I'm close to the final revelation.

I stop the car at the Hamilton gates. I roll down the window and pant, "I'm here for Poppy Taylor."

The burly six-foot guard in his forties peers down at me. "Poppy? Do you have the penthouse number?"

I reach for my badge, but it's missing. I groan in frustration.

"I'm Detective Brooks, NYPD. Let me in."

"You mean Penelope, daughter of Mr. Alexander Taylor?"

Rush was right about Poppy's wealthy background. The guard

mentions her father first. He doesn't even flinch when I say I'm a detective.

"Yes, that's her," I say. "Tell Mr. Alexander I want to see her."

"And you are?"

"I just told you. Detective Brooks." None of this is by the book, and I don't even know what I'm doing. In a perfect world, I'd already be driving the Camry straight through the gate.

"You don't look like a detective to me."

"What did you say?" I'm about to pull out my badge when he reaches for his gun. He doesn't draw it—just a warning.

"I'm afraid that's not enough to let you in. I'll need to see an arrest warrant."

"Calm down," I say, raising both hands in the air, glancing sideways at the gate's camera. What if he's just crazy? Or this city really is corrupt to the bone?

"I thought so." He frowns at my silence and pushes his luck, pointing the gun at me. "I can't let you in. Hamilton Estates values the privacy and security of its residents. Now please drive away and make way."

I clench my fists, frustration boiling inside me. I have to play every card. I don't have time for this mess.

I'm just worried that a killer teen from a powerful family might be slipping away. They've probably seen my car on their security feed by now.

"How about you kindly ask if I could speak to Mr. Alexander Taylor himself?" I try to soften my voice. "I have serious allegations against his daughter and would like to clear them up. I'm only worried about Poppy's safety and would love to help if I can."

It strikes me as odd when I see the guard's face soften. Maybe that's how it works. Rich people are used to people changing their tone as long as you show the right respect.

"You'll need to call someone above your pay grade, Detective, if you want me to let you in," he says. "I don't have the authority to call

Mr. Taylor directly anyway. A maid would answer my call, then she'd have to talk to a couple of other people—if they even think it's important."

I can't calm down. My head tilts forward, watching the gate. My foot taps like it wants to stomp the gas. My knuckles are white on the wheel.

"Don't do that, please," the guard says, strangely sincere. "The gate won't budge anyway."

"You tried?" I raise an eyebrow, trying to inject sarcasm into the situation.

"I don't drive," he says with a suppressed laugh. Nice to know we're both just doing our jobs.

"And I've never seen anyone crazy enough to give it a shot."

He wins me over with that one.

"I'm crazy," I say with a smile. "But even I don't feel like doing it."

He lets a smile break through. "I appreciate your honesty. I'm sure if you call the right people, you'll get inside, Detective."

I nod and check my phone. To my surprise, Johnson has been calling. A lot. I didn't realize I'd put her on mute.

I pick up.

"Did you do something stupid, Kiddo?"

"Not yet," I say, eyes still locked on the gate.

"Pity. A public screw-up would've made it easier to pull you off the case."

Her raw honesty almost wins me over, too. What is with everyone knowing exactly what to say today?

"Rush told me all about this Poppy Taylor," she says.

"I thought he would."

"Have enough evidence to warrant her arrest, or am I going to waste my time coming over?"

"Indisputable evidence," I say, swallowing hard. "Though I obtained it without permission."

"We'll discuss your rogue behavior later. Stay where you are. I'm coming."

"Okay."

"And Kiddo?" Her final words twist the knife.

"Don't you dare talk to the press before I arrive."

CHAPTER 28

Twenty minutes later, Johnson's SUV stops beside my car. The engine purrs like a satisfied beast. Two men occupy the back seat—not cops, not in uniform. Just shadows behind tinted glass.

Johnson beckons me to the passenger seat.

"No police backup?" I slide in, the leather seat cool against my back.

"We're civilians today." Johnson's voice carries that familiar mix of silk and steel. "The NYPD isn't knocking on Taylor family doors—not yet."

Corruption has a smell—cologne, cigar smoke, and polished leather. I breathe it in, steadying myself.

Just breathe. Get inside. Find Poppy. Arrest her—Johnson be damned.

"The Taylors are old friends." Johnson keeps her eyes on the road ahead. "Alexander Taylor owns most of New York's cloud data servers."

"Including NYPD's data?"

Her smile tightens. "Smart girl. Now you see why they don't get police visits without an ironclad case."

"I have all the evidence on my phone—"

"It's useless, trust me. If any half-decent lawyer finds out how you obtained it, you have no case. I looked into it—I've got everything on my phone too."

"You made Kat give it to you?"

"Kat's drowning in alcohol, like usual. Rush sent it to me."

"How did he get it? I didn't give it to him."

"He broke into Kat's house after you kicked him out of your car."

"So we're not different after all. You ordered him to break in without a warrant."

She just smiles—as if she'd ever admit we both do what we have to.

"Here's a piece of advice, kiddo." She taps my thigh like a general giving orders with a smile, then mouths without speaking: *"If you're going to do something wrong, do it really well."*

I'm not sure what she means. Is she implying I can break the law as long as she doesn't know about it? I glance at the backseat shadows.

"And who are they?"

"That one's a cop. That one's press." She jabs her manicured finger at each one without turning around.

"Of course. Press."

"I've arranged two squad cars around the corner. If you're right about Poppy, they'll come arrest her."

"You don't say."

"Don't get clever, kiddo. If she's guilty, she's going down. I just don't need some trust fund lawyer breathing down my neck until retirement, making me wish I'd picked a career in tax evasion."

Johnson drives toward the gate.

The guard who blocked me earlier watches us pass. His eyes slide right through me now.

It's like I never existed.

CHAPTER 29

The driveway winds past pristine hedges. Johnson checks her lipstick and straightens her blazer in the rearview mirror.

This isn't just a villa—it's a monument to wealth. I ignore the sprawl of luxury and zero in on the marble stairs and the double oak doors waiting at the top.

A maid answers our knock. Her black and white uniform is crisp as paper. Her gaze slides from my wrinkled jacket to Johnson's immaculate suit.

"Commissioner," she bobs her head. "Are you here for Mr. or Mrs. Taylor?"

"Either would be lovely." Johnson's voice drips honey. "Though if they're occupied, I can return."

"Is Poppy here?" I cut through their country club waltz.

The maid's spine stiffens. "Only friends call her Poppy. Are you a friend?"

"She's with me, Carmen," Johnson slides in like oil on water. "Is Victoria—"

"Sara!" A woman's cry splits the air. I almost forgot Johnson's first name is Sara. I haven't seen anyone on a first-name basis with her until now.

Victoria Taylor appears at the top of the stairs, her Chanel suit wrinkled like she slept in it. Not what I expected. Her mascara runs in black rivers down pale cheeks like she's been crying for hours.

She throws herself into Johnson's arms. "Thank God."

Whatever show they're pulling, I'm not taking the bait. I try to peek past them, through the foyer and up the stairs, looking for movement. For evidence. For escape routes.

"What happened?" Johnson catches Victoria in her arms.

Alexander Taylor appears, clutching his phone like a drowning man's rope. His salt-and-pepper hair is wild, and his five-thousand-dollar suit is creased at the sleeves.

"I've called everyone. Every contact I have."

The words hit sideways. Is this a father's panic—or did he just admit to orchestrating his daughter's escape? That phone could've reached a lot of people who make problems disappear.

"Poppy's gone." His voice splinters. Unlike his wife and the maid, he meets my eyes directly. "She went to shoot photos in Bedford-Stuyvesant yesterday. That rough neighborhood near Brownsville."

"It was for a photography class," Victoria chokes out. "I told her not to go."

Brownsville. That's where Kat lives. Was Poppy watching me this whole time? Following me? Playing both sides?

"Poppy always calls me during the day. Sometimes five times or more to let me know she's okay." Alexander swipes at his phone screen. "Then nothing since yesterday."

"Why would she call you this much, Alexander, if I may ask?" Johnson's voice softens with curiosity.

"She met this friend a month ago," Victoria's words slice through my thoughts. "Wouldn't tell us about him. Said he understands her like no one else does." Her voice breaks. "I think... I think he kidnapped her."

A month ago. Right when she bought the tripods.

"Why didn't you call me?" Johnson asks, while my knees threaten to give out. I don't believe a word they're saying.

But who could fake it this well?

"We thought we'd wait a little. It was my idea," Alexander avoids Victoria's accusing gaze. "She is nineteen, Sara. Girls get wild sometimes. She could have been in Cancun, for all I know."

"But you knew about this friend, Alexander!" Victoria snaps. "I told you we had to know who he is."

"Stop it, Victoria." Alexander holds out his phone toward Johnson. "I was about to call you now. Look what I've received from her phone just an hour ago."

I step closer to look. Alexander shows it to me too. "Just this, and then her phone went dead."

A single message glows on the screen. The blue bubble contains just three words:

Help me...

My stomach drops. The room tilts. For a moment, I can't breathe.
The cages. The tripods. The cameras. The recordings.
It all slides into focus with sickening clarity.
I came here hunting a killer.
But Poppy Taylor isn't the Comedian.
She's his next victim.

CHAPTER 30

Maddie, my only friend,

I'm writing this from the new basement. It's spacious and dark—just the way I like it. It has everything I need for my masterpiece.

And I, the greatest Comedian of all, laugh at you while I write this.

Do you know what comedy really is, Maddie? It's laughing at someone else's pain.

Oh, this human race. So beautifully broken. So deliciously tragic. I adore it.

Don't get me wrong. Laughter can be medicine—unless someone's laughing at you. And I'm laughing at you, Detective.

Poppy didn't have to buy those tripods in cash or use her real name, but I made her. Just a little touch of genius—my signature.

Did your eyes light up when you went to arrest her? I can picture it perfectly. Hope flashing across your face. That desperate fire burning in your gut. You wanted to look into my real eyes. You wanted to cry in my arms.

Admit it, Maddie. You wanted it.

I know more about you than the police ever will. You and I, girl—

cut from the same cloth. Those secrets you can't tell them. Can't even whisper to your reflection.

But don't worry. Failure is just one step closer to closure. That slap in the face? Oh, I know—it stings. But pain is part of the transformation.

And I'm not heartless, Maddie. I left you more clues.

This time, forget the evidence. Trust your gut.

Because every artist needs a fan.

And you're my biggest fan—the same way I'm yours. You just don't know it yet.

Now excuse me. Sweet Poppy Taylor is ready for her money shot.

CHAPTER 31

Back in the Yellow, the fluorescent lights flicker overhead while the coffee machine gurgles. The sounds match the furious pressure building in my skull.

My six-star, underground accommodation comes with premium water features. The leaky pipes create a calming sound that no pricey meditation app can match.

I swallow back tears. I never cry in front of anyone. Johnson's voice cuts through the static of the phone.

"The killer calls himself the Comedian. He knows how to blend in, earn trust, claims to be a photographer. Real or just bait, we don't know. He's the type women feel comfortable talking to. The man neighbors always describe as 'seemed so normal.'"

It's a solid read on him. But this shift to charm in his personality scares me. If he could charm his way in, why spend years hunting in shadows? Maybe, as Homer suggested, the Comedian vanished all these years because he evolved. That's what he said in his letter.

How do you catch a killer whose personality changed this much?

The coffee machine gurgles, probably plotting my murder. Given my track record with identifying killers, it's probably innocent.

Back at the mansion, I urged Alexander to track Poppy's dead phone. He owns the biggest data cloud company in New York, so he should be able to help. He dodged the issue. Instead, he tossed around fancy words about untraceable privacy software on her phone. Even he can't crack it, he claims.

He owns half the city's servers, but can't track one phone Please.

If I believed that, he'd probably try selling me the Brooklyn Bridge next. At a special detective's discount.

When I asked why a father would lock his daughter's phone, he quickly gave his reason. He said his family is at risk for blackmail because of his job. Everyone in this city keeps their story crisp and ready for display.

I took a different approach. I asked Officer Johnson to see if any cops saw Poppy near Kat's building while I was there. The Comedian showing up in that neighborhood wasn't random. It was choreographed. Now I can't shake the feeling he's watching me, turning my every move into his next scene.

I trust no one in this case anymore. Not the killer, not the victims, not their families, and not even the cops at the door.

"Oh, no, the Comedian is not a woman," Johnson keeps explaining to the deputies on the phone. "That's Detective Brooks' fault. She got it all wrong. It's her first individual case, you know."

Nice. I've been upgraded from incompetent to merely mistaken. Progress. I should add this to my résumé: Detective Brooks. Slightly better than expected.

I feel like I want the basement to swallow me whole. But how deep into the earth can I hide when I live in a basement six feet under already? Even the dripping faucet feels calmer than this disaster of a case.

I stand up, shaking off my helplessness, and head to the bathroom. On my way, I wonder if the NYPD was as keen to find a killer who took the five nobodies, including me, six years ago.

Poppy Taylor. A rich girl? Is that why the Comedian picked you?

Something tells me he wants all eyes on him this time. This won't end well.

I fight the urge to scream and pull my hair. I lock myself in the bathroom and listen to Johnson's muffled voice outside.

I stare at my reflection, uneasy, then splash cold water over my face. When I look up, the mirror's fogged, and suddenly I don't see the present me anymore. I'm seeing myself six years ago, trapped in that basement. The memories I've buried. The truth I can't admit.

How can a detective who can't remember her real personality catch a killer?

What if I'm not just a victim? What if I'm as guilty as the Comedian?

Or worse. What if he rewired my brain, and I'm just his puppet on strings, dancing exactly how he wants me to?

I look just like I feel. Like someone who chased the wrong suspect for two days, living on regret and vending machine crackers.

Johnson's voice suddenly fades away. I fear she's left without discussing recent events or what I want to do next to catch the Comedian.

But wait. She's still here, on the phone now with Sam, her husband.

"No, I can't," she says, her voice drifting down. "No, she doesn't know."

The words hit like ice.

I ease the door open when her voice grows distant. She's moved up to the alley. I quickly put my phone under the basement kitchen's only window. It's where concrete meets pavement above. I lean in to hear her words to Sam. I used to care about privacy. That was before all this.

My detective skills have devolved—from hunting serial killers to eavesdropping on my boss.

I freeze as a shadow falls across me.

"We need to talk."

I spin around.

Johnson watches me. Her eyes are hard as stones.

CHAPTER 32

I stand tense at the kitchen sink. I know I'm being foolish. My stress will give me away. Johnson's footsteps are silent as usual. I just hope she didn't see me set my phone to record.

"Maddie," Johnson says, using my name for the first time. "I want you off the case."

I saw this coming. Johnson has reasons to fire me. I've broken rules. But she's not innocent. Her careless handling of the crime scene shows she doesn't care. Also, her dismissive attitude shows that catching the Comedian isn't her main concern. I could go to the press with what I know. Maybe that's why she's being nice instead of ordering me out. So I fire back.

"If I hadn't used Kat behind your back, we wouldn't know about Poppy, Commissioner. Taking me off now isn't smart."

"Don't justify your disobedience," she says. "Poppy's parents would have reported her missing anyway."

"Would they?" I meet her eyes, searching for any flicker of doubt. "They don't seem the type to me. If they were so concerned, why didn't they report the suspicious man she met? Or that she suddenly stopped her five daily check-ins? And what nineteen-year-old calls her father five times every day, anyway?"

Johnson shakes her head, burying her hands deeper in her expensive coat.

"You're a mess," she says flatly. "Everything is a mess. These people have their reasons. Not everything fits your conspiracy theories."

She looks at me like I'm something she found stuck to her shoe.

"You're not even half the detective you think you are."

"Yeah?" I brush off the insults. Dealing with Johnson toughens you up quickly. "Even if they reported her missing later, how would you know it was the Comedian who took her?"

I step forward, pressing my point. "And how would you have learned about the tripods, about him filming the girls? That he befriends his victims before taking them? That he's someone we'd normally trust? Above all, that he made Poppy buy those tripods under her name a month ago, leaving me a clue to his identity?"

"You mean leaving you breadcrumbs to nowhere." Johnson's voice rises. "I told you he's using you. His letter said he wants you to try to catch him one last time and fail."

I take another step forward. "Why can't you ever give me credit for my work?" Another step. Fury drives me now. "Or is it because this time you couldn't claim it for yourself, Commissioner? Or should I call you Sara? Because I'm rich and you're my friend—not the law to me?"

If I'm getting fired, I might as well burn every bridge on my way out.

"Stop talking. Stop moving. And listen," Johnson holds up her hand like a traffic cop.

She takes a deep breath. Something shifts in her eyes. Not softness exactly, but a glimpse behind the mask.

"Some cases we can't solve, Maddie. Some killers we can't catch. It's not that we don't try, but we're not built to grasp that kind of darkness."

She glances at the rusted filing cabinet in the corner.

"That cabinet holds the ghosts we couldn't put to rest. The monsters we couldn't cage."

Johnson's voice drops lower.

"You looked into his eyes, Maddie. You breathed his air. He got inside you somehow. I see it when you work. You don't follow rules because, deep down, you don't think like us anymore."

I don't step back, but I stop advancing.

"You're stuck between two worlds. Not fully a cop, not fully a killer. You understand him in ways we can't, and that makes you dangerous—especially to yourself."

Her words cut deeper than I want to admit.

"Go back to med school. Be a doctor. Save lives instead of chasing what almost took yours."

"I know I don't play by the book," I say, the words escaping before I can stop them. "But he wrote that letter for me. And like you said, only I came this close to him. I can catch him, Commissioner."

Johnson shakes her head. I'm a hopeless case to her. She turns and walks away. Then, she stops at the stairs but doesn't look back. I hold my breath, hoping she'll say more. The moment feels like six years of darkness.

Then she speaks the word everyone thinks.

"You can stay," she says, and I hear her gulp. That doesn't sound like her. "But you have to tell me what really happened in that basement six years ago."

I feel like I might faint. Her words send me to a world I never want to visit again.

"I thought so," she says, shaking her head again when I don't speak. "You're fired."

And without another word, she slams the heavy basement door behind her.

CHAPTER 33

SIX YEARS AGO...

I can't see clearly. Everything is a blur. The drugs rush through my veins. A bad headache makes everything smear like watercolors soaked in rain. I can see the basement door. It's open—just a crack—but that's enough.

I crawl on all fours. My limbs feel heavy and strange, like they don't belong to me.

Behind me, I hear screaming—girls' voices blending together.

"Maddie, no! Please, no!"

The words are confusing and clear at the same time. I think I understand, but my mind won't let me figure it out. It won't let me admit it to myself.

I keep crawling. The concrete scrapes my elbows raw. My knees leak hot blood, but I barely notice.

The sliver of light from the door grows closer. Is it freedom? Escape? I can't tell anymore.

"Maddie, don't do it, please!" a girl shrieks behind me.

I try to count—were there four of us? Three? Did one die yesterday? Was it two girls? My memories flutter away like startled birds when I reach for them.

My head feels heavy. Foam drips from my mouth onto the floor. I push myself forward. Every inch feels like a marathon.

Here I come. I can't do this anymore. I need to leave this darkness.

"Maddie, no!"

I don't know if I'm going to do it—but I know I can never tell.

CHAPTER 34

I wake up suddenly, the screams of those girls echoing in my ears.

My head spins with questions: lies dressed as truth and truth hidden behind lies.

I want to call Homer, and that scares me. Why do I need him now?

He understood the Comedian better than anyone, but something feels off. Maybe even dangerous.

Johnson's words ring in my head, along with the slam of the door and its finality.

Was she really taking me off the case, or was this a test?

I could have told her what happened six years ago, but would she have kept me on?

I need to focus. I need to prioritize.

The clock is ticking on my badge. What must I do before they strip it away?

The answer lies in Johnson's words. The Taylors had reasons for not calling the police earlier.

What reasons?

A father checking on his daughter five times a day is not protection. It is surveillance.

A rich girl buying camera gear and sneaking into rough neighborhoods is not rebellion. It is something else.

The Taylors are hiding something. Something big enough to risk their daughter's life rather than call the police.

Whatever it is, my chance to find out fades the moment Johnson makes my removal official.

I rush out of the Yellow and slide into the Camry.

It is still my car, at least for now.

Thirty minutes later, I arrive at Hamilton Estate. Lorenzo, the guard from before, is at the gate again. His eyes look different this time. He tells me he gave me his name earlier, but I can't remember. My memory gaps might be worsening. I need to see my therapist when I have time.

I am glad no one has told him I am off the case yet.

"The first time you came, I didn't know Poppy was kidnapped," he says, waving me in easily. "She's important to us all. A special girl."

"How so?" I ask, squinting to read his face. Lorenzo gives me a look I don't fully understand.

"You better let her parents tell you."

Definitely a suspect.

The driveway feels different now. It feels less like a fortress and more like a path to answers. I wonder how the Comedian managed to cross paths with Poppy. Is he rich? Powerful enough to get close to her?

The maid opens the door. Her eyes are cold as ice.

Of course. She is a suspect too.

Just before she speaks, Alexander Taylor appears behind her.

"Detective," he says, shaking my hand politely. I struggle to find my words. Something about him feels different. He seems more composed. Was his nervousness earlier just an act?

"Any news about Poppy?"

"Actually, no. But I have questions," I reply with a shrug. "About Poppy."

Victoria suddenly appears, right in my face.

She looks like she hasn't slept since I saw her. She has definitely been crying since I last saw her.

"We're the ones with questions! Where is my daughter? Who kidnapped her? Is it true he's a serial killer?"

Her questions crash over me, and I have no answers. Now I see why people like Johnson turn cold-hearted. Did she have to deal with moments like this when she was younger?

But I am not Johnson. The Taylors think I am just doing my job. They do not realize how much I want to save Poppy.

"Better another time, Detective," Alexander says, pulling Victoria close. The maid looks eager to shut the door in my face.

I catch the edge of the door and look into both of their eyes.

"Look," I say, taking a deep breath, "I'm not just a detective." My face twitches. My toes curl. "I was the killer's victim six years ago."

It takes longer than I expected for them to process it. At first, it seems like they don't believe me, especially the maid. People see my face and assume I'm strong and put together. I often have to remind them that is not true.

Finally, Alexander opens the door fully.

Victoria's anger fades. For the first time, she really sees me. Not as a detective. Not as an intruder. But as someone's daughter. Some-one's victim.

She wraps her arms around me before I can step back.

I don't like being touched unless I have clearly signaled that I want to be.

But it has been years since anyone held me like this. Like a mother would. Like mine never got the chance to. I think I like it, but I do not want to cry.

"Maybe we should show you her studio," Alexander says softly. "It will give you a better idea of who my daughter is."

CHAPTER 35

The studio sprawls across the entire top floor. As Alexander fumbles with the keys, Victoria wraps her arm around my shoulders. It feels like she is afraid I might disappear next.

The space beyond the door takes my breath away. Three walls of windows flood the room with light, but the arrangement feels strangely controlled. Expensive cameras sit in perfect order. Post-it notes cover every surface—some fresh and others faded with age. There are lists, ideas, and quotes about transformation, along with several calendars marking the same events over and over.

It's uncannily similar to how I'd arrange my own space.

"She has a system," Victoria says quietly. "Everything has to be in its place. When it's not, she spirals."

I understand completely. The room screams of someone trying to control the chaos inside them.

A psychology textbook lies open on her desk, with sticky notes sprouting from its pages like weeds. Next to it, photography magazines are dog-eared and worn. The contrast hits me.

"She was brilliant at psychology," Alexander says, his voice a mix of pride and pain. "Full scholarship to Columbia."

Victoria walks toward a wall of black-and-white portraits. "Until last semester, she focused on something else," she says. "Now, photography is her passion." The portraits are all of women, each with haunted eyes. "Psychology was just to fix her dad," she adds with a brittle laugh. "Just a little joke."

Alexander's jaw tightens.

I glance at him. I will not pretend I do not notice the tension, but I will not jump to conclusions either. I wonder if her fixation on older men has anything to do with him.

Focus, Maddie. Follow the evidence. The truth, not your assumptions. If you had done that sooner, you would have known the Comedian was not a woman.

"But photography," Victoria says, brushing one of the portraits with her fingers. "She said it captured the truth, especially in places people usually look away from."

"The underbelly," Alexander adds. "That's what she called it."

"Underbelly?" I repeat. Poppy reminds me of the girls who were in the cage with me. At some point, we all realized we had specific passions. None of us was shallow or directionless. Why did I never mention that to the police?

"Homeless shelters. Addiction clinics. Places like that," Victoria adds. There is pride in her voice.

"Places where I had to send bodyguards to collect her," Alexander mutters.

"She wanted to show their humanity, Alexander," Victoria replies. Her response is practiced. It is an old argument.

"Peru last summer. Brooklyn's worst neighborhoods this fall. Always with that camera. Always chasing her 'authentic moments.'"

"All of it stopped when she met him," Victoria says. Her voice drops. "Someone who finally understood her vision."

"You mean someone who knew how to spend my money," Alexander says bitterly. "Three weeks of equipment deliveries. Professional lighting. Multiple cameras."

"I know the police searched the studio and found no trace of him," I say, "but did she ever describe him? Did she say where he lived or how they met?"

"I tried asking. She kept him a secret. She said he was different and that Alexander would scare him off, like the others."

So this was not the first time Poppy had been drawn to older men. I worry I am projecting my own issues. I am like her. But I never get taken anywhere. I am the one who drags people into the rabbit hole of my mind.

I wonder if Ivy Williams shared those traits. Profiling the Comedian may not lead to his capture, but understanding the kind of girls he targets might.

"The other men never changed her like this one did," Victoria says. "She was becoming someone else. Rebellious, volatile, overly joyful one moment and devastated the next."

"No description at all?" I press. I am desperate now. I even consider asking if he wears masks or uses cages, but Victoria looks too fragile for that.

"This generation lives on their phones," Alexander says, waving his hand. "You can't tell what they're doing anymore. We don't even understand the apps."

I stop believing him entirely. He runs a tech company but complains about understanding technology?

"But she still called you," I say to Alexander. "Five times a day?"

"That was my idea," Victoria admits. "She wouldn't answer my calls—but she'd always answer his. They say girls love their fathers more."

I do not know what that means, but I am sure they are hiding something. That is why they waited to report her missing.

"So Poppy never dated anyone her own age?" I ask. I am done holding back. This girl's life is in real danger. Time is slipping away. One photo of her—vacant smile, lost eyes—claws at something inside me.

"Not really," Victoria says, stepping closer to the photo.

"Remember that history teacher in ninth grade, Alexander? How she used to stay after class..."

"That was different," Alexander snaps. "She was just—"

"Looking for you," Victoria finishes. Her voice holds years of blame. "In every older man she met. Because you were always too busy being embarrassed by her to actually show up."

The air in the room turns cold. Did she just say he was ashamed of his daughter?

"I was protecting her," Alexander says. The cracks in his polished demeanor begin to show. "While you encouraged every wild impulse. Every fantasy. Just like your mother did. Just like—"

"Don't you dare," Victoria cuts in. Her fists clench. "Don't make this about genetics when you are the one who—"

"Please," I interrupt. "Your daughter is running out of time. I need to know why you did not call the police immediately." I take a breath. "And why you felt embarrassed by her, Mr. Taylor."

Alexander will not meet my eyes. I can tell his reputation, his shareholders, his empire are more real to him than his own child.

"You would not understand," he says finally.

"I get paid to understand what most people can't," I reply.

"Poppy is bipolar," Victoria says at last. "She always has been. Her condition is severe." She swallows hard, but finishes her thought. "It's not the first time she's felt overwhelmed and disappeared."

"With strangers she loved more than her family," Alexander adds.

"That's why she had to call so often?" I ask.

"Yes," Victoria says. "And when she doesn't, we assume she's having an episode. Her last psychiatrist warned us to keep a close eye on her. This could be dangerous. But Alexander—"

"Was tired of being embarrassed by her behavior," I finish for her. I do not judge them. I know how hard this must be. I know what it's like to not feel seen. To be told you are too much. Sometimes, even your own parent refuses to look at your light.

But someone else always does. He calls himself the Comedian.

"I should have called the police myself," Victoria whispers. Her regret is heavy. "Not just when she texted for help. I'm sorry."

"It's okay," I say softly. I lie. I pretend I am strong.

I excuse myself with polite words.

The walk down the stairs feels like a descent into purgatory. Even the maid, who once glared at me, now looks at me with pity. Does she know I see myself in Poppy? In all the girls the Comedian took?

I step outside and climb into the Camry. I pass through the gate. Lorenzo gives a small nod.

Once I am clear of the estate, I pull over and park on a quiet side street.

Only then do I let myself cry.

CHAPTER 36

I feel your pain. But don't worry—I'm closer than you think. I'll always be there for you, until death do us part.

Watching you cry in the car breaks my heart. After all, you're the only one who really knows me. If you just gave in and remembered everything...

Did I tell you how busy I've been with Poppy? She's quite the fighter, Maddie. Just like you. I think she might be the first to actually transform. Would you believe me if I said I may not need to kidnap another girl?

Poppy is perfect. And that means the time you have left to catch me is running out.

But don't stress. I promised I'd take care of you too, once I'm finished.

Maybe I should start mailing you these letters. Or slip them under your basement door. I hope that wouldn't spook you. I just want you to know that you're not alone.

Does anyone else send you letters, or even ask how you are?*Does anyone really know you? Does anyone care?*

Cheer up, girl. You're much closer than you think.

Profiling the girls is a good start. I'll help you find me from that angle.

If you'd only remember what happened, Maddie. We made a deal once—and you're not keeping your end of the bargain.

CHAPTER 37

The streets of New York feel strange to me, like I haven't been outside in years.

I don't own a car. I walk everywhere. Now, seeing the city through a windshield feels surreal. The buildings blur past like they belong to a place I've never visited.

I used to wonder if the Comedian should have killed me like the others—if life on the other side would feel less empty than this one. My therapist helped me stop thinking like that.

Watching the city through dirty glass doesn't help. I feel stuck. I want to roll down the window and scream, but nobody would care.

I've spent years in this city without real friends. I'm still young, but I feel ancient.

The Comedian grabbed me just a year after I moved to New York for med school. I never had time to become a city girl. I never had time to feel at home.

The car's leather seat feels cold through my pants. My fingers are freezing on the wheel. Rush's car isn't taking me anywhere useful. I need help, but I don't know how to ask. I need love, but I've never really felt it.

The Taylors' conversation keeps echoing in my head. Poppy's story matches mine—and every other girl the Comedian took.

After leaving, I called Ivy Williams' parents. Then I forced myself to look through the files of the girls who died six years ago. Their faces in those photos turned my stomach. Young women. Bright smiles. No idea what was coming.

It all makes sense now.

The phone rings. It's Johnson.

"Victoria called about Poppy's condition," she says. "Good job, kiddo. I'm briefing the press on our findings."

I'm used to her attitude by now. Johnson stealing credit is like New York rain—inevitable.

"Did Victoria mention that Poppy matches every girl he's taken so far?" I ask.

"What do you mean?"

"I called Ivy Williams' family. She had a disorder too—severe BPD."

"No way Ivy was borderline," Johnson scoffs. "I'd remember that from the file."

"Her parents were probably embarrassed. Like the Taylors," I say. "Ivy fit the profile—nineteen, student, unstable relationships, fear of abandonment."

"That narrows it down," Johnson admits, her voice grudging. "Let me guess—she dated an older man too."

"Bingo. A month before she died. Told her sister, but there were no pictures or anything traceable."

"Just like Poppy. So that quote in the basement was about Ivy's condition?"

"'If you don't know who you are, you can be anyone you wish to be,'" I recite. "Fits most mental disorders—identity issues."

"The bastard's been mocking us from the start," Johnson says. "Handed us his victim profile on a silver platter."

Her words hit hard. I don't know how to answer.

How do you deal with a killer whose every move is so carefully planned?

Even worse—does this mean we have almost no chance of saving Poppy?

CHAPTER 38

"Wait!" Johnson breaks the silence. "You actually read the files from six years ago? Thought you couldn't even look at the girls' pictures."

She's right, but I pushed through. "Desperate times, desperate measures."

"Kudos, detective."

It's the first time she's called me that.

I don't know why, but I can't accept compliments. I've never felt like I deserve them.

"Look," I say, keeping my voice professional, "the key isn't figuring out who he is. It's about who he takes. Nineteen or so. Smart. Driven. Psych or art students. All with mental disorders. Rebellious. Drawn to older men."

"Vulnerable women act tough sometimes," Johnson says. Her voice sounds worried—maybe she's just practicing for the cameras. With her, sincerity always feels fake.

"And now," I add, "he's focused on the same profile, but with rich girls."

"He wants attention," I explain. "Last time, nobody gave him the spotlight—or the press coverage."

Johnson lets the silence hang, then says, "Did any of this trigger your forgotten memories?"

"No."

The lie makes my palms sweat instantly. My heart pounds so loud I worry she can hear it.

More silence.

She knows I'm hiding something, but I'm not telling. Not now.

"Here's the plan, kiddo," Johnson says. Her voice sounds different—almost vulnerable. "I won't pressure you about your memories, as long as it doesn't hurt the case."

"I promise—"

"Don't interrupt me. Just listen. You're back on the case. You did good work, and frankly, I need you as alert as you are right now to help find Poppy."

Johnson asking for my help feels like Christmas—except instead of gifts, it brings anxiety.

I get it. Poppy is rich. Her father is powerful. Thousands can die every day, but not his daughter. Or all hell will break loose.

Who knows what will happen if Poppy is found dead?

Maybe The Johnson will lose her precious job.

"Thank you, Commissioner," I say, trying to make her trust me. "I'll report only to you."

"Good. Go back to the Yellow and wait for my call," she orders. "Tonight the force is searching every basement in the city. I'll update you."

It would make more sense for me to join the manhunt, but maybe she doesn't want me stealing the spotlight if the press shows up.

It's already after sunset, and I'm tired. I can wait until morning to continue my investigation.

"And, detective," Johnson adds, not leaving without one last punch in the gut, "please send me a report first thing in the morning. Why haven't you mentioned that the Comedian's profile matches Professor Homer? That makes him a suspect."

She hangs up.

My jaw drops.
It's not like I haven't thought about it.
I've just ignored it.
Why?
I'll have to figure that out.
But when I take one last look at myself in the mirror, I realize—
I've been wearing Homer's coat all night.

CHAPTER 39

Pulling into the quiet alley, I kill the engine and sit there in silence. The sudden stillness presses against my eardrums. Homer's coat lies on the passenger seat where I tossed it.

I cannot stop staring at it.

How did I miss something so obvious?

I get out and begin walking away from the basement. I need to move. I need to think.

The night air is sharp in my lungs. My breath forms small clouds that vanish quickly, like erased evidence.

I keep thinking about Gabriel Homer. He is a charming psychologist in his forties. Oddly, he lives in a psychiatric institute. He uses a pipe and a cane, even though he does not need them. They are props. What more do I need to make him my number one suspect?

Ah, yes. It is called indisputable evidence.

I think about Poppy and Ivy liking older men. It reminds me of the men I have liked over the years. There were two people. One was Dr. Alan Reeves, the physical therapist who helped me heal after the kidnapping. The other was Michael, an older nurse at the ER where I ended up after a panic attack three years later.

Both relationships crashed the moment they became intimate. With one touch, their faces vanished. In their place, I saw a golden mask and heard laughter echoing off concrete walls.

I stop walking and press my palms against my eyes.

What is wrong with me? I have been wearing his coat like magical blinders this whole time. Johnson, with all her attitude, saw through it before I did.

Sirens blast nearby. There are too many tonight, even for New York. I hope they find the right basement.

But no sirens can stop my irrational curiosity about Homer. Am I actually attracted to him? Or is it something else? Something worse?

Of course he has a spell on you, Maddie. He is the Comedian. You have been his captive for days, and he fits the pattern. You are drawn to older men, for whatever reason.

I wrap my arms around myself, the cold sinking through my clothes. I really miss my dog. What I need tonight is simple: Stray and his uncomplicated love. He is the only guy in my life with no hidden agenda. He does sneak off with my chicken sandwiches when I am not looking, though.

I see him in my mind, waiting. His hopeful eyes watch the door. His tail thumps when I come home. He has his automatic feeder, but dogs do not understand "Mommy is hunting a serial killer." They only understand gone.

I turn around and start walking toward my car. I want to drive back to him. But when I check my pockets for the keys, they are gone. I search the car. Nothing. How could that be? I remember Rush giving them back yesterday. Maybe I forgot.

I call him.

"You owe me an apology," he says flatly.

"I didn't think you were the salty type, Officer," I say, softening my tone.

"You kicked me out of my car after I saved your life. With all due respect, Detective."

"I'm really sorry, Rush." There is no point in being formal now. "I shouldn't have done that."

"Apology accepted." He sounds more relaxed now, like he is munching on popcorn or something. Easy to please, I guess.

"Listen, do you have my keys?"

"Yes. I pocketed them when I left the car in the hood."

"Thank God. How can I meet you to pick them up? I need them."

"What about Johnson's orders to sleep in the basement?"

"I imagine she would cut me some slack tonight. We actually had a relatively good phone call."

"I didn't know such a thing was possible with The Johnson." More munching. "But I get it. You miss Stray. Can't blame you. He's cute."

"And loyal," I say, wondering about this new, calm side of Rush.

"I can be loyal. I will prove it."

I laugh. "How?"

"I'll come over and bring your keys. How about that?"

"I was thinking I'd drive by your—"

"No. I'm already on my way. I need to get my car back too."

"Okay." I guess I can wait a little, then go see Stray. But then my annoying detective brain kicks in. "Hey, Officer," I say, shifting my tone back to formal. "Can I ask where you were today after I left Kat's place?"

His footsteps pause. "Do I have to answer that, Detective?"

"I could make it an order, but since you saved my life today, I'm asking out of curiosity. As acquaintances or something."

"I appreciate that. Off the record?"

"Don't worry. I don't tell Johnson everything the way you do."

"Alcohol."

"What?"

"I went to AA. Johnson doesn't know. That's why I've been on edge. In the hood, I wanted a drink. I went to get one, but I stopped at the last minute. That's why I nearly shot those thugs. Thank God I didn't."

"I didn't know," I say, genuinely surprised. "I'm really sorry."

"No, you're not." He pauses. "I'm not the killer, Detective. I'm trying to help you catch one. And I risked my sobriety for you today."

I think I've reached a new personal low. I made a recovering alcoholic risk his sobriety to rescue me. I should start a business: *Maddie Brooks—Ruining Lives Since Birth.* We are not accepting new clients at this time.

"I'm on my way, Detective. Thirty minutes, and I'll be there." He hangs up.

I stand there feeling like the worst person alive.

And why?

You are trying to hide your doubts about your your Prince Charming, Homer. *You need to investigate him further. Not just for you, or for the memory of the girls who died. For Poppy. You can still save her.*

I walk for thirty minutes, punishing myself in the cold. Sirens echo across the city. I need the pain. I need something to wake me up and stop my personal feelings from clouding my judgment.

But when I return to the alley to meet Rush, my heart freezes.

Homer stands at the Yellow's door, swallowed by shadow, waiting.

CHAPTER 40

Homer stands at the Yellow's door like he belongs there. I cannot pinpoint his demeanor, but he looks too comfortable, like he lives nearby or has done this before.

I squint at him in the dim light, trying to remember if his build matches the Comedian's. My memory fails me again. Another critical detail lost in the fog of trauma. Convenient.

Maybe if I slapped a golden mask on his face, everything would come rushing back.

"Look who showed up at my doorstep." My voice sounds steadier than my pulse feels. Inside, my heart is doing an Olympic-level gymnastics routine.

His smile is practiced perfection. "I'm sorry, Detective." He presses his lips to the pipe. "I'm having dinner with colleagues nearby and thought I could come by and ask for my coat back."

"You could have called first." The words tumble out, a flimsy shield against the storm in my head. My eyes strain to see through his calm expression. The pipe is unnecessary, and the cane is just a prop. His well-fitted outfit hides who knows what.

I study his face, hunting for traces of a golden mask that may have never existed. I want proof that I am not just paranoid. I want some-thing to explain why Commissioner Johnson sees what I refuse to.

"I drove by on a whim," he says, shrugging with casual elegance. "You know what? I think I've overstepped. I'll call you tomorrow and schedule a proper time to collect it."

"It's in the car." I do not know if I can let him leave yet. I also do not know if I should let him stay. It feels like playing Russian roulette with every chamber loaded and still hoping for the best. "I haven't worn it since yesterday. I can get it for you."

"Thanks, I appreciate it. Also..." Homer sighs and taps his cane against the ground. He looks into my eyes with his usual concern. "I heard today was rough for you. I thought I'd check in."

So it is not about the coat. Dr. Perfect is ready to play his game. People reveal themselves when you stay quiet and give them enough rope to hang their lies.

"Who told you?" I keep my distance, maintaining a three-foot gap —the same rule they recommend for wild animals at the zoo.

"I have contacts in the force. Old connections." His eyes never leave mine.

"What kind of contacts?"

"I'm sure you know I've consulted with the NYPD before." He leans against the wall and crosses his legs, settling in. I am not sure if this is good or bad, but I have definitely baited him into a longer conversation. Or maybe he baited me.

"You mean with Johnson?"

Something flickers across his face—surprise or irritation, maybe— but it vanishes before I can name it. "Yes. Sara consulted me on two cases. You won't find much in the official records."

First-name basis with the Commissioner, yet no documentation of their work together. Sure. Nothing suspicious about that. Just another day in the cesspool of NYPD secrets.

"And why is that?" Let's see what kind of lies he is selling today.

"Professional disagreements."

"Don't stop there." I lean against the doorframe, pretending to be relaxed. "I've got all night."

His smile tightens. This part of the conversation probably was not in his script. "I testified that two patients were not insane. They walked free. Johnson never forgave me."

"Were they guilty?"

He shakes his head. "They did strange things, sure. But murder? No."

"Aren't you worried about letting unstable patients live among the general population?"

"Look around, Detective." He gestures at the city with his cane. "You can shoot someone here, and no one notices. Do you see anyone sane?"

I bite back a smile. His logic is oddly satisfying, even if not socially acceptable. But I keep a straight face.

"Are you saying we should all live in asylums like you, to protect ourselves from the world?"

"I believe insanity is not an easy diagnosis." His eyes light up with academic passion, and my stomach flips. "What if what we call insane is just different? Maybe even genius?"

"Oh, I get it. You live there because you're a misunderstood genius." I am not sure how that came out. I want to corner him or provoke him, but I end up leaning into his thoughts. I play along with the color of his cards.

God, I am terrible at this. Rule number one: do not flirt with your prime suspect.

"I have my reasons for locking myself up in a cell with my patients," he says. His voice is quiet now. He actually sounds sincere. There is a shadow behind his words, a real weight.

I tilt my head, unable to speak for a moment. I want to read between the lines. Then I notice him rubbing the place on his finger where a ring once rested.

The moment stretches, and my silence is unbearable. I cannot go back to the car and grab the coat. I cannot invite him inside. I cannot even walk past him. I am frozen—body, heart, and soul.

What is your secret, Homer?

Only the sound of distant sirens pulls me out of his spell.

"Johnson is really scouring the city for the killer tonight, isn't she?" He looks up, following the sound.

"How do you know that? Did she already tell you?"

"No," he says casually. "It's all over the news."

"Great." I grit my teeth and close my eyes.

"I know," Homer says. "It was too easy to announce that the NYPD is looking for him tonight. Even the Comedian could hear it."

"Right?" I open my eyes, giving in a little to the way his mind works. "Why would she do that?"

"Probably to calm Alexander Taylor. It's a bad move for the case, but a good move to show the elite that she's doing everything she can to save Poppy."

"I guess the case details are public too?"

"Johnson has not stopped talking about her discoveries the last two days." *"He even makes finger quotes when he says 'her discoveries.'"*

He definitely knows how to win me over. Maybe it is best to step back and prepare better for next time.

I take a step toward the car. "I should get your coat." It is better if he leaves now. I need time to think.

"Wait," Homer says suddenly. "Would you grab a bite with me?"

CHAPTER 41

I cannot remember the last time someone I liked asked me out. The few men who have approached me since were creeps. They had boundary issues and wandering eyes. Then again, if Homer is the Comedian, he is the biggest creep of all. I almost laugh at the thought.

My mouth goes dry. Fight-or-flight kicks in, but my body chooses a third option—freeze.

"Ah." I cannot stutter here. My response has to be crystal clear or I will fall into his chains of charm and strange logic. "I'm not sure that's a good idea."

"We can discuss the case." He leans forward slightly. "I think I can help you narrow the Comedian's profile by a lot."

"I appreciate that, but maybe we will not need to." I point upward at the sounds of sirens echoing across the city.

The smirk on Homer's face sends my thoughts spinning. He leans in a little closer, and even with space between us, I feel like he towers over me.

"We both know they will not catch him tonight."

The space between us shrinks. The alley reeks of damp concrete and something else. Maybe it is his cologne. Maybe it is just male confidence.

I have never heard anything with so many possible meanings in one sentence. Is this when he admits everything? Will I have to fight him hand to hand?

Is he confessing?

Is he taunting me?

Is heI know I haven't fought in a long time. But maybe I have been saving all my strength for this. If he is the Comedian, I will not let him win. I will not need an arrest warrant or a self-defense excuse. I will kill him in cold blood, and I know I am good at it.

"He has been two steps ahead of everyone so far," Homer continues. "Does Johnson really think she will find his new basement tonight?"

I notice how his eyes reflect the dim streetlight, how his presence fills the narrow alley. Something flutters in my chest—a feeling I do not want to name. There is no way he thinks this way unless he is the Comedian. Or the killer is one of his patients he released.

This is not a real date, Maddie. It is a game.

He knows you are onto him. He is rushing his plan. He skips the charm, the fun month of getting to know me like the others. He is going straight for the kill. The walls are closing in on him. Take the chance, Maddie. Play the game. He is just as vulnerable as you are right now.

My pulse hammers in my neck like it is trying to punch its way out.

I need leverage—something personal. My eyes drop to his left hand, to the pale line on his ring finger. The mark where a wedding band should be.

"Are you married, Professor?"

Homer follows my gaze and straightens. "Ah, this." He rubs the spot again. Something in his voice sounds sincere. "We are in the process of divorce."

"I see."

"But let me clarify. I was not asking you out on a date, if I misspoke." He backpedals quickly.

Interesting move.

"Good, because married men should not ask someone else for a date." I watch his reaction closely.

Something flashes across his face. It is not guilt or anger, but a raw pain that stops me cold. It disappears just as quickly, replaced by his composed mask.

"Of course," he says quietly.

I am a bundle of mixed feelings—hurt, curious, guilty. I am stumbling through a game with rules I do not understand. The way he produces such authentic emotional responses throws me off balance. Either he is the world's best actor, or there is more to his story than I realize.

"Frankly, I am starting to think you do not know why you are here. First, it is the coat. Then, my well-being. Then, a dinner?"

My brain adds: Next, it is me in a cage?

"Yeah." He lets the pipe dangle from his lips and rubs the back of his head. He looks like an embarrassed teenage boy now. "I think I am really out of my element today."

The sudden shift makes my skin crawl. It is like watching someone try on different personalities to see which one works best. I have seen this before. In interviews with sociopaths.

"It is okay. I would like to discuss the case with you further. You have good insight into things. But," I check my watch, "I am waiting for Officer Rush. I am not sure why he is late, but he was going to bring me my keys so I could spend the night with my dog."

"Yeah, I know." Homer's smile changes. The serious psychiatrist becomes a playful college kid, like someone ready to admit he crashed his dad's car. The sudden boyishness feels calculated, like he is trying on a new mask.

I squint, all accusing eyes and no words. Silence demands an explanation. The air between us thickens.

"Rush actually sent me to give you the keys." Homer's tone is cheeky, almost too casual for his persona. This is his fourth reason in a few minutes for why he is here. What is really going on? "Do not take this the wrong way, but your tense conversation made him worry he might slip and drink if he went outside again."

"How do you know that?" My voice sharpens. I am supposed to be playing along, but my patience is running out faster than Rush's sobriety. None of this feels honest.

"Rush is one of my patients at the institute." He says it like it is nothing. Like he is commenting on the weather. "He pretended not to know me in the car because I am treating him off the record. No one in the NYPD should know he still struggles with addiction."

Great. My backup is an alcoholic who secretly sees the man I suspect might be a serial killer for therapy.

Why do I feel like the only outsider in this strange little family of Mama Johnson, Papa Homer, and Little Boy Rush?

I gulp. "I guess it is not really my business. I have been hard on him today, but I had no idea."

"It is okay, Detective." Homer reaches out to pat my shoulder. The brief contact sends electricity up my spine, like I touched a live wire.

"I left you the keys inside." He gives me that empty smile people exchange in elevators. "Enjoy your night. Call me whenever you want to discuss the case."

"Wait!" I step forward, confused again. "How did you get in?" I point toward the basement's locked door.

"Rush has the keys," Homer says, already disappearing into the shadows. "He told me to leave them inside with your apartment keys. He said you can return them if you still want him on the case."

Perfect. The suspect talks to my colleagues, arranges my schedule, and has access to my home.

"I should go," he says, checking his watch.

"The coat—"

"Keep it. It suits you." He stops at the edge of a puddle. "And by the way, I convinced Rush to let me leave you a surprise inside. I think you will like it."

A surprise? My stomach drops like I missed a step on a dark staircase.

He walks away, melting into the darkness like he belongs there.

I stand alone in the alley, feeling like the only sane person in a city gone mad.

The keys feel unnaturally heavy in my hand.

I approach the Bilco doors and unlock them with trembling fingers. The metal is cold against my skin, like touching a corpse.

What waits for me inside? A trap? A message? Another body?

I pull the door open just enough to peek inside.

And then I hear it.

Barking.

The sound hits me like a physical force. It is familiar. Impossible. Heart-stopping.

It is my beloved dog, Stray.

CHAPTER 42

SIX YEARS AGO

The basement is a world of silence, broken only by the occasional whimpers of defeated girls. Darkness swallows everything, thick and absolute, with no sense of walls or space. I am barely conscious, drugged and defeated, when the first sound comes.

A scratch. A soft scraping. Then a blurry image.

First, a wet nose—moist and quivering. Soft snuffling breaths break the silence, a tiny condensation of warmth in the cold darkness. Each exhale is a faint, humid whisper against the concrete. Then two bright and curious eyes stare back at me, but the dim light does not reveal the rest of it.

I'm too drugged to realize it's a dog. I tense. My muscles coil, wondering if this is another one of the Comedian's twisted games.

But the nose keeps moving. Sniffing. Exploring.

Slowly, a scruffy dog appears. Just past the puppy stage, lean and wiry, he seems to have found his way into the basement somehow. The puppy is too cute to be the Comedian's doing. He would never tolerate such a beautiful soul nearby.

He's not fully grown, but no longer a helpless puppy. His eyes are different from anything I've seen in this cage. Not predatory. Not calculating. Just pure, unfiltered curiosity.

I call him "he" the moment I realize he is a boy. I feel flattered he chose me over the other girls, but then again, my cage is still in the middle, and I'm not bleeding like the others.

Even so, I am too weak to move.

But this random stray cares. He wiggles through the impossibly narrow gap, all ribs and matted fur, looking more lost than threatening. Our eyes meet. His tail gives a tentative wag, as if he's asking for permission to exist in this nightmare.

I push through the pain and reach through the hole in the floor to bring out some of the food. He's reluctant to eat. He keeps licking my face. I can't feel his love, but I want to. Only when I place the food in the palm of my hand does he finally eat.

"Stray." The name comes out like an imminent fate. Like he was always meant to be called that, no matter who found him. "Where did you come from?"

Trying to find his way in this darkness is futile. But he must come through a crack in the walls or something. And if that crack exists, however small, it means there is hope.

Just my luck. Hope arrives as a mangy mutt in a serial killer's basement.

But when Stray finishes eating, he leaves.

Only to come back later. Was it every day, twice a day? I can't tell through the blurriness of my exhausted mind.

At first, I think he comes to eat, which I don't mind. But then, when there is no food, he still comes. He just sits there, keeping me company. When a tear rolls down my cheek, he whines softly. No demands. No judgment. And he disappears in a flash when the Comedian's footsteps return, as if he can smell evil.

At some point, the girls stop talking to me. They think I'm in cahoots with the Comedian. My cage is in the middle. I get twice the food. He hasn't operated on me yet.

That's when they start to hate Stray, too.

But Stray never hates.

He is just who he is.

Some nights, he presses closer to me, as if I can shield him from the darkness of this world.

Even as I leave, I find him strolling alongside me. He guides me through the dark streets he knows well, but I'm too tired. I collapse, thinking I will never see him again.

When I wake up in a hospital, the nurse says someone found me and brought me in. She smiles and says, "We sent your dog to a shelter nearby. Don't fret, you'll see him before long."

CHAPTER 43

Stray looks at me like I am about to pull a gourmet meal out of this basement's sad excuse for a kitchen. The metal cabinets have more rust than actual food, but challenge accepted.

Some canned beans. A package of slightly stale crackers. Half a jar of mustard that looks like it survived the apocalypse. Perfect.

"Fancy dinner, buddy," I mutter, mixing the beans with a splash of mustard. Stray wags his tail, either impressed by my culinary skills or just happy to be eating something that is not concrete and despair.

I, myself, would kill for a glass of wine right now, but I have Stray instead—and that is enough.

The apartment keys catch my eye. They sit there like they are apologizing for interrupting my gourmet bean feast. Then I notice another key. Rush's. A duplicate for the basement.

My stomach twists a little, thinking about him possibly being the one who spied on me last night. He has keys I did not know existed. But I cannot deal with that kind of headache right now.

Maybe Stray can help with his terrible investigative skills. I scratch behind his ears and lean in close.

"Who came into the apartment to get you tonight? Was it Rush or Homer?"

Stray's ears perk up the moment I pantomime Homer's cane and pipe. Not just a casual twitch—this is a sharp, alert reaction that makes me narrow my eyes.

"Seriously?" I lean in close enough to smell his doggy breath. "You like Homer?"

He confirms it with a spin around himself, tail wagging like we are talking about his favorite chew toy.

I switch tactics.

"What about Rush?" I say, imitating Rush's intense stare and pretending I have a mustache by holding my finger under my nose.

Stray's ears flatten. A low, barely audible growl escapes him as he turns away, pressing his warm body against mine, like he is seeking protection from the very idea of Rush.

"No?" I nudge him gently with my elbow. "Remember when he brought you that steak?"

Another firm huff from Stray. He stays still, his whole body rejecting the idea like I just offered him a bath. He is not budging. I wish I had Rush's photo of them together from yesterday in case I messed up the imitation.

"You don't know who I'm talking about, huh?" I roll my eyes. "You are absolutely the worst detective assistant ever."

I push the thought aside and kneel until we are at eye level.

"Do you at least like me?"

Stray licks my hand and nudges his forehead against my legs, his eyes never leaving mine.

"Turning into a cat now, huh?" I laugh and scratch his chin.

And just like that, nothing else matters. Not the Comedian. Not Rush's keys. Not Johnson's impossible expectations. Just me and this furry traitor who has clearly chosen Homer's side.

Later, with Stray curled up in my lap, I notice a folded piece of paper on the floor. Rush has left me a handwritten note: *Johnson doesn't know. Homer's idea btw. Hope this proves I'm not the killer.*

I assume he means Stray, right? I cannot help but smile at the smiley face at the end of the note. It is like finding out the school bully secretly volunteers at an animal shelter.

But the note is also placed over a book. One I have never seen before: *The Sky Below and the Earth Above* by Professor Gabriel Homer.

I cannot say I didn't ask for this. I crack it open with one hand while the other keeps stroking Stray's fur.

Stray's ears shoot up. His eyes lock on the pages. His tail thumps like he is reading along with me.

"What, you're a scholar now?" I smirk. "Though a pipe and coat would look brilliant on you." I ruffle his fur.

In the background, the news plays on my phone. The NYPD's search for Poppy continues.

Guilt gnaws at me. I should be out there—doing something, anything. But Johnson's orders hang over me like a bad hangover.

Back to the book. Homer's writing is dense and overly academic. The kind of prose that makes your brain hurt after a few pages.

It feels repetitive, hammering the same point over and over about mental illness being a social construct.

This must be Homer's personal copy. It is filled with handwritten notes in the margins. Little comments, clarifications, arguments with himself. Like he is having a conversation no one else is invited to join.

His theories about how society defines "normal" and "insane" are plausible. But his view of the insane as creative and misunderstood feels risky.

I like some of it. But I do not fully buy it. Especially not from a man who chooses to live in a psychiatric institute. That is what I call commitment.

Eventually, the words begin to blur. My eyelids grow heavy.

Stray's warmth. The background hum of sirens. Homer's academic rambling. My exhaustion.

I drift off, hoping Poppy will be found, safe and sound, when I wake up—if I wake up the same person again.

CHAPTER 44

Morning light seeps in, and I stretch in bed, feeling Stray's warm weight against my leg. It is the first good sleep I have had in a long while.

But it does not last.

My phone blares with breaking news.

NYPD'S COMEDIAN SEARCH FAILS.

Bold headlines describe a frantic search. Police have checked every basement in New York—empty or not. They found nothing. Still, they promise not to stop.

Johnson's words to the families of Ivy and Poppy have sparked outrage. She tried to apologize, but it only made things worse. Now, many believe Poppy might be gone for good.

The Taylors are dominating the news. Alexander Taylor appears in video after video, criticizing the NYPD. Victoria Taylor, her makeup smeared with tears, offers financial rewards on social media. She pleads for any information that might lead to her daughter.

Poppy is still missing. And the Comedian, fully aware that he is the target of a citywide manhunt, will now be more cautious than ever. Did we really believe it would be easy to catch him? The entire city is on alert, yet he remains out of reach—a phantom.

I am at a loss. I did not expect the police to find him quickly, but I hoped they would uncover something—anything—to move the case forward. With their efforts falling short, I am left grasping at air. Where do I go from here?

I try to ground myself by preparing breakfast for Stray. I mix his favorite meal—wet food with a scoop of kibble. He bounces around with what looks like hysterical joy. He must really like the basement, I think, watching him leap across the room.

Suddenly, he stops. He stands by the desk and rests his chin on a book that Homer left behind.

I freeze.

"Hey, buddy," I say, ruffling his ears. "What's the matter?"

He lets out a soft moan, almost nostalgic, his nose pressed into the book.

"You have to be kidding me." I frown, half amused, half confused. "Do you actually miss Homer? You barely know him."

Stray paces in tight circles, whining gently. His tail droops low, dragging against the floor. He glances at the door, then back at me, his eyes sad and expectant. It is the unmistakable look of a dog who misses someone.

I take a deep breath. Maybe Homer used some psychological trick to win Stray over. Or maybe it has something to do with the book itself.

I reach for the book slowly. Stray steps aside, almost politely.

"You want to read with me again?" I ask.

He almost nods. I open the book, and he peeks underneath my hand, his eyes locked on the pages. His behavior is strange, even for him.

I know people can disguise handwriting. I never truly expected the Comedian to slip up. But part of me still hoped for a clue.

Then.

Suddenly.

I hear a knock.

At the door.

The sound is sharp and sudden. I wince. Stray retreats behind me, his breathing loud and fast. I freeze, torn between running to grab my gun or opening the door.

Before I can decide, the knocker vanishes. I hear footsteps fading down the alley.

I stay frozen, paralyzed by hesitation. Why am I not chasing whoever it was? Is it fear? Or am I just trying to protect Stray?

Through the window above the sink, I see the figure retreating.

The long coat.

The same one that covered the intruder's shoes two nights ago.

What is wrong with me? Why can't I move? Am I remembering something?

But it is not a memory that freezes me.

It is what the intruder left behind.

It lies near the basement door.

Another letter.

But I am still holding the original one in my hands.

This is not the same letter.

My heart pounds.

Is this what I think it is?

Is this what I have been waiting for?

Everything suddenly feels like it is happening too fast, and I am not sure I am ready.

This one is different. Not worn or familiar. It is sealed. A fresh envelope. Crisp. Waiting.

My name is written on it.

My hands begin to shake as I reach for it. Stray whines beside me, his nose twitching. He senses the dread in the air.

It is clear now.

The Comedian was here two nights ago.

And whatever is inside this envelope, I know one thing.

Everything is about to change.

CHAPTER 45

What the hell is going on, Maddie?

Who the hell said Johnson can be involved?

I don't like this woman. I don't want her to be part of the investigation.

Calling me a "killer"? "Insane"?

She has no idea who she is talking about. She is not worthy to even talk about me.

If you are going to mention me on the news, at least get it right.

I am the Comedian. The Cager. The Architect. The Surgeon. The one who brings truth.

My work is a masterpiece, and you are letting them mock it.

I am insulted, Maddie. Truly angered. Deeply disappointed in you.

I reached out to you. I offered you a connection. A chance to understand. To wake the world up and set these women free.

But now the NYPD tells everyone I am some idiot?

I left you clues. All over the place. And you still cannot see them.

What the hell happened to you?

We had a deal.

You are not holding up your end.

Do you want me to tell them what you did?

My headache is splitting me in half again. I warned you. I do not want my darker half to rise.

You have one hour.

Or Poppy dies.

If you do not do exactly what I say, she dies.

You made me do this. You stupid bitch.

This is your last clue.

Miss it, and you will never see me again.

To find me:

Tread lightly.

I'm like you.

I'm down too.

Alone and out of love,

Where the basement's below

And theasylum's above.

CHAPTER 46

I grip the letter so hard my knuckles turn bone white.

The Comedian's poem—or whatever it is—burns into my vision like acid:

To find me, tread lightly. I'm like you. I'm down too. Alone, and out of love, where the basement's below and asylum's above.

My fingers tremble as I dial Johnson. Each ring vibrates through my skull. My pulse beats so wildly I can feel it in my eyeballs.

"I told you I'd call you, Detective." Johnson's voice sounds worn, like someone who has not slept in days.

I cut in. "Did your search include abandoned psychiatric facilities with basements?"

"Not specifically. But abandoned buildings are abandoned buildings. We checked Manhattan, Brooklyn, Queens, and the Bronx."

"You're absolutely sure?" I pace the basement while Stray shadows me. His nails tap a nervous rhythm on the concrete. When I stop suddenly, he bumps into my legs and tucks his head under my knee. He wants reassurance I am not sure I can give.

"Yes, Detective. I am." Johnson scoffs. "Would you like to take over my job while you're at it?"

"Just bear with me for a second. What about psychiatric facilities that are still operating?"

"Of course not," she says. Her impatience scrapes across my ears. "The search criteria included abandoned buildings with basements. Besides, it would be damn hard for him to operate out of a functioning facility. He would be—"

"Your search was compromised from the start." I raise my voice over hers.

"What do you mean compromised?"

"The Comedian has been watching us this whole time. He's been stalking the Yellow. I found another letter slipped under my door minutes ago."

Johnson goes silent. I can almost hear her brain working, grinding through the implications.

"A sealed letter. Addressed to me," I continue. "He's angry that the media is making him out to be some run-of-the-mill psycho. He wants people to see his work as a masterpiece."

I am practically gasping now, my chest heaving like I have run a marathon.

"He gave me a written riddle. A one-hour deadline to find Poppy. Or she dies."

"A riddle? Another quote from Homer's book?"

"No. It's something he made up. A weird poem. But the meaning is clear."

I read it aloud, the paper shaking in my hand like dry leaves.

"It means we could still save Poppy." Johnson exhales. There is a flicker of hope in her voice, though it is buried beneath layers of fatigue. "So we should search basements in asylums?"

"That narrows it down. But which one? New York is the city of asylums." My head throbs with every possible lead. "If I go with my gut, the line about the basement below and the asylum above reminds me of Homer's book. *The Sky Below and the Earth Above.*"

"I had my suspicions about Homer too," she says. "But it is not him."

"How can you be so sure?"

"He has an airtight alibi."

"What kind of alibi?" I narrow my eyes until the edges of my vision blur.

"His wife. She went to see him right after she saw you. He's staying in a facility with surveillance cameras everywhere. I checked it myself. He was there all night."

"In a facility?"

"I don't have time to explain. Just—"

"He was waiting for me at the Yellow when I got back. He asked me to dinner yesterday, Commissioner. And now, suddenly, he has a perfect alibi with a wife he never mentioned? That makes him even more suspicious in my book." I force the words out, my throat tight with disbelief. "We already know the Comedian isn't working alone. It's still possible—"

"It is not him, Maddie. For God's sake." Johnson's voice explodes through the phone. "I take responsibility for that. Do you think I don't want to catch the killer? Focus on the location now, or send me the letter and I'll handle it myself."

By the time she handles it, Poppy will be dead. These riddles are meant for me. They are custom-built for my brain. I am the only one who can solve them in time.

"Maddie." Johnson sounds like a drowning woman grabbing for driftwood. "My entire career is hanging by a thread. I need to save Poppy just as badly as you do."

I appreciate her honesty, no matter how self-serving it may be. My hands shake so badly I have to grip the phone with both. I close my eyes and let the Comedian's words play through my mind like a twisted nursery rhyme.

Stray's cold, wet nose presses against my wrist and pulls me back to the present. His eyes meet mine—deep, brown, and full of unshakable devotion. I press my fingers into his fur and draw strength from the solid weight of him.

This time, it hits me hard. The answer is so obvious I feel stupid for not seeing it sooner. I still don't fully understand the "tread lightly" part, but the rest is clear.

"Commissioner, I need backup right now," I say. My voice sounds calm, even though I am trembling inside. "That includes Officer Rush and as many officers as you can spare."

"Only if you tell me you are confident you know where Poppy is."

"I know exactly where to find her." My grip on the phone is so tight I am surprised it does not shatter in my hand. "I just hope I'm not too late this time."

CHAPTER 47

Stray remains in the basement after a quick pat and a promise I will return soon. Leaving him behind hurts like tearing off a limb, but Poppy needs help right now.

Minutes later, I am in jeans and sneakers—the fastest outfit change of my life. I take the metal stairs two at a time, my heart pounding harder with each step.

I slam the Yellow's door behind me just as the first backup sirens wail at the corner. The sound prickles my skin. We are moving. Finally.

Rush's Camry is waiting. I fling open the passenger door, slide in, and drum my fingers on the dashboard. Johnson actually sent backup. Rush arrives a second later, yanking the driver's door open and folding his lanky frame behind the wheel.

"Did you bring the documents I asked for?" I ask.

"Here's the file on all the double basements under asylums, just like you asked." He drops it in my lap. "Old archive stuff—never digitized."

"Look." I pull out the Comedian's letter, my voice sharp. "It says, 'basement below and asylum above.' This isn't just about abandoned buildings."

"So they could have saved a lot of time if they had searched basements under asylums."

"Not exactly. Give me a minute to figure it out. For now, just drive."

"Where to?"

"No solid lead yet. Just go."

"I like that logic." He hits the gas.

"Listen." I scan the letter again. "Homer pointed out that Ivy's crime scene had a double basement, right?"

"Yeah, but the ceiling was broken through. It made it one big space."

"What if he didn't break the ceiling this time?" I tap the line that says tread lightly. "It means he is hiding below. Using only the lower part. Quiet. Hidden."

"Changing his whole setup?" Rush raises an eyebrow.

"Desperate times, desperate measures." I say it between breaths. "Smaller cages. Basic cameras. Whatever keeps his 'masterpiece' alive."

"So yesterday, he could've been right under the NYPD's feet. Them stomping around above him."

"Exactly." I snap my fingers.

"But wouldn't blueprints show a lower basement?"

"Not always. Most were built in the early 1900s for flooding. They were sealed off when drainage systems improved. I skimmed the files."

"Forgotten spaces, then?"

"Yeah. Perfect hiding spots that don't exist on modern records."

"Wish I could vanish like that," Rush mutters.

"The problem is we have too many options." I straighten up and point at his phone. "Call Kat."

Rush puts the phone on speaker. It rings three times before Kat answers in her gravelly voice.

"Was about to solve my problems from the bottom of a vodka glass," she says in her semi-Russian accent. "Unless you've got someone else's problem I can borrow to silence my mind."

Someday I will sit down with her and figure out why she is like this. Whatever darkness she has seen must have been enough to break most people.

"Kat, we need locations of undocumented double basements under asylums in New York," I say. "Places that do not exist on paper anymore."

"I see." Kat's tone shifts instantly. "Those old tunnels and basements won't show up on modern blueprints. They're buried in pre-1930 archives—planning documents, sewer maps, and all that."

"How do we access those? We don't have time to dig through records in person."

"You don't need to," Kat says. I hear her keyboard come to life. "History nerds love digitizing this stuff. They do it for free. I'm hacking into databases now. I'm pulling scans from historical societies and old building photos. You can spot extra cellar doors and flood vents in the old pictures. Stuff the city forgot about."

Rush and I exchange a glance. Better to let her ramble. It keeps her sharp.

"Bingo Salamaningo!" she shouts.

"What did you find, Kat?" My pulse is racing so hard it hurts to breathe.

"These pre-1930 archives are gold. Bodies found. Bootlegging. Hidden morgues. Some serial killers even used these places as graveyards."

"Where the bodies were never found," Rush adds, slowing to keep pace with the backup cars.

I elbow him hard and mouth the words don't encourage her, then turn back to the call.

"What exactly did you find, Kat?"

"Five possibilities. Asylums with double basements no one knows about anymore," she says. "One in the Bronx, two in Brooklyn, one in

Queens, and—wait, maybe six? No, five. The last one's in Manhattan."

"Five is too many." I glance at my watch. "We have less than an hour left to save Poppy."

"I know it's a rabbit hole." Kat sighs. "Tell me how to narrow it down. I'm all yours, Alice."

A thought hits me so hard I look at my reflection in the mirror, like I'm asking myself for permission. Sometimes, instinct is all we have.

"Kat?" I swallow hard. "Does the Empire Institute have a double basement?"

"It didn't come up in my search," she says, "but I'll dig into their private records."

Rush gives me that look. "It can't be Homer."

"Why not?"

"He saved my life. Got me sober."

"He was also the first to notice the double basement at the crime scene. He always knows exactly what to look for. And he's always absent when the Comedian strikes." The suspicion keeps churning inside me. "Stray had the weirdest reaction to Homer's book yesterday. Like he recognized something. It's like Homer hypnotized him. Everything that man does is calculated."

"Like what?"

"Have you ever seen him lose his cool? He's always too calm. Like he is enjoying some private joke. I don't care what alibi Johnson says he has."

"If he's the killer, why would he give you the clue about the double basement?" Rush's defense of Homer makes my skin crawl.

"How should I know? He's playing some sick game. Just like the letters. He's following a twisted plan, and I'm not playing along the way he wants."

"Both of you, stop." Kat cuts in. "Maddie's right."

"What?" The word catches in my throat.

"The Empire Institute built a lower basement for flood control in

1928," she says. Her voice hits me like a blow. Even Rush looks stunned. "They sealed it off two years later. No one working there now knows it exists."

"That's it." I slam my hand against the dashboard, hard enough to sting. "Rush, get us to the Empire Institute. Now."

CHAPTER 48

The Empire Institute's gothic spires loom against the darkening sky as we approach. Rush flicks the sirens back on, their wail echoing off stone walls while we race up the curved driveway. There is no point in stealth now. We need full cooperation from everyone around us. They need to know a killer is here.

Our convoy—six patrol cars strong—screeches to a halt at the main gate. The light from the guard booth shines on a startled face. A heavyset security officer steps out, his hand drifting toward his hip.

"NYPD!" I slam my badge against the gate before Rush even stops the car. "Open it. Now."

The guard plants his feet. "Medical facility. You can't just—"

"Open the gate!" I slam my palm against the metal, making it ring. "Every second counts."

Rush appears beside me, calm and composed. "We're here about Professor Homer," he says, flashing his badge. "Department business."

Something shifts in the guard's face. He nods and hits a button. The heavy iron gates creak open.

Rush revs the engine too soon, scraping the Camry's side mirror as we squeeze through. The backup units follow, fanning out across the circular drive.

"Shit," I mutter, reaching instinctively for my waist—empty. I left my gun at the Yellow. Amateur move.

"Rush, your gun." I extend my hand as officers begin scrambling around us.

He hesitates. "You're not in the right headspace—"

"Not a request." I keep my hand open. "I'm the primary on this case."

Reluctantly, he unholsters his service weapon and places it in my palm. It feels heavy—too heavy. Like the weight of responsibility. I am also not sure it is legal to use his weapon, but who cares at this point?

The phone in my other hand crackles. Kat is still on the line.

"Alice? You there?"

"Yes. We're at the Empire Institute."

"Good. Listen carefully. I'm looking at the original blueprints from 1892. The building has had six owners, been renovated fourteen times, and had three wings torn down."

"Cut to the chase, Kat."

"The lowest basement isn't on current maps. It was reportedly flooded since 1957." Kat's voice crackles. "But they installed drainage in the east wing in 1986."

"So it could be dry?" I'm already moving. Officers fall in behind me.

"Maybe. And listen—there's a service tunnel from the boiler room. It vanished from blueprints after 1960."

Rush pulls up the building's evacuation map on his phone. "There." He points to a red square labeled MAINTENANCE in the east wing. "That has to be the boiler room."

We storm through the front doors, past stunned nurses and night staff. A heavyset orderly tries to intercept us.

"You can't just—"

"Police emergency." Rush hesitates, but when I glare at him, he flashes his badge. "Stay out of our way."

The interior of the Empire Institute blends sterile modernity with faded grandeur. Fluorescent lighting throws harsh shadows across marble floors and ornate crown molding. The halls are mostly empty. Only the night shift moves between rooms.

"East wing," I say, jogging forward. "We're looking for maintenance access."

Kat's voice returns through the phone. "Take the service elevator down to B1."

The elevator reeks of antiseptic. It crams us together like sardines. We descend in tense silence, the only sound the mechanical whir of old cables.

The doors open onto a utility corridor. Exposed pipes run across the ceiling. The air is thick with humidity, and emergency lighting casts everything in a sickly yellow glow.

"This way." Rush points, following the building map.

A heavy door marked AUTHORIZED PERSONNEL ONLY blocks our path. Rush looks like he is about to call for help when I raise the gun and aim for the lock.

The trigger jams. I glance back. Rush steps in, flips off the safety, and shoots.

The lock bursts apart with a loud crack. He hands the gun back to me without a word. I appreciate it more than I can say. I must have looked awful—shaking so badly it seemed like I forgot how to shoot.

Rush and the others look at me with concern, but none of them stop me.

"Kat." I press the phone closer to my ear. "We're in the boiler room."

The space is cavernous. Massive machinery hums and clanks, heating the entire complex. Steam hisses from overhead valves, creating clouds of white mist. The temperature rises ten degrees, and sweat beads instantly on my skin.

"Spread out." I direct the officers. "Look for an access point. Hatch, door, anything that leads lower."

"It should be against the east wall," Kat says. "Behind the main boiler."

We fan out, flashlights cutting through the haze. The concrete floor is slick with condensation. Every step is risky.

"Here!" an officer calls from behind a large water tank. "I've got something!"

We hurry to him. He has found a metal hatch set into the floor, its wheel rusted in place.

"This has to be it." I holster Rush's gun and crouch down. "Help me open it."

Three officers grip the wheel. Their muscles strain against decades of rust. It screeches, then turns slowly. A quarter turn. Then a half.

The hatch finally pops open with a wet, sucking sound. A thick wave of stale air rolls out, heavy with the scent of mildew and standing water.

I shine my flashlight inside.

A ladder drops into darkness. The bottom three rungs are submerged in black water.

I curse under my breath.

There is no way anyone lives down there.

CHAPTER 49

I am hitting concrete so hard my knuckles are going to bleed, but I do not care.

All I can think about is Poppy. Another girl. Another victim. Another name I will carry like excess weight for the rest of my life.

"Maddie, stop!" Rush's voice sounds distant, even though he is right behind me. He feels miles away. In another universe where I am not a complete disaster.

My breath comes in ragged gasps. The Empire Institute's sterile hallway stretches in front of me like an accusation. I have nothing. Zero. The Comedian is playing me, and he is winning.

Something snaps inside me like a bone breaking. I feel wrong in my own skin. Sweat slicks my palms, and my pulse hammers so loud I feel it in my fingertips, my temples, my throat.

Pure desperation floods my body with adrenaline. I am beyond reason now. Not even all the liquor in Kat's veins could slow me down.

"I need to get into Homer's cell," I announce to no one and everyone. My voice sounds strange. Disconnected. Like it belongs to someone else.

I dash past the officer. I am lost and trying to find my way back, relying on scraps of memory from when I first arrived. The feeling drags me back to the cage, to the girls, to the night he let me go.

Eventually, I reach the elevator to the main floor. That is where Homer's cell is. When the door opens, nurses try to block my path.

Big mistake.

I unholster my gun.

"Move," I growl. I actually point Rush's gun at them. The metal is cold. Perfect. As cold as justice needs to be.

No one moves.

Then they step aside.

Nothing about me says I am not mad enough to shoot someone. Forget my therapist and all those wasted years of trying to fix me. I am whoever I was made to be.

If you don't know who you are, you can be whoever you wish to be.

The cell door swings open. Almost too easily.

It is empty inside. Pristine and elegant. Like Homer.

Not a single thing out of place—which means everything is wrong.

Why is he not here? Of course. He is in some basement with Poppy and who knows how many others.

The room is full of books, cabinets, papers, and gadgets. I start throwing everything left and right. I am not searching. I am destroying.

That is what happens when you do not know what you are looking for.

Outside the cell bars, Rush and the officers watch me. They caught up. Hands hover near holsters. I can feel the weight of their judgment. Like I am the one who belongs behind bars.

But Rush makes a subtle gesture—stand down. Let her work. She is close.

And then, of course, Professor Gabriel Homer appears.

He stands there with his cane and pipe, looking at me calmly. Not provoked. Not upset. Not even surprised.

"What are you looking for, Detective?" he asks, as serene as a therapist.

"Stay away from me." The words shoot out like a bullet. I want to scream that I do not even know what I am looking for. But if he is the Comedian, I will find something.

"You know you don't have a warrant to search my space, right?" His tone is light, almost bored. I cannot tell if he is still calm or starting to shift.

"Consider this a warrant." I wave the gun and yank open drawers with my free hand.

What am I doing? I am waving a gun like some unhinged cop in a bad thriller. But I cannot stop. I will not stop.

Not until I find something.

Homer speaks again like we are discussing the weather.

"Why me? How could you believe I kidnapped you six years ago?"

"Because I'm desperate!" I shout. I know how I sound. I know what I am confessing. There are so many reasons to suspect him. Like the double basement under his office. But Poppy is running out of time. "You are manipulative. All of you. Every last one of you. And I can't leave another girl behind. Not again."

A thick silence settles over the room. But I keep searching.

"So is that what happened in the basement six years ago?" Homer's voice softens, though there is something sharp underneath. "You left them behind when he let you go?"

"Shut up."

"I thought we had a deal. You would tell me everything that happened. No secrets."

He taps his cane gently against the floor. I see something new in him now.

"And I think you lie all the time!" My voice breaks. "I think you know more than you say. I still believe you are the Comedian. Or at the very least, you know who he is. Your answers are too perfect. Your alibis too convenient."

"I do not know who he is," Homer replies too quickly. "But it's okay, Detective," he adds, as if offering comfort. "It is not your fault that you left the girls behind. You did nothing wrong."

"It. Is. My. Fault." Tears blur my vision. They soak the files I am rifling through. "You don't understand. You don't know what happened."

"No one is blaming you." Homer's voice is unbearably calm. "There was nothing you could have done. Let it all out. Destroy everything if you must."

My phone buzzes. It is Kat. I do not answer. I do not think she can help anymore. I am beyond help. I am at the bottom, sinking in black glue, unable to tell up from down.

Kat gives up.

But then Rush's phone rings.

He answers. Listens. Eyes locked on me.

"Kat has something important to share," he says gently, trying to hold me together. "I'm putting her on speaker."

Her voice crackles through.

"I found it."

"Found what?"

"The double basement I missed earlier. There are six, not five. The sixth is in Brooklyn." Kat sounds sure of herself now. "Barely any water damage. It was shut down over some shady legal stuff tied to the basement's use."

"So?" I'm shaking. "What makes it the one?"

Kat gulps. Loud. Clear.

"It's under the Yellow."

CHAPTER 50

The fluorescent lights in Homer's office keep flickering, casting strange shadows across the walls. I rub the back of my neck—a nervous habit I've developed after years of chasing nightmares.

"Under us?" My stomach drops like I've missed a step on a dark staircase. The realization that Poppy has been beneath my feet for days makes me want to vomit. "This whole time?"

"The older blueprints show a sealed sub-level from 1921," Kat's voice crackles with urgency. "Buried after some illegal patient experiments. Sorry I missed it the first time."

"'Tread lightly,'" I mutter. The Comedian's cryptic message suddenly makes sense. "He wasn't talking about the police. He was talking about me."

"Walking all over Poppy's trail for days," Rush says quietly. His voice slithers through the air like guilt given form.

Homer stands in the doorway. For once, I see something real behind his carefully composed facade. His eyes are distant. His shoulders sag. This doesn't feel like an act. It isn't the usual cryptic calm. It looks like fear.

Could I have been wrong to suspect him?

For the first time, I see a man who looks genuinely shaken.

But I'm already moving. I shove past the officers crowding his office. There is no time to second-guess myself. No time to dwell on mistakes.

I jump into the driver's seat. This time I'm driving.

"One thing I don't understand, Detective," Rush says as he climbs in, fastening his seatbelt with shaking hands. "How could the Comedian risk getting caught like this?"

"I think he's mocking me. Or maybe he wants to be caught." The words taste bitter. "All I know is I need to find Poppy first."

Kat's voice returns through the speaker. "The basement's entry isn't inside the Yellow. There's a private staircase that bypasses the entire building."

"And no one knew about it?" I swerve between two cars.

"It's only accessed from the morgue," Kat replies, her typing never stopping. "Not the public one—an old one. It's locked off. Like a brick wall was built over it. Someone made sure the past stayed buried."

"Asylums have morgues?" Rush asks.

"Like I said, shady stuff happened here a century ago. The morgue was a cover."

I do not want more details. Not now. "Just tell us how to break through that door, Kat. We're almost there."

Twenty minutes later, the asylum looms ahead, a monument to forgotten secrets and hidden horrors. I don't drive through the alley this time. I come from the main street. As I pull up, I wonder how I never bothered to check it before—or why I never questioned the Yellow's setting and how closely it resembles the Comedian's crime scenes.

Maybe I've been in over my head since the beginning. Maybe I've missed the obvious again and again. But part of me senses something else. Something deeper.

Something about me tells me the Comedian has been pulling the strings all along—like a puppet master watching me dance to his tune.

Maybe Johnson is right. Maybe he planted himself in my mind

six years ago. Maybe he's been inside me ever since, cultivating the perfect victim to torment.

The thought makes my skin crawl more than any basement ever could.

CHAPTER 51

The morgue smells like forgotten secrets. The metallic taste of fear coats my tongue. My boots stick slightly to the floor with each step, the tacky surface reluctant to release me. The cold seeps through my clothes and settles in my bones—the kind of deep chill that feels like it will never leave.

Johnson is already here. According to Rush's dispatch, she ordered her men to break through the wall.

But it turns out the Comedian had already done that and covered the opening with a rusty old cabinet. It was hidden at the far end of the most abandoned corridor in the Ashwood wing.

According to Homer, who followed in his own car, the morgue may have been left as the asylum's dark secret—buried behind these walls for nearly a century.

And yes, based on his research, he admits that most nurses and doctors in asylums—and even some hospitals—know nothing about certain wings or floors. If they do not have a reason to go there, they avoid them. Places like this creep people out for a reason.

Behind the cabinet, the hole in the wall opens into full darkness. My flashlight cuts through layers of dust that hang in the air like blood clots. Story of my life—always uncovering what others want to keep hidden.

Eventually, I find a spiral metal staircase descending into blackness.

As I step down, the surface beneath my boots begins to give. It feels soft and spongy, like I am walking on something rotten. The soles of my shoes sink slightly with each step. The floor seems to exhale beneath my weight. I try not to think about what might be decomposing in the walls, the floor, or the air I am breathing. I keep going until we reach the first sub-basement level—the one closest to the Yellow.

"Spread out," Johnson orders. Her voice is sharp and clipped, but I can hear the tremor buried under her usual authority. Even The Dick folds when he meets the unknown.

A chaotic mess of flashlight beams dances across the room, making everything harder to see. But then I find it. Another massive metal cabinet, like something from a horror movie set. This one is not blocking the morgue's entry like before. This one blocks the stairwell to the next level down.

"Here." My voice cuts through the noise. "Help me move this."

Before anyone reaches me, I find myself capable of dragging the cabinet aside. Either I have gotten stronger, or the Comedian made it easier in case I came alone.

Another spiral staircase disappears into the dark.

My heart hammers against my ribs. The pulse in my ears is so loud it drowns everything out. I cannot move. My legs refuse. It is as if they already know what my brain does not—that whatever is waiting down there may be worse than anything I have imagined.

What if we are too late? What if she is barely alive? What if he is down there, waiting?

I have spent six years running from this moment, and now I have to walk straight into it.

"We're not backing up now, Detective!" Johnson snaps. Her voice hits the back of my neck like a gun cocking.

"Shut up!" I yell. I know I am overstepping, but I do not care.

A short silence follows. But in the distance, more officers keep murmuring.

"All of you. Quiet."

They freeze instantly. The flashlight beams stop moving. Even Johnson shuts her mouth mid-command.

The air that rushes up from below feels thick. It carries more than cold—it brings a weight of human suffering that crawls across my skin. But that is not what I am listening for.

I do not want to show Johnson who is in control. I do not care about the authority in the room. I am not trying to hide a panic attack, or even prove I am the only one who gives a damn.

I want to hear her breathe.

Poppy.

Through all the usual basement sounds—resonating pipes, distant water flow, street rumble above—I can hear it.

She is breathing.

Too loud.

It is as if she is hooked up to a speaker.

My entire body locks into place. The sound hits like a jolt of electricity. Goosebumps shoot up my arms.

She is alive. She is here.

Every cell in my body screams to move.

"Poppy!" I fly down the stairs like a motherfucker.

CHAPTER 52

The cold hits first. The kind that creeps under your skin and makes a home there.

I squint into the darkness, disoriented and blind. The officers' flashlights bounce wildly around us, more confusing than helpful. There is no sign of the Comedian's signature light bulb—no eerie spotlight hanging above his victim like in the other scenes.

But I can hear her. Poppy's breathing. Ragged. Amplified. As if someone put a microphone to her lips.

"This is Commissioner Johnson, NYPD!" Johnson's voice booms into the dark, echoing off invisible walls. "Show yourself or I will shoot!"

I almost snort. "He's not here," I whisper, just loud enough for her to hear. "I can feel it."

Rush appears beside me, the light from his phone casting strange shadows across his face. "Kat sent these," he says, showing me yellowed blueprint scans of the building.

I trace the faded lines with my finger, following the layout of this underground nightmare.

"Left," I say, pointing toward the direction where Poppy's

breathing is loudest. "The Comedian told us to 'tread lightly.' He wasn't being poetic. We've been walking right above her this entire time."

Then I see it. A cage. Not red like the others. Smaller. Black.

Our flashlights converge like spotlights, and there she is.

Poppy Taylor.

Alive.

She's strapped to a chair, bolted to the floor. A wooden box—ancient and stained dark—encases her entire head. Only her mouth is visible through a narrow slit cut across the front. Her lips are pale and trembling with each breath.

The room falls completely silent.

I circle the cage, but there's no way in. Black wires coil around her like snakes, disappearing into the box over her head.

My hands shake as I reach through the bars. "Poppy, can you hear me?"

She tries to nod but stops with a whimper. She manages only a faint "yes" through her drugged lips.

I want to tear the box from her head, rip the wires away like parasites. Free her from this nightmare.

But I freeze as Homer's voice cuts through—sharp and urgent.

"Don't touch it, Maddie. The box is rigged to her pulse. One wrong move could trigger a shock strong enough to stop her heart."

His flashlight flickers across the wires, revealing a tiny blinking sensor taped to her neck. Crude, but deadly. A kill switch I can't remove without tools—or time we don't have.

My stomach twists. I'm so close, yet helpless. Her shallow breaths taunt me through that slit in the wood.

"We need specialists. Someone who can disarm it." My voice breaks as I grip the bars. "I'm here, Poppy. I'm Detective Maddie Brooks. It's going to be okay. I won't let you die. I promise—"

Homer grabs my hand to quiet me. His grip is surprisingly firm for someone who once claimed to need my protection.

"Stay back, Maddie," he whispers in my ear, careful not to startle

Poppy. "She might not even know we're here. That's a sensory deprivation box. It's meant to shut her off from her surroundings. To
weaken her senses."

"And how the hell do you know how the box works?" I snap,
yanking my arm free. "It's a recreation of old psychiatric treatments.
They were banned for a reason."

"Banned? Like your book?" I laugh bitterly, the sound ragged,
close to a sob I refuse to let out.

Homer's face shifts. The clinical mask drops. His eyes darken—
not with malice, but with something closer to guilt. His shoulders sag
under invisible weight. He runs a trembling hand through his hair,
his gaze fixed on the device.

"Are you sure he isn't one of your patients?" I ask, my voice like a
blade.

The question hits him hard. I see it in the way he flinches. A
terrible possibility takes root in his mind: what if his own unorthodox
theories inspired this? What if his writings became the Comedian's
bloody blueprint?

The weight of that thought seems to age him on the spot. His face
collapses in on itself. He looks older. Vulnerable. Human.

"And what are the wires for?" My voice cuts through the silence.

"Periodic electrical shocks," he says, barely audible. "Psychological
manipulation at its most extreme."

He swallows, slipping into lecture mode like it's the only way he
knows how to survive this.

"English, Professor." I grab the bars until my knuckles turn white.
"Talk to me like I'm not sitting in your goddamned classroom."

Homer takes a breath. His eyes meet mine with devastating
clarity.

"He thinks she's insane. And he believes he's treating her."

CHAPTER 53

Homer's words hang in the air for a full minute. Too many thoughts spiral through my head, and it feels like my skull is about to split from the pressure. Understanding his motives—as an amateur surgeon using banned techniques—shows progress. But like everything else with him, it still doesn't explain enough.

A couple of specialists arrive. Homer moves to block me from interfering or talking to Poppy. He claims we need to keep her as calm as possible. Just having us nearby, he says, will help her feel safer.

"You don't want to mess with her survival right now," he warns. "You have someone who, unlike you, saw the Comedian's face. She spent days and nights with him. Messages. Conversations about photography. Just be patient for a few hours, and she'll be able to tell you everything."

Homer's words offer clarity, but they also deepen my doubts. Is he involved? I still believe he is. But to what extent, I'm not sure.

Rush and Johnson stand behind us. They're making calls and coordinating hospital logistics. They're handling the usual police work that follows in cases like this. Rush glances at me in the flickering lights, and I can see it clearly. He's proud of me. And for once, I don't flinch from it. I'm slowly warming up to this man.

Johnson, on the other hand, is laser-focused on salvaging her career. She's already calling the Taylors, alerting the press, managing her narrative.

I take a deep breath and step back. I agree with Homer. I wait while the specialists speak tensely to one another, untangling the intricate web of wires. One thing becomes clear—they believe they can free Poppy alive.

With surgical care, they manage to release her from the chair inside the cage, though the box on her head remains. They extract her without disturbing it. The process is slow and dangerous, but they pull it off.

They place her gently in a new chair they brought. They ask her to stay quiet and breathe slowly. I watch her closely, secretly proud. She's the only girl I've managed to save.

Everyone helped. It was a team effort. But it means something deeper to me. It lifts a part of the weight I've carried since that night six years ago.

And then I see it.

In the shadows.

A white, shiny object stuck to Poppy's dress, crisscrossed with medical tape.

"What the hell is this?" I shove past the specialists before they can stop me.

"Maddie!" Homer's warning comes too late.

The tape seals an envelope to her clothes. It says: *For Maddie, XO.*

The specialists try to pull me back, but when I show them what I see, Johnson, Homer, and Rush freeze. They stop the others and join me, their eyes locked on the envelope.

I pull it off Poppy's dress.

She whimpers softly, but I cannot help myself. Maybe I need psychological treatment now too.

I rip the thick envelope open. Inside is a set of letters—all written in the handwriting I know too well. The Comedian's.

I begin to unfold them, and I can feel everyone's eyes on me. Rush. Johnson. Homer. It's too late to stop. Whatever these letters contain, I need to know.

Dear Maddie Brooks,

CLICK—CLICK—CLICK—RECORDING—CAPTURING—COLLECTING.

AND THEN:

Maddie, Maddie, Maddie,

MY MASTERPIECE IS *about to begin...*

NEXT:

Yo Maddie! ('Dear' sounds so nineties, right?)

Then:

Maddie, my only friend,

I'm writing this from the new basement...

I can't stop reading. Each letter feels like a window into someone who has been watching me far too closely.

Maddie, I feel your pain, but don't worry. I'm closer to you than you think...

And finally, the last one I read before my knees nearly buckle:

WTF is going on, Maddie?

But there is one more letter.

My hands tremble as I lift it. I can feel Rush, Johnson, and Homer watching me. Do they know what it says? Or are they just as scared as I am?

I unfold it carefully. The handwriting is the same.

Maddie, my better half,

I didn't want it to come to this.

But you've been slow, and you've underestimated me.

It seems that my gentle manners aren't getting me anywhere.

I'm left with no other solution but to remind you what happened that night...

CHAPTER 54

SIX YEARS AGO

The basement swims around me in a fog of hallucinations and fear. My tongue feels swollen and dry, stuck to the roof of my mouth like sandpaper. I cannot see straight. Everything blurs at the edges. The floor is cold and hard beneath my palms as I crawl toward that sliver of light. My knees smear blood across the concrete. Each scrape feels like hot glass dragging across my skin.

The door—it is open. Just a crack. Enough.

Behind me, the screams echo off the walls, bouncing like trapped birds. The other girls' voices tangle together in desperation.

"Maddie, no! Please, no!" They know what I'm doing. The weight of it crushes my chest. Each breath is a battle. I hate myself for leaving them, but if I stay, I will die. We all will.

I think he is hiding in the farthest shadows, but I hear his voice. He likes this—manipulating the lighting so we never see the walls. Endless black on all sides. It makes the space feel infinite, our fear eternal.

"I'm done, Maddie," he says softly, almost tenderly.

I am too exhausted to look toward him. I save my energy for

crawling. But then he hurls something toward me. It lands with precision, just inches in front of me.

The golden mask.

It lands with a soft thud. Its hollow eyes stare up at me.

"I used to enjoy this," he says. "But not anymore."

I do not know if the mask is meant to stop me. I could crawl around it with my bleeding elbows and knees. But I am afraid to provoke him. The door could slam shut at any second. If he changes his mind, I am trapped forever.

"People in this city," he mutters, "they've gone numb to violence." He lets out a bitter laugh. "And so have I. But they never get enough. They always want more."

He groans and curses. His headache again. He says it feels like it's splitting his soul in half.

I hear scalpels scrape against the wall behind me. The sound pierces through the drugs and slices my brain with pain. His footsteps shift. He is reconsidering. I freeze.

"Look at all you beautiful cocoons," he says. Something about the way he says *cocoons* unsettles me. Like it means something else. His tone twists the word, makes it sound like an insult.

"All I want is to—"

He stops. I think I moved without permission. I do not know what he wants anymore.

"Do you know how many times I tried to operate on you, Maddie?" His voice softens, even through the voice changer. "So many times."

I do not understand what he means. I hesitate. Should I keep crawling?

"I just can't break you," he says. "Last night, you bit the back of my scalp when I tried to sedate you. When I strapped you to the bars for filming, you never gave in. You kicked me. You never begged. I'll give you that. It's like you're me. My better half. I feel like you understand me."

The girls are silent now. They listen to him speak about me. No wonder they stopped talking to me. They thought I was special. Turns out my strength is what kept him from hurting me—unlike the others.

I change my mind. I have to crawl around the mask. His fascination with me might buy my freedom. I can always come back for the girls. I tell myself that. I promise I will. But even now, it feels like a lie.

"Don't you dare leave before I tell you to!"

His voice explodes behind me. The other girls gasp. If this room wasn't soundproofed, the whole world would hear. The floor tiles are soft, spongy. Maybe that's how he mutes the noise.

"You're my last hope, Maddie," he says, quieter again. "That's why I'm letting you go."

My heart thunders against the concrete. The mask catches the light. I cannot believe what he might be implying.

"Put the mask on," he says. His voice is soft again. Like we are friends. No, we are not. You are a monster. Just let me go.

"Please."

I have no choice. My trembling hand reaches for it. I grab the mask, but I cannot bring myself to wear it.

"Maddie, don't put it on!" another girl screams. Annie—or maybe Sadie. Maybe Amy. Not Kelly. Kelly is dead. She was killed yesterday with a hammer while trying to escape. Right? I remember because he made a joke. Said Kelly was the first to be *killed*.

I am too drugged to think straight.

"Don't do it!" That is definitely Annie. I recognize the slight Southern twang in her voice when she's scared.

"I'll come back for you," I mouth. I cannot turn around. The mask slips over my face. Cold. Heavy. Wrong. It smells like metal and sweat and something else. Something I will later recognize as power.

Its cold interior burns my skin.

"Go be my protégé," he says, pleased now.

I want to scream. But I cannot risk it.

Now the girls scream louder. "Don't do it, Maddie!"

"Good girl," he whispers. "You're now my protégé. Only a strong soul like you can complete my masterpiece."

His delusion slices into me. *Protégé? Apprentice?* Is that how he sees me?

"You don't have to come back," he says. "With the mask on, you'll find a way. You'll continue what I started. Don't say I didn't teach you. You've seen it all. This time, make it count. Make them see you, Maddie."

I hiccup, trying to hold back sobs. He cannot make me into a copy of him. I want to assure the girls, but I need to get out.

"Go now. I set you free so you can laugh forever!" His voice lifts like he's performing in a Broadway play. "Before I change my mind."

I crawl faster. My elbows burn. My knees scream. I do not look back. Every inch forward takes everything I have. My vision is going dark again. The drugs are winning.

I ignore the girls' screams.

I ignore my own.

The mask is tight against my face. My knees and elbows leave trails of blood. The drugs might stop me at any second.

"Don't do it, Maddie!"

The stairs appear ahead. The same ones I stumbled up that night.

Each step costs me. The drugs turn my limbs into lead. The stairs wobble. I almost fall.

I cannot crawl anymore. I have to stand.

Stray waits at the top. Eyes wet. Barking softly.

I push to my feet. My knees buckle. I scream. I move anyway.

Fresh air hits my lungs. It is cold and sharp and burns my chest.

I stumble forward. The mask blocks my vision.

Where the hell am I?

I rip it off. I gasp. The world spins.

Stray's bark keeps me moving. His sound fades.

I collapse.

The mask clatters beside me.
"I'll come back," I whisper.
Then the blackness takes me.
Stray's yips cut off.
And the darkness claims me.

CHAPTER 55

THIRTEEN YEARS AGO

I'm thirteen years old, returning to the orphanage I left just six months ago. The Gothic building ahead looms dark and solemn, but I love its strange beauty. I wish it would wrap me in its embrace again.

Behind me, my adopted family waits to get rid of me. This is the second family to reject me after adoption.

The first was a suburban couple who wanted a trophy daughter and got a damaged one instead. Now, this family—one that clearly thought I came with an off switch—has given up too.

Mrs. Madeline Stray, the social worker, meets me at the top of the stairs. Her white hair frames a kind, weathered face. She radiates warmth and motherly care. Weary, I let her hug me while looking over my shoulder at my soon-to-be-former adoptive parents.

"I'm sorry. We've tried," my adoptive mother says. "But her erratic behavior is threatening the peace of our family."

Mrs. Stray nods silently. She cares more about me than she does about them. Her hand moves gently along my back, checking without asking if I've been hurt—again.

"I mean, look at my husband," my adoptive mother adds. "Look what she did to his hand."

Mrs. Stray looks—and understands instantly.

"She almost bit off my fingers," my angry, pathetic adoptive father says. "This little—"

Mrs. Stray's glare stops him mid-word. She knows what really happened.

"I'll have the papers ready tomorrow to terminate the contract," she says. "I'll see you in court."

I listen as my adoptive family walks away. Mrs. Stray leads me back inside, to my old room. She takes care of me for the rest of the day, never pushing me to speak, never asking questions. She respects the silence.

"You had to break his fingers, huh?" she says with a smile as she buttons my uniform.

I say nothing.

"Just like the family before." She smooths the collar of my clean shirt. "I'm glad you came back, though."

I still say nothing, but I smile. This is my home. It always will be.

"No wonder the other girls called you Maddie Breaks," she says. "You break everyone who even thinks about breaking you."

I like that. I lean forward and kiss her on the cheek.

"I have a better name for you," she whispers into my ear. "We'll call you Maddie Brooks."

I raise an eyebrow as I lean back.

"Breaks will scare off the boys. And you want a boy in your life someday, right?"

I nod, too shy to smile, even though I want to.

"Maddie Brooks it is, then." She pats my shoulder and stands. "I'll get the papers done."

"Thank you," I say, gripping her hand with both of mine.

"I'll find a way to get you into med school, like you want, Maddie Brooks." She walks toward the door, then turns back.

"By the way..." Her voice softens, but it's still made of iron.

She doesn't know—and neither do I—that one day, I'll crush a man's skull in a bar.

Eventually, Mrs. Stray dies of old age, after making sure I go to med school. I thought I would miss her unconditional love forever—until a little mixed-breed puppy found his way into my cage.

He became my new Stray.

Now, I hear voices calling me back. Johnson. Rush. Homer. They sound far away, like they're trying to wake me up. I know I've fainted after reading the Comedian's last letter. I know I've saved Poppy. I know I'm proud of that.

And I also know I'm tired.

So I let myself rest a little longer.

I'll catch the Comedian when I wake up.

CHAPTER 56

I wake up with a gasp. My head pounds like someone took a sledgehammer to it.

The ceiling above me isn't the Yellow's water-stained concrete. It's smooth. White. Institutional. A fluorescent light buzzes somewhere overhead.

What happened to—? Recent memories hit me all at once.

The double basement. Poppy's alive. The Comedian's letter in my hands. Those terrible words swimming in front of my eyes. Truth crashing over me like a tidal wave.

Then I fainted. I fell into a memory I thought I had hidden too well to ever resurface.

The screams of those girls. The mask. My escape.

Then nothing. Just darkness. My knees gave out. And I hit the floor.

Now I'm back. Back in the real world.

"Try not to move too quickly." A familiar voice breaks through the fog in my brain. "Your system is still processing the shock, Maddie."

I turn my head and instantly regret it. Pain shoots through my temples.

Homer sits across from me in a leather chair. A notepad rests on his knee. He holds a pen like it's a scalpel.

I'm lying on a therapy couch. The room feels warm and professional. Not like his elegant office at the Empire Institute. This space is simpler. More clinical.

"Where am I?" My voice sounds like I've been gargling gravel.

Homer leans forward and offers me a glass of water. "You're safe," he says. "That's what matters right now."

I take the glass. My fingers tremble as I raise it to my lips.

Outside the window behind Homer, I see treetops and a strip of gray sky.

"Poppy," I blurt. The memory rushes back—the cage, the medieval torture device, the letter. "Did we—?"

"She's being treated," Homer answers carefully. "Fingers crossed, the damage to her nervous system is minimal. Soon you'll be able to speak with her."

Relief washes over me, but only for a moment. I know too well that surviving is just the first step. The real battle happens afterward. The war in your head. The years of silence. The way trauma rewrites you.

At least now we'll catch the Comedian. Poppy isn't just a survivor. She's a witness. She saw him. Really saw him. He couldn't have charmed her with a mask on. I'm so close this time.

I try to sit up. The room spins.

"The letter," I say through gritted teeth. "Did you read it?"

Homer's expression shifts. His practiced calm fractures slightly. "Yes," he says. "Johnson did too."

I try again to prop myself up, but my skull feels like it's splitting apart.

"I went through all the letters again and again," Homer says, pointing to a pill beside my water glass. "Most were handwritten. He probably wrote them on a whim. One was typed. It looks like he used his phone."

"He was watching me. Documenting every move." I swallow the pill and wash it down with water.

Homer nods. "That also explains why he said he had written to you before."

"He didn't plan to send them. He only sent one to Johnson after Ivy's abduction. Then another when she embarrassed him on TV." My headache begins to ease. I lock eyes with Homer. "Now you know what I've been hiding."

"I do," he says. "The Comedian described it all in detail. You fainted beside Poppy after reading it."

"You told me it wasn't my fault. You said I was drugged. That I collapsed trying to get help." I narrow my eyes. "You said the same thing at the Empire Institute. Did you already know what happened?"

"No," he replies. "Just a clinical hunch. It started the first time I asked you not to lie about that night."

"What gave me away?"

"Classic signs," he says plainly. "Eyes drifting up and left. Jaw tightening. Voice sharp and clipped. That's where the brain goes to invent a story. Most people don't realize they're doing it."

"But you didn't push me." My throat tightens. Tears threaten. "Why?"

"Truth heals when it's found willingly. Not when it's forced. Otherwise, it just becomes another wound."

"Remind me to carve the opposite of that into the Comedian's skull." I swing my feet to the floor and press my palms into the couch. "Because I'll force the truth from him if I have to."

Homer doesn't laugh. "I know it's not easy, Maddie. The Comedian let you go to be his apprentice—"

"I'm not his apprentice," I snap. My pulse pounds. The idea makes me sick. "And I never will be."

"Of course not," he says gently, tapping his pen against the notepad. "But it explains why you've felt stuck. Why you've carried guilt for so long."

I nod slowly. "His voice stayed with me. Every day. The thought that he saw me as his legacy—it poisoned everything."

"I understand. But why didn't you tell the police back then?"

I don't meet his eyes. "I was afraid it would stain me. People say they understand, but once it's in their head, they always wonder. They'll smile at you in person, but when they're alone, they'll judge. They'll ask why the Comedian thought you were like him."

I lift my gaze. "They'll come to their own dark conclusions."

"I don't blame you," he says. "I would've done the same."

I believe him. He's been accused of believing in patients the world dismissed as insane. He gets it.

"Thank you," I whisper.

Homer gives a tight smile. Something unreadable passes between us.

"I owe you an apology," I admit. "I suspected you might be him."

"I know," he says. He brushes something from his pants leg. People do that when they lie—or when they're about to say something important. "According to your profile, I fit."

"You do," I say with a half-laugh. The fog clears a little. But now something new settles in. "Do you think the trauma made me a worse detective?"

"I don't," Homer says. "You've done great work. Johnson only doubted you because of your memory gaps. But after saving Poppy—and saving Johnson's reputation—I think she's changed her opinion."

"Tell me about it." I roll my eyes and smile.

The room smells faintly of bergamot and paper. The clock ticks slightly too fast. I think Homer once said that reminded him of his father's office. Or did I always know that?

I study him more closely.

"Well," he says, brushing his pants again. "I think you should rest."

"I won't rest until I speak to Poppy. I want everything she knows."

"You've had a major breakthrough," Homer replies. "Poppy's alive. No new girls have been taken. One day of rest won't hurt."

"You're right," I say, forcing myself to agree. "I should call my therapist. He helps me untangle things."

Something flickers in Homer's expression.

I reach for his coat on the couch—then stop.

The room suddenly feels off. Too familiar.

I scan the space. The lighting. The smell. That mahogany desk. The brass lamp. The medical books stacked by height. The cracked window.

My heart skips.

I've been here before.

"Come to think of it..." Goosebumps rise along my arms. I stare at Homer. A strange laugh escapes my chest. "This room looks exactly like my therapist's office."

"It does," Homer says without flinching.

"But my therapist's office is uptown. Near my apartment—"

"Where is your apartment, Maddie?"

My stomach drops. Why can't I answer that? "It's near—" I pause. "It's... near the office."

"We're in your therapist's office now," Homer says. "And it's not uptown."

"What are you talking about? It's in—" I stop. He's right. This is my therapist's office.

"Who is your therapist, Maddie?" Homer stands closer.

"What?" My voice cracks. I try to stand, but I feel lightheaded.

He's too close. It's not his face I see, or the mask. It's me—staring at the other girls—wearing the golden mask.

"Can you remember, Maddie?" Homer's voice is calm, but I don't want him near me. "Where do you think we are?"

I sweat beneath a mask I'm not even wearing.

"We're in the Ashwood Asylum," he says. "We're above the Yellow."

"No," I whisper. I shake my head, trying to stay upright. "I need to leave. I need to see my therapist. He's been helping me for years."

Homer doesn't step aside. He blocks the door.

"Who is this therapist, Maddie?" He grabs my arm. His touch feels wrong.

"Let go of me!" I squirm. I'm looking for something. Anything that makes sense. "Why does it matter?"

His voice hardens. "Why do you think you felt like you knew me when we first met?"

I narrow my eyes. "I didn't feel like that. You confuse me."

"You did." His grip tightens. I can't break away. "Because we've known each other for six years."

The words slide under my skin like cold knives.

"Because I am your therapist," Homer says. "I always have been."

CHAPTER 57

Now Homer's words feel like toxic air. I can't breathe. The fluorescent light above us flickers, casting uneven shadows across his face.

I stare at him. His face is both familiar and suddenly wrong, like a photograph where someone has been edited out.

"Is this a joke?" My voice comes out smaller than I intended. "Did Johnson put you up to this to get me off the case?"

Homer doesn't blink. His eyes stay steady and clinical, the way a coroner might examine a body.

"It's not a joke," he says. "You've been a patient in the Ashwood Asylum for almost six years now."

A chill runs down my spine and spreads like ice water through my veins. My mouth goes dry.

"That's impossible." Even I can hear how thin and unconvincing my voice sounds. "I've been investigating the Comedian. Johnson assigned me the case. I've done real detective work."

"You've never been a detective," Homer says. His voice is quiet but firm, like a doctor delivering bad news. "Although you've always wanted to be."

No. This isn't happening. He's lying.

A harsh laugh escapes me—sharp and brittle like glass breaking on concrete.

"So what have I been doing all this time? Imagining crime scenes? Making up evidence?"

Homer pulls a thick file from his desk. The folder is worn at the edges, overstuffed with papers. My life reduced to a manila folder. My stomach turns just looking at it.

"Your name is Madison Brooks. Six years ago, the Comedian kidnapped you and four other girls." He opens the file. The pages crinkle loudly in the silent room. "Someone found you unconscious in an alley. Stray barked until they found you. Even as a puppy, he wouldn't leave your side. He kept barking for days."

I remember. The barking. The cold pavement. The feeling that the world was ending and only one soul had noticed.

"After a long investigation, you were released. The sole survivor."

"So?" My toes curl inside my shoes. Memories begin to stab through the fog in my mind—sharp, jagged, and impossible to hold.

"Then, you smashed a man's skull in a bar with something like a hammer," Homer says. "It mirrors what you saw the Comedian do to one of the girls who tried to escape."

The image returns with a sickening jolt. The weight of the barstool. The crack of bone. The blood.

I remember Mrs. Stray telling me to break anyone who tried to break me.

The air suddenly feels too thin. I'd never connected the two moments before. But now something deep inside me goes still, like prey sensing a predator nearby.

"NYPD wanted to charge you with assault," Homer continues, flipping to another page. "That's when I was called in."

"You?" The word slips out, barely a whisper.

Homer nods once, like a judge delivering a sentence.

"I convinced the court that you weren't well. You were diagnosed. They agreed not to prosecute. You were transferred to Ashwood Asylum."

His voice speeds up, trying to pull the bandage fast.

"In here, you created a new life. You built a detective persona. A mission. And for years, you've been my patient. Healing. Breaking. But never truly leaving."

"No." The word scrapes up from somewhere deep in my chest. "No."

My head throbs like it's splitting in half. I feel unmade. I feel like him—the Comedian—dissociating, splitting, denying.

I start counting on my fingers. I need to anchor myself to reality.

"I almost solved the case. I worked so hard. I've been to crime scenes. I stayed in that awful basement. I didn't tolerate all of that for nothing."

"We made up the Yellow," Homer says. His voice is calm. "It's not real."

"We?" My breath shortens.

"Johnson and I. We created the Yellow. It's an unused basement in the asylum. It gave us a way to monitor you. We told you that you'd been transferred from the NYPD to a secret unit. But the transfer was from upstairs to downstairs."

I grip the edge of the chair. My knuckles go white.

"Oh really?" I sit forward, fire rising in my chest. "So you and Johnson designed this fake world just for me? And you didn't know about the double basement underneath?"

Homer looks away for the first time. A tiny crack in his wall of calm.

"I'm sorry for that. We didn't know. The idea that the Comedian hid Poppy there never crossed our minds."

His sincerity only makes this worse. Because now I know he's telling the truth.

"No," I repeat. It's all I have left. "I am a detective." I jab my chest. "I earned this. I worked for this. I gave up six years to catch him. You don't get to take that from me."

Homer says nothing. He just waits, eyes steady, watching me run out of ways to fight.

My head pounds with unbearable pressure. Finally, something inside me cracks. A warm tear slips down my cheek.

"You're no different from him," I say, pointing at Homer with shaking fingers. "You cared more about your methods than my truth. You used my delusion to prove your point. You let me think I was sane so you could show the world that insanity is just a myth."

"I know," he says softly. "And I'm sorry for that."

He stands and walks to the door.

"How about we go for a walk, Maddie?" he says. "I want to show you something."

CHAPTER 58

Staring at Homer, the silence stretches so long that voices from down the hall drift into the room. Mistrust settles in my chest like concrete.

Every instinct tells me to refuse—to scream, to run, to pretend none of this is real. Rejection pulses through me like a second heartbeat. But under the denial, curiosity flickers like a weak flame refusing to die.

"Fine," I mutter. "Just remember, I've crushed someone's skull before."

"And rightfully so," Homer replies, his tone softening slightly. "He was a wanted killer in three states, anyway. Now follow me, please."

He opens the door and motions me forward.

The moment I step into the hallway, something clicks.

My legs feel leaden. Each step demands conscious effort. The buzzing fluorescent lights drill into my skull. Goosebumps prickle my skin, and I catch myself hugging my arms across my chest like a shield.

I know this place. The pale green walls, the squeaky floors, the barred windows I thought were just in nightmares.

"After your kidnapping," Homer explains as we walk, "you developed what traditional psychiatry calls Dissociative Identity Disorder. But your case defies simple labels."

"I'm special. What a shock." Sarcasm is all I have left when everything else feels like it's falling away.

"This is exactly why I wrote that banned book," he says with restrained frustration. "The human mind doesn't fit neatly into diagnostic boxes. Your mind created a version of you—a detective—someone who could stay in control and hunt the Comedian when the real world became too painful."

"Is that even a common diagnosis?" I ask.

"Not in this form. But your history made you particularly vulnerable." His voice gentles. "Losing your parents in that crash before you turned two. Cycling through failed adoptions. Each rejection fractured your developing sense of self. Mrs. Stray was the only real constant you ever had."

Her name lands in my chest like a weight.

"So I was already broken before the Comedian got to me."

"Not broken," he says. "Adaptable. The psychiatric world likes labels. But what you've done is adapt. The detective persona was your mind's way of surviving."

"But I fit his victims' profile perfectly," I say.

"I'd say you were overqualified." Homer nudges me with a small smile. "You resisted. And it messed with him."

Before I can reply, a nurse passes us and smiles like we've known each other for years.

"Morning, Maddie," she says cheerfully. "I still wear that teddy bear necklace you found."

I stop. "She knows me?"

"Everyone here knows you," Homer replies quietly.

"What necklace is she talking about?"

"You find lost things for the staff and other patients. That's your detective side coming through."

This can't be my life. But the evidence stacks higher with every step. Around the corner, a woman in a pink sweater talks to herself. When she sees me, her face lights up.

"Detective Brooks!" she calls. "Go get that bad boy!"

Homer gives me a look that says, "Just go with it." I nod politely but feel like an impostor wearing someone else's skin.

"That 'bad boy' would be the Comedian, by the way," Homer whispers. "They all know your mission."

I suddenly understand how easy it was to send me out after the Comedian. I've been rehearsing the role for years between these walls. It didn't take much for my brain to continue the act outside. But accepting that means accepting this version of reality—something I'm not ready for yet.

"This is your room," Homer says, stopping at a heavy door with a small window. I try not to gasp. It looks exactly like the maid's room at the Yellow. They've recreated it downstairs—probably to make me feel safe. Or in control.

A wave of nausea rolls over me. My vision tunnels. I grip the wall for support. The bed. The desk. The barred window. It's all familiar and horrifying—like learning your childhood home was actually a cage.

"I lived here for six years?" The words barely leave my mouth. I can't look inside. I'm afraid that if I do, I'll never leave again.

"We have an open policy on this floor," Homer says, almost like a tour guide. "Your door stays unlocked most of the day."

"Part of your experiment with insanity, I assume? Letting every patient live out their fantasy?"

"Not every patient," he says. "But you were never dangerous. Most on this floor aren't."

"What you did is still wrong." My face tightens with anger. "I don't care what your intentions were. I understand why your book was banned. Why no one trusts you."

"I'm not here to defend myself," he replies. "But letting you chase the Comedian wasn't my idea alone. Johnson and I were pressured. Borderline threatened."

He stops walking. So do I.

"Johnson was about to lose her job," he says. "And I was about to lose my wife."

He hesitates.

"But... I'll get into my personal life later."

I blink. "When you say threatened... by who?"

"The mayor."

I frown. "What mayor?"

"New York's mayor. Sam Willet."

I tilt my head. "As in... Johnson's husband?"

CHAPTER 59

"No," Homer frowns, clearly confused by the connection I made. "Sam is just the mayor. Where did you get that idea?"

"She's always calling him," I say, narrowing my eyes.

"Ah, I get it now, but you're wrong." He pieces it together. "Sam, being a slave to the powerful, forced Johnson to let you investigate after Ivy Williams was taken."

"Isn't that illegal?" I ask. "I could sue him."

"Don't take this the wrong way, Maddie," he says, "but you were worried that people wouldn't understand why the Comedian let you go. Sam might even call you 'insane' and say you escaped from the asylum." Homer pauses. "Sam didn't care about catching the Comedian—until Ivy. After the Comedian wrote to Johnson, Ivy's family urged Sam to include you. But it was already too late. Setting everything up and making sure you believed it took time."

"Even knowing my condition?" I ask, pushing aside the ethical nightmare for now—I want the truth; justice can come later.

"They didn't care—you were bait—a link to the Comedian—someone he specifically asked for in the letter."

"Then why was Johnson such a bitch to me?" I press, digging into the cracks of his story.

"I'm not saying Johnson is easy to deal with, but in your case? She was trying to break you."

"Yeah, I got that. I asked why."

Homer says, "She wanted to show Sam and the Williams family you were unstable. This way, she could quietly bring you back. Sara tried to play both sides. She wanted to keep her job, follow orders, and still protect you."

"How noble," I roll my eyes.

Homer pauses, the kind of pause that means he's deciding whether to tell me something or not.

"She's not as cold as you think, Maddie," he finally says. "She has another reason for protecting you—one I can't tell you yet. Please don't judge her fully."

"That's rich coming from you," I shoot back. "Sam, Johnson, you, the Comedian—you're all the same. You all have your agendas. I'm just a pawn in this puppet show of a psych ward."

"If you weren't so damn good at pretending to be a detective, we could've brought you back in a day," he says, almost amused. "But it turns out you're a real detective—and now you're close to saving this city from a very dark soul."

"Takes crazy to catch crazy," I mutter.

"Which proves my point," he says with a smug half-smile.

I ignore the bait. "What about Rush? Where does he fit into this circus?"

"Gregory Rush was assigned by Sam Willet," Homer explains. "His job was to watch you, take care of you, and make sure you didn't figure anything out."

"Because if I did, I could blow the whole thing up." My eyes lock onto his. "Mayor—NYPD—mental health system—it'd be a media bloodbath."

"You still can," Homer says. "I won't stop you."

"You can't stop me," I fire back, before circling back to Rush. "His shift makes sense now. He was anxious around me, then helpful, and finally... oddly supportive. But what about his alcoholism? Another act?"

"No, that's real—I'm his doctor," Homer admits. "Sam black-mailed him too—said if he didn't comply, he'd never work again."

"And Kat?"

"She doesn't know anything," Homer says. "She doesn't want to. She's moved on from her NYPD days. Now, she seeks off-the-books work to feel useful and avoid relapsing. Johnson hires her often."

"That's why she called me Alice," I murmur. "We both fell down the rabbit hole."

Then a question rises up in my throat like bile—my heartbeat stutters. "What about Stray?"

Homer arches an eyebrow. "What about him?"

"You don't allow pets here, do you?" My voice is soft now. "Or is he just a delusion? A hallucination I hold onto because I can't let him go?"

CHAPTER 60

Homer's mouth curves into something almost resembling a smile. "Follow me."

I walk behind him through the asylum. We stop at a plain door. A brass nameplate shows a different doctor's name.

I hear frantic scratching and excited whines from the office. They sound so familiar that my chest aches and my heart races. Homer quickly twists the handle. The door barely opens before a furry missile launches through the gap.

Stray vibrates with joy. His tail wags so fast it's a blur. His ears perk up and twitch as he circles me. I hear his nails clicking on the floor. He whimpers, as if he can't believe I'm here. His warm breath puffs against my legs.

I drop to my knees, wrapping my arms around his neck. "Hey, boy," I whisper against his fur. "At least you're real."

But then Homer walks into the office. To my surprise, Stray breaks away from me. He trots after Homer, tail wagging. Then he sits beside the desk as Homer takes a seat. The betrayal stings more than it should.

A bitter jealousy twists in my stomach, sharp as a knife. I sit across from Homer. More pieces fit together in my mind. The puzzle forms a picture I wish I could unsee.

"You took him in after I was hospitalized, didn't you?" I say flatly. "That's why he was excited when I was reading your book."

"I held him in my lap many nights while I wrote," Homer says, stroking Stray's head—his fingers vanish into the fur. "And let's not forget he saved your life by barking until a stranger found you."

"Why didn't you send him to a shelter?" The words come out sharper than I intended.

Homer glances down at Stray, who looks back at him with complete adoration. "Look at him—he's too cute for that." He softens. "I always intended to return him to you, once you were ready to leave here."

The implications crash over me like a wave—I grip the armrests of my chair to steady myself. "So that night... when I was upset about Poppy and you waited for me in the alley—you were at my door because—"

"Just making sure you were all right," he finishes. "Also, when Rush told me you'd need the apartment keys for the dog, I brought Stray along."

"That's why Rush always hid the keys from me, isn't it? You didn't want me to decide to go home and discover I actually live here."

"Yes." The word is small but definitive.

"And meeting me at the Empire Institute—that was to avoid triggering my memories if I had met you here?"

"True," Homer ruffles Stray's fur.

"But the Comedian does know about you—how?" My fingers drum against my thigh, a nervous habit I didn't realize I had.

"I think he knows about everyone and everything—not sure how—but he enjoys it more than anything."

"Which means he is one of us, right?" The thought sends chills down my spine. My gaze is sharp and defiant. This isn't a faceless monster in the dark. It's not a myth or legend. It's a colleague—a friend. It's someone I've seen in these halls. Maybe even someone who has smiled at me or said my name.

"Or someone connected to us—I agree," Homer says.

"Are you ready to know what I've discovered about the Comedian?"

"I didn't know I was still considered a detective on the case," I reply. "Unless you guys really need crazy detectives."

Homer gets right to the point without commenting on my current situation.

I must admit, I don't fully understand my situation. I've just gone along with it. Everything I've heard makes me want to retreat. I wouldn't want to talk to anyone for weeks.

I think my drive to find the Comedian in this wild world matters most. As I told Rush in the car earlier: drive now, think later.

Homer tosses a file onto the desk. Inside, there are pictures of Poppy and Ivy from the crime scene. The shiny photos reflect the fluorescent light, making the horror in them seem to glow.

Then he says, "I think I know what the Comedian means by calling his work a masterpiece."

CHAPTER 61

"Since Ivy's murder scene, I felt like I should have known what was going on," Homer says. "But I couldn't place it at first."

"I'm listening."

"But after seeing that medieval contraption on Poppy's head, everything clicked." He spreads a set of historical photos on his desk. The sepia images are shocking. Men and women are strapped into strange devices. Their faces show pain, and their bodies twist in odd ways.

My stomach churns. "What am I looking at?"

"These are old ways doctors treated mental illness in the 1700s and 1800s," Homer says, pointing at the first photo. "Ashwood Asylum and the Empire Institute in New York used secret treatments that were not allowed."

"They called this treatment?" My body recoils as Homer flips through thick, sticky pages in old textbooks. "They were killing them."

"Mental illness used to be a mystery, like witchcraft or magic from another world," says Homer. "And these methods, believe it or not, were considered state-of-the-art at the time."

Stray tries to jump onto the table to look, but I stop him—he shouldn't see something this awful.

Homer stops turning pages and points to an image that makes my toes curl.

"Cages?"

"Yes." His gaze holds mine, like he's checking whether I can handle this next part.

The photos of patients in cages are disturbing. People are squeezed into metal boxes that barely fit them. Some sit upright in a 'tranquilizing chair,' while others huddle painfully.

"This is called the Belgian cage," Homer says, pausing on one image, his voice tinged with disgust. "It was used well into the 20th century in some places."

He points to another. "This is a drip cage. Patients were held still while cold water dripped on their foreheads for days."

I stare at a red-painted cage that looks eerily familiar. "Why red?"

"To hide the blood, the crimson paint worked well. It made cleanup easier and helped staff deal with the trauma."

If these images weren't right before my eyes, I'd think Homer had a wild imagination.

"All these cages are in basements. Why?"

"Doctors kept their 'worst' patients underground—away from the public eye," Homer explains. "Basements were soundproof. If a patient died during treatment, they could be buried quietly—no questions asked. Most of this was done in the name of science."

"Just like the Comedian's setup," I say absently, as if I am talking to myself.

Stray whines softly next to me. He senses my distress. I want to bury my fingers in his fur and feel something warm and real. But I still don't want him to see the photos.

"What about the masks?" I point at the doctors in the image— they're not comedic smiley masks, but various other types.

"Doctors often wore them in surgeries," Homer says. He opens another folder. Inside are pictures of doctors in face coverings. Some are simple cloth, while others are fancy metal. "Some say it was for sterilization. But mostly, it was to stop patients from recognizing them outside the asylum."

He reaches for my shoulder, and for the first time, I let him. "I need you to be calm for the next two photos—okay?"

I nod—words don't come—I hate when people ask you to brace for something you haven't even seen yet.

Homer takes out two pairs of photos. The first shows a woman with a wooden box around her head, just like the one we found on Poppy. He places them next to a photo of Poppy from the basement.

This is a sensory deprivation device—it calms patients by blocking out sight, sound, and feeling, reducing mental and emotional stimulation. It was once used to treat what we now call bipolar disorder.

"Like Poppy, her parents worried she might get overstimulated. Still, she jumped into another wild adventure."

"And this," Homer says, moving the second pair forward—one is from Ivy Williams, and the other is an old clinic sketch. "Trepanation is drilling holes in the skull to ease pressure on the brain." He taps the image gently. "Doctors believed it released 'bad energy' or calmed restless minds. It was like early neurosurgery that claimed to heal."

"Like Ivy Williams," I whisper, the realization hitting hard. "He drilled into her skull... to treat her—it wasn't murder."

"Not intentionally," Homer says. "He thinks he's curing them, just like I said in the basement. He's trying to recreate old psychiatric treatments that were banned long ago."

"So he is crazy." I feel sick.

"I wouldn't say crazy—psychopath or a sadist, maybe," Homer replies. "The level of detail, the timing, the planning... it's too structured to be pure madness."

"Then why cure his victims using old, forbidden methods?"

"Not victims, but patients." Homer hesitates—his tone shifts. "Only women."

I gasp as I remember the Comedian's first letter: "Now I'm setting them free—not just my victims—but all women in the world."

"Yes—the Comedian truly believes he is curing madness in women." Homer opens another book. "Now pay attention, Maddie—because this next part is what the Comedian is all about."

CHAPTER 62

"The so-called madness in women," Homer begins, "was never really about madness."

Why do I have a feeling that I'm not ready to hear any of this?

"For centuries, female suffering was misunderstood—misdiagnosed—sometimes deliberately." Homer's voice turns clinical. "Women who grieved too long, spoke too loudly, or desired too much weren't seen as complex. Instead, they were labeled as unstable or dangerous."

He pulls an old book off the shelf and opens it with care, the spine cracking like old bones.

"Doctors didn't grasp depression, trauma, or grief. So, they called it hysteria, a name they could control."

I see where this is going, and I wish I didn't. Sometimes, when the puzzle pieces fit, they can be too sharp to hold.

"The word hysteria comes from the Greek word **hystera,**" Homer says, diving into lecture mode, and I don't mind—I want to know.

"Hystera..." I echo, frowning. "That means womb, right?"

"Yes," he says, almost apologetically. Their logic is absurd. They thought the uterus could move through the body like a ghostly organ. If a woman felt chest pain, they believed her womb was pressing on her lungs. If she cried for no reason, they said it had migrated to her brain."

"Are you seriously not making this up?" I ask—I know he's not, but it still sounds impossible.

"The cure for hysteria involved experimental treatments. Mostly done in the basements of asylums."

"Like Poppy and Ivy," I murmur. "Crazy women—crazy doctors—inhumane surgeries."

"You've seen enough," he says. "I don't think you want to see more—but what I haven't told you yet is the underlying concept behind those treatments."

I wait—I'm not going to guess.

"They were all designed to dull the mind—erase the symptoms—and force women back into submission."

"Submission," I repeat, hollow.

"It was never about health," Homer says. "It was about control. The fewer senses a patient could use—sight, hearing, touch, even thought—the less she could resist. Silencing the soul was the path to a cure."

"You sound like a witch doctor."

"And witch doctors they were."

"He's copying these old treatments?" I ask. "To cure them by... silencing them?"

"He's resurrecting an entire ideology that revives a dark age of ignorance. It wraps itself in science, but every method stems from one thing: hatred and fear of women."

I can barely take it in—my stomach turns—I can only listen and hope the next sentence won't somehow be worse than the last.

"But then," Homer continues, "in the late 1800s, one doctor proposed a final, permanent cure."

He swallows hard—he looks like a man ashamed of his profession.

"What kind of cure?" I ask, already suspecting the answer.

He meets my eyes. "The hysterectomy."

I want Stray with me, but he's gone from the chat. Now, he sits under the window, staring at a sliver of sky. It's like he knows something we don't.

"They believed removing the womb would remove the madness," Homer says. "No uterus, no hysteria. Surgery erased women. They were sedated, cut open, and sterilized. This often happened without consent and sometimes without anesthesia. They believed this restored order and made women obedient again."

I blink, too stunned to speak. "And they got away with that?"

"They were praised for it," Homer replies bitterly. "Academic journals praised it as revolutionary. Hospitals promoted it, too. Wealthy families spent a lot on it."

"But the Comedian didn't do that kind of surgery—"

"He is going to," Homer says, cutting in.

He opens the book to a chart with sketches, dates, and procedures. He doesn't need to say it. I see it clearly: the last phase before a full hysterectomy was sensory deprivation.

That's what he did to Poppy—the same thing he plans to do again.

"I guess he has one last victim lined up."

"His masterpiece," I whisper. "But why?"

"I wish I could tell you," Homer says grimly. "It could be anything —a mother, a sister, even a cult. It might be some twisted belief system. As psychologists, we often label things. But some cases..." He trails off. "Some don't fit any labels."

"And I'm the one he couldn't break," I say quietly, my eyes drifting toward the gray sky beyond the glass. "So now he wants me to complete his work."

"Maybe," Homer says. "You're his breaking point."

"Good—then I need to see Poppy."

"I'm afraid you can't."

"Why? She's the only one who saw him—she's our only lead."

"Not for at least twenty-four hours. She's still unconscious. I hope she doesn't fall into a coma. Johnson said you can keep playing detective if you have a plan."

"I don't have a plan—my only plan is to go out there."

"Good," Homer says. "Actually, I think you're more qualified than ever to go out and catch the Comedian now."

"How so?"

"I'll let Officer Rush explain that part—he's waiting for you in his car." Homer opens the door and points at the elevator.

"I can leave the hospital? Just like that?"

"And you can take Stray with you, too—now go before I change my mind."

CHAPTER 63

The elevator makes its descent. Each floor ticks by with an electronic *ding* that feels like a tiny needle jabbing my eardrum. Stray squirms in my arms, his nails digging into my forearm through my sweater.

I see my reflection in the shiny metal doors. My face is pale, and dark circles sit under my eyes. My hair hasn't been styled properly in years. I look exactly like what I am: a mental patient being granted temporary freedom.

The elevator shudders to a stop at the ground floor, and my heart rate spikes. I almost expect sirens to go off as soon as I step outside. Orderlies in white will rush in and pin me to the ground. *Patient escaping. Code red. Sedate on sight.*

When the doors slide open, the antiseptic smell of the main floor hits me like a slap. It's stronger here. I smell bleach and industrial cleaner. There's also a medicinal scent that burns my nostrils.

A nurse with frizzy gray hair appears.

"Maddie! Congratulations on the conditional leave." She talks to me like I'm a five-year-old at the zoo. I'm not a child; I'm a psychiatric patient going outside for the first time in years.

"Thanks." It's the only word I can force past my lips. My anxiety kicks in. I think the problem with knowing who you are is that it's too hard to become whoever you wish to be. "I should go."

I push through the double doors and step outside. The air is shockingly crisp. And suddenly, I understand why I couldn't recognize the city earlier in the drive. I've never really *been* out. Not for years.

Stray probably knows his way around more than I do as I scan the parking lot for Rush's Camry.

I feel like a fish out of water. The streets I imagined running through now feel suffocating and alien. Stray looks just as overwhelmed. His nose twitches at the flood of new scents. His ears turn toward every passing car.

A car horn blares. I flinch.

The Camry stops in front of me, its dented bumper and scratched paint reminding me of the past three days. Rush leans over the passenger seat and yanks the door open. The metal hinges squeak in protest.

"Detective." His voice carries across the courtyard—too loud, too cheerful.

I notice he shaved his mustache, leaving his upper lip naked and strangely vulnerable. Without his facial hair, he looks five years younger. He seems less intimidating too—more like a college kid pretending to be a cop. I smile, but Stray still doesn't trust him.

"Easy," I mutter. "Officer Rush is one of the good guys."

I slide into the passenger seat. Stray jumps into the back. He positions himself as far from Rush as possible. His eyes lock onto our driver with unmistakable suspicion.

"Still playing hard to get, huh?" Rush glances back. "Did you forget about that steak I brought you?"

Stray answers with a sharp bark that makes Rush flinch; I hide my smile.

"I think he's mad about the mustache," I say, running my finger under my nose in demonstration.

"Do you think so? I thought it was time for a change." His eyes glance at my face, then look away.

"You look cute without the mustache," I admit, then immediately regret the honesty. "But don't get cute with me."

A smile pulls at the corner of his mouth. "I'm not really into crazy girls anyway."

Even though the word *crazy* slices through me like a blade, there's something different about Rush now. The anxious officer I met is gone. He was worried that this wild girl might crush his skull with a hammer. This version of Rush seems more relaxed, more real. Like revealing who I am lets him drop his own mask, too.

"I'm into Mad Men," I say, nudging him playfully. Not sure if I'm nervous or if knowing you're crazy is the most underestimated kind of freedom.

Rush reaches into his jacket and pulls out a folded sheet of paper. "I think Professor Homer told you about this."

"He said you'd explain it. Something about an advantage I have now that I'm officially crazy."

"Your official Certificate of Insanity." He hands it to me.

I open a document that seems to be from the government. It has embossed seals and several signatures. It resembles a birth certificate —names, dates, and formal statements. But it reflects my struggles with reality and my tendency to dissociate. All couched in clinical language that basically says I'm nuts.

"Is this for real?"

"I asked the same thing. But apparently, there is such a thing." Rush winks.

"Look, baby," I say to Stray, holding up the paper as he moans in sympathy. "Mommy is officially cuckoo."

"A Beautiful Cuckoo, though," Rush says, smiling slightly. It gives me a flutter in my stomach.

Was he always this flirty? Where did he get that idea?

"So how is this to my advantage?" I ask.

"Easy," Rush taps the wheel. "You go overboard, do whatever you need to do to catch the Comedian. If things go sideways, you pull out the certificate and get sent back to the asylum."

"Huh?" I think it over. It's a wacky, borderline absurd idea. But... you can't jail the crazies.

"Mad times, mad measures," Rush says, taking a curve. I still don't know how to feel about this. "So where to, Detective?"

"I wanted to see Poppy, but Homer told me the situation," I reply. "And since that's the case—and we don't have any actual leads at the moment—there's something else first."

Rush glances at me, one eyebrow raised. "What's that?"

"I need to visit the parents of the four girls I left behind in that basement."

The words taste bitter on my tongue. "Annie, Kelly, Sadie, and Amy."

"You sure?"

"I'm sure," I say quietly. "I should've done this six years ago. I owe them that much."

CHAPTER 64

Welcome back, Maddie.

I'm glad they finally told you who you are. I've tried so many times, but you're stubborn. Sometimes I admire that—sometimes it drives me mad.

This is my last letter. Not that I'm sending it. I've already given you too many details.

Poppy's surgery was the hardest. I left because it was killing her. I never wanted to kill the girls. That wasn't the point. Torture them? Maybe.

Soon you'll understand. History will remember my masterpiece—uncovering one of the city's darkest secrets.

I didn't invent the mental illness angle. They did it before me, years ago. It has always been the same. Who cares for the mad?

Everyone wants to stay away. Only the wicked and shadows draw near. They exploit society's broken, hypocritical system.

I'm just a continuation of an inevitable darkness. And I'll be its end, too.

This time, I'm done playing fair. No more hints. No more help. I've already given you everything you need. The final clues are in place. The end is coming—and I will win. One way or another. You've finally taken the bait.

I admire you visiting the parents, though. But I don't think you can handle what you will discover.

Right now, I'm staring at my last girl—the one who will complete the masterpiece and end this hysteria.

She's rich. She's famous. I can't believe I didn't choose her sooner.

CHAPTER 65

The Camry's windows are down as we drive through Queens. Cold air blows on my face. Nothing can make me feel colder inside. Rush keeps glancing at me, worried.

"You sure you want to do this?" he asks.

I nod as we drive. The neighborhoods shift around us. We pass middle-class homes, decent cars, and hardworking people. There are no gates or secrets here, just folks trying to live another day.

I feel guilty for leaving those girls behind. Their families won't forgive me, but that guilt drives me. It's not just about catching a killer now. It's about avenging four women who deserved so much more than being abandoned by the only one who got away.

"Closest house is Annie's parents' house," Rush pulls up to a modest two-story home with faded blue siding. "Do you want me to come with you?"

"No," I straighten my outfit and take a deep breath. "I can handle it."

But I'm not. I never was.

I'm the one who lives while everything around me dies.

Footsteps approach, and the door swings open.

I see a man in his fifties. The tiredness in his eyes speaks volumes. This is Mr. Callaghan, the factory foreman. He's been working double shifts since Annie died. He hopes to avoid thinking about what happened.

"Can I help you?" he asks, guarded but polite.

"I'm Detective Maddie Brooks—I'm handling your daughter Annie's case." I wouldn't say I'm an unstable young woman with a bad memory and weak morals. That wouldn't be right, would it?

His face changes instantly—rage floods his features.

"You!" The single word holds six years of grief and anger. "Get the hell off my property!"

I take a step back—not from fear but from respect for his pain.

"Robert?" A woman's voice calls from inside. The clatter of dishes and the smell of baking waft through the house. Mrs. Callaghan steps out, wiping her hands on a dishtowel. She looks much older than in the photos from six years ago. Lines map her face, and flour dusts her apron. This domestic scene feels surreal in the current situation. "Who is it?"

"It's her," Mr. Callaghan points at me. "The one who left our daughter behind."

"Robert, please," Mrs. Callaghan places a hand on his arm. "Not on the porch."

"She's working with him," he continues, shaking. "Has to be—how else did she escape when our Annie didn't?"

"That's enough, Robert," she says firmly.

Mr. Callaghan shakes his head in disgust. He mutters under his breath. The pain is too much for him. With one last glare, he retreats deeper into the house. A door slams shut, sharp and final. Then he asks, "Why are you here, detective?"

"Please call me Maddie—this is more of a personal visit," I gulp. "I'm here to apologize."

Mrs. Callaghan's face pales.

"Come in," she says after a moment.

The Callaghans' living room is simple yet cozy. Family photos cover the walls. Many capture Annie at nineteen, a moment frozen in time. I take a seat when Mrs. Callaghan points to a chair. I see there are no pictures of Annie from her younger years.

"I heard you became a detective to catch him," she says.

I nod. If you don't want to lie, just let people assume.

"Do you remember Annie?"

I nod again—yes, I do, ma'am. She warned me, "Don't do it, Maddie—no!" That's the last I recall, but I keep it to myself.

"Did she say anything to you?" Mrs. Callaghan's eyes brim with tears. "About us? About me?"

"She said she loved you very much."

The lie slips from my lips easily, as if I've rehearsed it. It's funny how comforting lies are often the most predictable, like those in every cop movie.

I don't actually remember Annie saying a single word about her family during our time in those cages.

Mrs. Callaghan's lips curve upward. She holds back her tears. She knows I'm likely lying—how could she not? But she accepts the gift anyway.

Grief changes people. It makes them accept fake comfort when real support isn't there.

See? Not all lies are bad, Maddie.

"Would you like to see her room?" Mrs. Callaghan asks suddenly.

The question catches me off guard. I'm not here as a detective. Still, maybe seeing her space will jog my memory. It's a strong hunch that I'm about to learn something I won't like.

Mrs. Callaghan takes me upstairs. The steps creak under our feet. These little flaws make this house feel more real than Victoria Taylor's mansion.

"It has been locked since then," she explains, struggling with the key in the door.

"Let me help," I offer, taking the key from her trembling hand—it takes effort, but the lock finally gives.

The smell of dust and stale air greets us as we enter. Annie's room feels like a shrine to her at nineteen. The layout is like Poppy Taylor's studio. It has neat organization, similar psychology textbooks, and a corner for photography.

Poppy had fancy gear and pro lights. Annie used a secondhand camera and a homemade backdrop. They shared the same passion but were in different tax brackets.

I spot medical textbooks on the desk and posters of bands I almost know. I wonder if we met at university. Would I have left her behind if she were my friend instead of a stranger?

"She was brilliant," Mrs. Callaghan says, running a finger along the desk. "But shy—never quite fit in."

"She took medication, right?" I ask, just to make sure.

She nods, then rests a finger on her chin. "It helped her fit in. The doctors said she had a chemical imbalance from birth. But honestly, she sometimes took too many."

"Why so?"

"She had to be cautious after what she discovered," Mrs. Callaghan says, her voice softening. Annie studied women with mental health issues who go missing. These women have a 63% lower chance of proper case investigation. Police often believe officers stopped their meds, left on purpose, or hurt themselves.

"Oh." I'm waiting for Mrs. Callaghan to make this clear.

"Annie said girls like her are easy targets," Mrs. Callaghan goes on. "Police won't search hard for them without proof—you know—because they are—"

"Seen as unreliable witnesses," I say. "Mad women, to be exact."

CHAPTER 66

The realization hits me hard. This wasn't random; it was calculated, planned, and strategic.

The Comedian didn't target women with mental health issues because they were easy; he chose them because they often went unnoticed. The system meant to protect them usually ignores them.

Girls who disappear by choice—girls whose stories are questioned—girls like me.

This wasn't about hunting prey; it was about exploiting a blind spot in the justice system. It was the perfect crime, hiding behind society's biases.

"Detective?" Mrs. Callaghan waves her hand, pulling me back to reality. I know why this happens to me: I'm just as unreliable as Annie.

"Are you okay?"

"I am," I muster a smile, the kind she'll see right through. Then I collect myself and gently touch her shoulder.

"I promise I will avenge your daughter."

She looks at me like I'm crazy—and I mean that. She's never

heard a detective talk this way. Usually, they say, "We'll catch the killer," or "Swift justice," or even worse: "We'll do our best."

I will destroy the beast who hurt her daughter. That's what a detective with a certificate of insanity says.

"I appreciate this," she says, looking as if she wants to collapse into my arms.

I stop at the bottom of the stairs and pull Mrs. Callaghan into a hug. she sobs in my arms like a grieving child. sobbing into my arms. Some moments don't need words. Sometimes, we just need to cry on someone's shoulder. It helps us feel connected and grateful.

As I look over her shoulder, I realize I've stopped in front of Annie's photo wall.

That's when I realize that I've found my next lead.

"Mrs. Callaghan," I ask while still holding her, "Annie was an only child, right?"

"Yes," she sniffs.

"May I ask why you don't have any pictures of Annie before she became a teenager?"

"Oh, that." Mrs. Callaghan pulls away and dries her tears. "Annie was adopted—Robert can't have children."

My heart skips a beat.

Adopted—like me.

I thank her and sprint back to the Camry, feeling pieces of the puzzle click into place with every step.

CHAPTER 67

I bolt back to the Camry, my mind racing. Rush looks up, going from bored to worried as I pull the door open, shaking the car.

"What happened? Are you okay?" he asks, quickly tucking away his phone.

"I need to check the case files again." I'm already clawing through the folder Rush brought along, papers spilling across my lap. "Annie was adopted."

"Okay?" His brow furrows, not yet seeing the connection.

"I was adopted, too." The files on my lap tease me. I see background checks and psychological profiles, but no adoption records. Those aren't usually in police files unless they're relevant. "Call Kat again."

Rush takes out his phone and dials. He moves slowly, as if he's holding something fragile. The mood in the car has changed.

"If you guys can't get enough of me," Kat's voice crackles through the speaker, "then why did you fire me?"

She's not wrong, but I cut in. "I want to know if the girls in the cage were adopted—like I was."

"On it," Kat responds. The sound of her typing fills the silence.

A minute goes by. Rush and I sit in silence, stunned. Stray pants between us, his silly tongue out. It feels like we're just picking dinner, not unraveling a conspiracy.

"Got it," Kat finally says, excitement breaking through. "Annie, Amy, Sadie, and Kelly—all adopted."

"What about Poppy and Ivy?"

"Also adopted."

"I see. Did you know the police often overlook cases of girls with mental disorders?"

"Not overlook, but wonder," Kat muses. "It's an old story. Attention is short, even from families. They often feel embarrassed by daughters who face mental health struggles." She pauses. "Professor Homer also sent me the historical context of the Comedian's surgeries."

"So what does all this mean, Kat?" I ask. "We have enough theories to fill a textbook on serial killers, but have zero idea how to catch him."

Kat exhales, then clears her throat. I hear ice clinking in a glass on her end.

"I do know what this means," she says. "But I worry that if I tell you, you won't take me seriously."

"Why would I do that?" I press. "You've seen cases like this before."

Silence—just her breathing—when she speaks again, her voice has lost its usual edge.

"These girls have mental health diagnoses, making them easy targets," Kat explains. "The system doubts them from the start. Ivy's guidance counselor ignored her when she said someone was following her. Amy reported strange cars outside her apartment. 'Production of violent content for distribution.'"

The car suddenly feels cramped, and the air feels thin. I pull Stray into my lap without thinking. Maybe I need comfort. Maybe I know deep down that I could have been one of those girls.

"Snuff films?" Rush's voice is tight again.

"Call it what you want," Kat says. "This killer is disturbingly smart. Why look for runaways or girls without support? Target women with mental health issues that make them seem unreliable. If they escape or speak up, no one believes them. The system's bias serves as the perfect cover."

"Shit." The word slips out of me. "Homer said the Comedian needs helpers. These setups, locations, and hidden cameras aren't just one person's 'masterpiece.'"

Rush runs a hand through his hair, looking troubled. "I get why you're following this thread," he says softly, "but shouldn't we be careful about how far we take these theories?"

I study his face—I can't tell if it's professional concern or something more personal.

"I'm not saying you're wrong," he adds, catching my look. "Just... extraordinary claims require extraordinary evidence."

"Listen," Kat says suddenly. "Johnson's calling—I have to go."

"Why is Johnson calling you?" I ask.

"She said she wanted me to look at something—I'll text you."

She hangs up.

Rush and I stare at each other for a beat.

"Why do you think Johnson is calling Kat?" he asks.

"I think Kat knows something we don't," I say. "But we'll find out soon enough."

Rush turns the key in the ignition. "So—we're still doing this?"

"It's the least I can do—to admit my worst nightmare to these families—and..." I glance out the window. "I have a feeling we'll learn more from these visits."

CHAPTER 68

The visits with Amy and Sadie's families feel the same. There's a lot of grief and pain beneath the friendly talk. Both families show similar patterns in the victims, but this doesn't help the case.

I often jump to conclusions. I wonder if the girls know each other or share a past in foster care. But none of that is true. They do share one thing: the frustration from their families. The stigma of mental illness shaped how police dealt with these cases.

In the Camry, I check my phone again. No text from Kat yet. I'm eager to find out if Johnson has made any progress in the case.

Rush worries that these interactions might hurt me. But they actually make me more determined to help these families find closure.

"Next is Kelly's house," I say. I recall she's the one the Comedian hit with a hammer when she tried to escape. Kelly was the first to be killed. The memory makes me sick—but I can't even throw up.

Rush's fingers tighten, almost imperceptibly, on the steering wheel. "Aren't three families enough for today?"

"We talked about this—why do you ask?" I slide my phone back into my pocket.

"I thought you might want to focus on the new discoveries—the adoption and organized crime angle." His voice is carefully neutral, but something has changed since our earlier conversation.

"An hour ago, you opposed our 'jumping to conclusions'—what changed?"

"Nothing." His eyes stay fixed on the road, unusually intense.

"Gregory?" I use his first name on purpose. I want to break down his wall. If anyone remains a mystery, it's him.

He swallows hard. "Did you know Kelly well?" The question comes out flat and emotionless.

"Not really?" I shift unconsciously away from him, tucking myself against the door. "Did you?"

"Me?" he scoffs. "Of course not. I was just curious if you remember anything about her. Maybe you can tell her mother, since you're sure she's the one who's dead."

I relax a bit. It's a strange thought, and I'm unsure of his expectations. Yet, his question brings to mind a specific trait of Kelly's. "She used to sing—that's all I remember," I say cautiously, surprised that the memory just surfaced.

Something flickers across his face—recognition, maybe even relief. "Did she have a good voice?"

"If you consider cats being strangled a musical genre," I mutter, chuckling uncomfortably. "You can be really strange sometimes; you know that?"

"What did she sing?" His tone sounds casual, but his shoulders are rigid with tension.

"Rush." I tap the dashboard, noticing we have arrived. "We're here —let me out."

He pulls up to the curb and parks. I grip the door handle and step out. Kelly's parents' house is right in front of us. It's a busy street, but nothing too wild could happen here anyway.

"Are you okay, Officer Rush?" I ask myself why I care. He wonders if his drinking led to his behavior or if he's hiding something. "Do you want to tell me something before I knock on that door?"

"I just wish you the best, Maddie." His eyes are strangely serene now. "I'll be waiting here if you need me."

There's a pause—something unspoken—hanging between us like static.

"Am I safe going in there?" I tilt my head.

He thinks for a beat. "Physically, yes." Then, after a breath—softer, "Emotionally... that's up to you."

"Okay, cryptic man." I slam the door, not sure I like this new version of him.

As I walk to the house, Kelly's song lingers in my mind. I wonder if she created it or if it's a twisted version of that Emilia song from the late '90s—"I'm a Big Big Girl in a Big Big World..."

Kelly's version had the same melody but warped lyrics:

I'm a mad mad girl in a mad mad world; it's not a bad bad thing that I'm crazy.

The melody stirs deep feelings—memories from the basement. Kelly sang in the dark. Her voice echoed through the concrete, especially when the Comedian was gone.

These memories make me wince. I suddenly recall more than before. Homer called these "anchors." They are melodies, words, or images that trigger deeper memories.

Did Rush mean to do that on purpose?—What does he know about Kelly that I don't?

I check my phone again, hoping Kat's message about Ivy and Poppy will save me from what's behind this door.

Nothing.

I shudder as I step onto the front porch. This visit feels heavier on my soul than earlier ones.

I knock and straighten my spine—I rehearse the introduction—it's always the hardest part.

The door swings open.

"Hello, I'm Detective Maddie Brooks. I'm—"

The words die in my throat.

Commissioner Sara Johnson is standing in the doorway.

Casual clothes—no badge—no blazer—just... her—at home.

We lock eyes for what feels like ages. My breath catches, caught between confusion and dread.

What is she doing here?

Why hasn't she said anything?

Before I can speak—before I can even think—my gaze shifts over her shoulder.

And that's when I see it.

A framed photo on the wall.

Two people are smiling.

A younger Johnson.

And next to her—a girl with familiar eyes and a crooked grin I will never forget.

Kelly.

My feet freeze—my mouth goes dry.

There is an inscription in neat, flowing script:

My lovely kiddo.

The shock hits all at once, slamming into my chest like a car crash.

Johnson wasn't just close to the case.

She was in it.

CHAPTER 69

"You're..." My brain short-circuits, refusing to form actual words. "Kelly's mother?"

Johnson's face stays blank as a poker player's, but her eyes change. The usual ice-queen coldness melts into something sharper. More personal. Like a wounded animal ready to bite.

"Adopted her when she was six," she says. "Could've had my own kid, but climbing the NYPD ladder seemed more important back then." Her mouth twists into something not quite a smile. "We all pick our poisons."

Who is this woman? Definitely not the Johnson I've been dealing with. This version actually seems human.

She steps back from the doorway. "Come in."

The apartment feels like a living memorial. Modest, middle-class, nothing like I'd expect from someone with Johnson's salary. Fresh flowers in a dollar-store vase. Mail piled on the counter. Candles flickering on the wall, like a shrine.

Kelly is everywhere. Her face watching from every surface, smiling from cheap frames. A teenage girl with Johnson's piercing eyes, always clutching a toy police badge.

"I don't live here anymore," Johnson says, running her fingers over a white sheet covering the couch. "Got a fancy brownstone in Upper Manhattan now. Where all the important people live."

The bitterness in her voice is thick enough to spread on toast.

"Seventy-Eighth Street," she adds. "The kind of address that makes people at the mayor's office pretend they care what you have to say."

She turns away from the sheet-covered furniture, shoulders stiff as a corpse. "Couldn't stay here after Kelly disappeared. Funny how my promotion came through that same month. Like the universe was trading one thing for another." Her eyes lock on Kelly's photo, something dark flashing across her face. "Come to think of it now—maybe they paid me out so I wouldn't dig deeper."

I bite back all my questions. Some revelations deserve their moment of silence. The grateful look she gives me says I made the right call.

My eyes catch on a fridge magnet shaped like a police badge, and everything else in the room disappears. Written across it in stark white letters, like a confession:

I'm a mad mad girl in a mad mad world...

The words punch me in the gut harder than any physical blow. Kelly's voice haunting the concrete basement of my soul like a ghost that hadn't died yet.

Johnson tracks my stare. "Kelly had it custom-made," she says, oblivious to the grenade she's just tossed into my brain. "She made up those lyrics herself when kids at school started calling her crazy, so they couldn't use it against her."

"Badass girl," I manage to say through a throat that feels stuffed with cotton. "Owned them by owning who she is."

Turns out being crazy is my superpower. All those years in therapy were just superhero training.

"She sang it constantly. Under her breath during doctor appointments. Full volume in the shower."

"I know," the words escape before I can stop them. My eyes

finally meet Johnson's. It's like staring into a mirror of pain. "I heard her. In the basement."

Johnson's face crumples like tissue paper in a fist. One tear breaks free, then another, carving wet paths down her stone-commissioner face. Her fingers fumble with her cigarette pack, shaking so badly she can barely grip it.

My own chest feels like it's splitting open. Even though she made my life hell, manipulated me, lied to me—I can't watch her heart shatter in real time.

Before I let my anger take the best of me, I reach for her hand. She doesn't pull away, so I tug her forward into an awkward hug.

Free therapy from Maddie, the mad girl, y'all.

"Did she..." Johnson's voice breaks against my shoulder, muffled and raw. "Suffer?"

All I see is the Comedian's hammer coming down.

All I hear is Kelly's scream cutting off mid-breath.

Blood pooling on the floor...

"I don't know. But I remember she was strong," I lie, because sometimes lies are kinder than truth. "Like her mother."

Johnson hiccups in my chest a couple of times but then straightens, composure returning like she's flipped a switch.

She pats my shoulder before reaching for her cigarette. She lights it with a practiced flick and inhales like she's trying to suck in courage with the nicotine.

I sink into a kitchen chair, giving us both space to rebuild.

"Rush mentioned your adoption theory," Johnson says, Commissioner-voice back in place. "From Johnson trying to lock me up to us playing detective duo. Talk about a workplace improvement." Another drag. Another exhale. "I called Kat, and she confirmed it. Poppy and Ivy were both adopted too."

The smoke curls between us, a physical manifestation of the darkness we're wading through. I should feel validated that my theory was right. Instead, I feel sick.

"Different agencies. Different years. Same outcome, but..." Her gaze oozes with worry—not for herself, but me this time.

"But?"

"I need to walk you through a few crucial details before I come to that." Johnson's tone is more practical—harsher than when we were in the Yellow. Whatever weight she keeps inside—it's going to crush her soon.

She kills the cigarette on the kitchen floor and ushers me to her study.

A laptop sits on the desk in the middle of the study. She reaches for it and turns it my way across the desk.

When I look at the screen, I'm not sure what I'm staring at for a moment. Then it becomes clearer. It's a tripod in a basement. The same exact brand Kat traced from Ivy Williams' crime scene—except this one is from Poppy's.

"You fainted after reading the letters, remember?" Johnson said.

Of course I do.

"After the paramedics saved Poppy and we lit the fast basement, we found this one tripod hiding in the dark."

"Of course," I wipe my forehead. "He had to complete his ritual and film her. But wait," I look again and realize that my mind blocked out the fact that it's not just the tripod he left behind—he also left the camera.

"Please tell me it isn't so."

"It is," Johnson reaches for the keyboard and clicks a button.

A screen pops up.

A movie of the Comedian, wearing his mask, and operating on Poppy.

CHAPTER 70

Watching the Comedian work on Poppy is a nightmare. There's blood, gloves, and the scalpel sliding across her skin.

Each cut, each stitch: visceral memories flood back from my own time in the basement. Flashes of pain. Of fear. I never saw what happened to me—I was too drugged. But watching this? It's worse than anything I ever imagined.

His golden mask glimmers in the harsh light. It hides his identity but shows a dark, inhuman pleasure.

I lean back, instinctively trying to put space between me and the screen. Between me and the guilt I still carry.

How will I ever move past what happened to those girls after seeing this?

But it's Johnson's behavior that puzzles me more.

I see her carefully lock the doors and draw the blinds. She's reinforcing our safety. "They could be watching us already," she whispers, her gaze shifting to the dark windows. The atmosphere thickens with unspoken threats.

"Why all these precautions? What are you afraid of?"

The last lock clicks. Blinds snap shut, plunging us into deeper gloom. The screen's blue flicker is the only light. It syncs with Poppy's muffled screams.

"What's going on, Commissioner?"

"We're not safe," she says, circling back to me. "I'll explain later." She advances the video to a specific frame near the end.

Her finger jabs at the screen.

"Look."

The Comedian's dead eyes stare out from behind the mask, directly into the camera. Green eyes? That detail doesn't fit my memories. But I have to focus on Johnson now.

"The camera—does it have more footage?" I ask, grasping at straws.

She nods, then pauses the video, retrieving a memory card from her desk. "Kat cracked it. But only off the record."

"Since when do you work off the record, Commissioner? What's going on?"

Johnson's response is dismissive; her tone is chilling. "This memory card might as well be a dispatch from hell. Every clip here will be etched into your soul forever."

"What's on it?" I ask, dreading the answer.

"Seventeen videos show kidnapped girls enduring the Comedian's 'treatment.'" Johnson's voice is sharp and cold, like a blade."

I gasp, a sharp intake of breath that feels like a punch to the chest. "Seventeen? Girls we didn't know about?"

"Many. This is only the beginning," she presses on, relentless. "Decades of torture, Maddie. These sessions on the memory card span back twenty years."

Overwhelmed, I clutch at my chest. "Twenty?"

Johnson flicks through the videos briskly, not pausing and not allowing me a closer look.

Girls in basements, behind bars—filmed from above, like animals in a cage. The quality of the footage shifts over the years. Each time-stamp shows more brutality, reminding us of past horrors.

"Kat didn't call you earlier because I told her not to," Johnson says, stopping the playback. "I can't trust the NYPD."

"Why would you not trust the NYPD?"

"You'll see for yourself soon." Johnson is now more determined to explain her findings. "Kat used image recognition software to find the locations." All abandoned asylums across New York."

"For twenty years," I'm not asking—I'm confirming, trying to understand the scope of what we're dealing with.

"*From King's Hospital to Bedlam Hospital, they all have dark pasts. Most are now shut down,*" Johnson says, *glancing around as if a ghost is with us.*

"*Here's what you need to know. Even I—Commissioner Johnson— thought snuff films were an urban legend. Me. Johnson. I never imagined it was real. But that's not the worst part.*"

"There's worse?" My voice is barely a whisper, bracing for her next revelation.

"They weren't just films," she explains.

"These were livestreams. Real-time horror shows where the depraved watched, paid... and even placed bets."

CHAPTER 71

My mind fits the pieces together, but my soul refuses to grasp the full monstrosity of it.

"What kind of person watches this?" I whisper, feeling the walls close in.

"These aren't your typical tax-paying citizens," Johnson says darkly as she pulls out random photos from a file—the images of torture are too much; I look away. "These are wealthy monsters with little sense of right and wrong—they spend their money on causing suffering."

My hands clench into fists, nails biting into my palms.

"I've met people over the years who hinted at this—they said it went back centuries—maybe longer—do you know what they did with patients who died or 'failed' treatments in the past?"

The Comedian's words ring in my mind again. He talked about freak shows and circuses. The rich pay to see suffering. He told me everything from the start, and I didn't want to believe it.

Johnson nods slowly, her expression grave. "It's an ancient part of human nature—taking joy in the suffering of the weak—especially if you can afford the view."

"Comedy," I whisper, "is just laughing at someone else's misery." I quote the Comedian's haunting letter.

"So Kat traced this memory card's origins? Confirmed it was a livestream? Isn't that... too obvious for a dark business like this?"

"Not on the dark web," Johnson counters. "It's a maze with no exits, full of traps and dead ends. Anonymity is built in."

"But then... why send us this memory card?" I ask. "It's like he's showcasing what convicts him—not hiding it."

"I don't think the Comedian is trying to commit crimes," Johnson says. "I think he's trying to expose them—or at least make some twisted point."

Rush barrels through the door, eyes blazing with urgency.

I almost wince, knowing Johnson can't trust the NYPD... but apparently, she trusts him.

"NYPD is on their way here," Rush tells her. "We've got to move."

"Why are they coming?" I ask, still not grasping the full reality. "And what's the problem if they do?"

Johnson's phone rings, cutting me off—she answers with a terse "Yes?" then her expression hardens.

"Rush is right—we need to leave—now."

The call ends abruptly—she meets my eyes with steely resolve. "This isn't about catching a killer anymore, Maddie—this is about staying alive."

A vague sense of dread settles into my bones, but I need someone to spell it out.

"Kelly's old car is out back," Johnson says as she and Rush head for the door. "We'll talk more on the move."

"I need to know what's going on," I insist.

Rush turns back, cues the video, and tosses me the phone.

It's a news clip.

And then I see him—Sam Willet—at a podium. He stands calm and clean-cut, like a man with nothing to hide. He declares a scandal about snuff films, conspiracies, and coverups.

He says Johnson orchestrated them—Johnson is the commissioner—his daughter's death left her unstable—she worked with disgraced Professor Gabriel Homer—they were carried out by a masked killer named the Comedian.

Then the screen cuts to black. His voice delivers the final blow. The real criminal, he says, is the one who fooled them all. The insane one. The one who claimed to be a victim to cover the perfect crime:

Maddie Brooks.

CHAPTER 72

Kelly's Honda Civic roars to life. Johnson drives through the dark streets, her voice rising above the engine's hum.

"We'll have to split very soon," she says. "My plan is to meet Kat, gather all possible info, and upload it to social media."

Rush sits in the passenger seat, tense. He turns to listen. Johnson is relentless. Her revelations and urgency fill the air.

"What about Maddie and me?" he asks.

"I'm sorry," Johnson says. "But I'd rather drop each of you off somewhere on my way to Kat."

"Why can't we come with you?" Rush presses.

"If we're all caught, it's game over. But if we split up, they'll have to work three times harder to find us. This buys Kat time and keeps our chances alive," Johnson says. "Kat's working on a way for each of us to pick up the data she's collected—sticking together isn't smart right now."

She glances in the mirror, her eyes locking with mine.

"What are you thinking, Maddie?"

"I'm thinking about what Homer said—that the Comedian thinks he frees women from their madness."

"So?" Johnson's hands tighten on the wheel, her focus razor-sharp. "Something doesn't add up. I think a powerful group is behind these videos. I see how the girls get picked, but the Comedian isn't so simple. He has a bigger message and a deeper motive. I just can't figure it out."

"I agree with Maddie," Rush says. Johnson guns it through a yellow light.

"I'm surprised you still give a damn about his motives after all I've shown you," Johnson snaps. "We're in grave danger—none of that matters."

"Of course it matters," I say, not meaning to argue, but something keeps tugging at me. "For example, how could it be the same Comedian for twenty years?"

Johnson jerks the wheel and nearly hits the brakes. Her face changes. Something just clicked.

"That's a damn good point, kiddo."

"Maybe the Comedian is just a role," Rush says.

"That would explain the change in methods—from six years ago to now," I add. "And the shift in tone—the man I knew wasn't theatrical like this—he didn't care about masks—he cared about silence."

"This also means," Johnson says slowly, "the Comedian who's killing now isn't the one you met before."

That realization chills me more than anything else tonight.

"Tell you what," Johnson says, continuing. "I'll drop you off here and stay in touch. Then, I'll drop off Rush. You both can call Kat while I head to her. This way, we can gather answers based on this theory. We still need to upload our findings publicly and immediately. Trust me: Gen Z will tear this apart faster than the courts ever could."

"I hope we're not dead by then," Rush mutters, holding onto the passenger door like it might fly off.

Johnson's phone rings again—she glances at the screen, then

frowns. "Why is Kat calling me again? She should be uploading by now."

She answers the call. Kat's voice comes through, loud but mixed with static. Only Johnson seems to understand.

"What do you mean?" she says, tension snapping into her voice. "Are you sure?"

Her eyes catch mine in the mirror. I see betrayal hit her hard. She looks at me as if she wants to apologize for everything: the lies, the chaos, the whole damn system.

"What is it?" I ask.

Johnson slams on the brakes. The car jolts violently, screeching to a stop at the curb.

She spins in her seat to face me. "Kat traced the videos—there's more—a lot more—it's not just what we've seen."

"How many?" I ask, already knowing it's going to be worse than I imagined.

"At least ninety videos so far," Johnson says. "But that's not the scariest part."

"Let me guess." The reel in my mind plays again. I see all the signs I missed. She traced it all the way back to the source—the company or the person producing these live streams.

Johnson swallows hard. "All the livestreams are hosted by... TaylorCorp."

"Of course!" Rush slaps a hand against the dashboard.

I should've seen the signs with Alexander Taylor. I should have listened when Olivia joked about Poppy liking older men. She said it to impress her dad or stepdad. I missed those connections. TaylorCorp often appeared in the investigation. The financial ties and security clearances mattered too.

Poppy told me that something was wrong.

She tried to.

And I brushed it off.

I didn't want to see what was right in front of me.

Even though I promised myself I'd never cry in front of anyone...
I can't hold it back now.

"Fuck it!" I shout, throwing the door open.

Before Johnson can react, I reach for her holster and rip the gun
from her side.

"Hey—Maddie!" she shouts, grabbing my arm.

I pull away, our eyes locking for a moment. "Do you remember
what I did to a man with my bare hands?"

She hesitates—just for a second—but that's all I need.

I slam the door with my foot and bolt into the street.

Behind me, I hear Rush yelling, "Maddie! You're crazy!"

I don't stop—don't look back.

"The hell I am."

Not the NYPD—not Willet—not even the devil himself can stop
me this time.

CHAPTER. 73

I don't remember grabbing the gun—just the pounding in my ears, and the way the world seemed to tilt when I stepped into the street.

All I know is I'm in the middle of the street now, running like a madwoman, waving the gun like I've done this before. Like I'm not two seconds from falling apart.

I don't.

But people don't know that—they see a gun, and they run.

Rush is yelling my name behind me—his voice chasing me down the sidewalk. "Maddie! Stop!"

I don't stop.

Can't stop.

Because this is it—no more therapy—no more talking in circles—no more hiding behind detectives and professors and so-called sanity.

My heart hammers in my chest like it wants out—I point the gun at the first car I see. 'Out! Out!' I shout.

The driver throws up his hands—but there's a woman in the passenger seat—two kids in the back—I freeze.

Not this one.

Not them.

The boy in the back stares at me, wide-eyed, clutching a stuffed dinosaur—my finger twitches.

I shake my head and wave them off. Then I sprint for the next car.

A sleek black Jaguar pulls up at the light—clean, fast, expensive.

A young businessman drives with Bluetooth in his ear—he's likely in the middle of a deal or something important.

I slam the butt of the gun against his window. "Out—now."

He hesitates, thinking the suit, the tie, the car will shield him from whatever's vibrating off me.

I drop the act, all of it.

I stick out my tongue, puff my cheeks like a blowfish, and cross my eyes for fun. Then, I drag my tongue across the certificate of insanity before stamping it against his window.

"You know what this is?" I snarl. "Full clearance to not give a single fuck!"

He's out in two seconds—no questions, no heroics—hands up, knees weak, briefcase abandoned. It's not the gun that scares him. It's the look in my eyes. It's the kind of crazy you don't fake. It fakes you —and they see it in my eyes.

People around me snicker and laugh at the unhinged girl I've become—I don't judge them because I'm too deep in my sea of pain, I'm afraid it's the only substance I can breathe.

I slide in, the leather warm, the engine humming like it's been waiting for me.

Rush throws open the passenger door and jumps in as I hit the gas. "Didn't know a certificate of insanity came with a cool upgrade."

I don't look at him. "You think they'll add 'carjacker' to my rap sheet?"

He chuckles, but it's tight. "Only if we live through this."

I swerve around a corner, pedal to the floor. The Jag eats pavement like it's starving, the city blurring.

We're heading for the Hamilton Estate.

Rush watches me out of the corner of his eye. "You have a plan?"

"Planning's for sane people."

"You're all in on this?"

"This isn't survival anymore, Rush—it's the final act—curtain's up."

He shakes his head. "Just so you know, Alexander Taylor being involved doesn't mean he's the Comedian—I mean, he couldn't have kidnapped his own daughter."

"Stepdaughter," I take the curve hard. "Also, he's old—fits the bill."

"You're saying Poppy dated her dad... and kept it a secret? Come on."

"I'm about to throw you out of this car, Rush—don't test me."

Rush exhales. "Okay, fine—but at least agree that Alexander Taylor could've just been the host of these videos—maybe he doesn't even know—maybe he knows and there are bigger fish."

"Whatever the truth is, he knows who the Comedian is—and who I am." I slam the wheel—my palms sting from the force. "I should've known when he looked at me the way he did—the handshake—calling me 'detective' without being introduced—he's known all along."

The Hamilton gates rise in the distance—tall, silver, cold. Like the gates of Hell.

Rush glances sideways again. "You realize if you pull up waving that gun, they'll shoot you before you get ten feet inside."

"Not when I make my offer."

"Offer? What offer?"

I grip the wheel tighter—no plan—no backup—just me, a gun, and one last desperate play.

I smile, but it's hollow. It doesn't reach my eyes.. "Devils love deals—and I've got one he can't refuse."

CHAPTER 74

The Jaguar speeds down the long road to the Hamilton Estate. Its engine growls beneath me.

I ease up on the gas as the gates come into view—massive, silver, and impossibly smug, like they're daring me to approach.

I slow down, scanning both sides of the property, my eyes searching for signs of trouble.

No police cars. No flashing lights. Not yet... but I can feel them lurking.

The doorman steps out and straightens his blazer. He squints at me, unsure if I'm here for a party or to cause trouble.

For the first time, I notice that he also meets the description of the Comedian.

If Rush is correct that the Comedian is a job, then why not have Alexander Taylor's bodyguard take on that role?

I remember my conversation with this guard about Poppy being a bit strange the first time I came.

"Detective Brooks?" His eyes bounce from my face to the Jaguar's hood. "Congratulations on the new ride."

He knows it's not mine. It means we're playing games.

"You know I'm no detective—so cut the crap."

"Pardon me?" Either he is a great actor, or he didn't understand.

"I need to speak with Mr. Taylor."

He starts to respond, the rehearsed denial already forming on his lips.

I don't let him finish. I stop him cold. "Show him this." I wave my certificate of insanity at the camera like a flag of surrender.

"Do you mind if I ask what this is?"

"It says I'm crazy." I smile, and it's probably the creepiest thing I've ever done—like a wolf showing its teeth.

The man stifles a laugh, his eyes flickering between curiosity and fear. "I'd rather you leave, detective."

"Okay then." I sigh. "Tell him the new Comedian is here."

The guard stiffens. Something in his whole being shifts. I can't tell whether it's inside knowledge or fear.

"Did you hear me?" I glare at him, letting my anger pour through my eyes.

"I did." He nods, almost with respect, then says something that makes Rush wince in the passenger seat. "Are you sure?"

His question sends shivers down my spine—but people can't see your spine, so you may as well hide it with a smile. "You want to know how sure I am?"

"I'd be honored if you tell me, detective." He laces both his hands in front of him.

I lean out, grabbing the side of the Jaguar's door, and whisper to him. "Ask the previous Comedian how his scalp feels?" My mouth goes sandpaper dry, but I chug through. "Does it still hurt like a little bitch?"

The guard stares at me longer than I thought he would. It's like he wants me to feel the impact of my words. Then, he picks up his phone and dials a number. I can't believe this is happening.

He answers the phone without a word, nodding at the camera, arms laced in front of him.

Thirty long seconds crawl by. Then, finally, the gates open.

"Not him," the guard points at Rush, who glares at me. I turn to him and mouth: it's okay.

Rush looks at me, confusion flickering in his eyes, as if I spoke a foreign language. I'm not sure what it means. Still, nothing compares to staring into the Comedian's eyes—whoever that is.

Rush opens the door, still keeping his eyes on me.

I look away, afraid it might be my last goodbye.

CHAPTER 75

The Jaguar glides down the long gravel driveway, the white stones crunching under the tires like bones. I can't help but smirk. Meeting my nemesis in a Jaguar? Talk about meeting the devil in style.

The Hamilton Estate rises ahead—grand, cold, and monstrous, like something too big to fit in the world.

It's too quiet—like the silence has been waiting for something to break it.

No one is trimming the hedges. There are no black-suited staff on the porch or security near the fountain. Just emptiness surrounds me. The giant house looms, as if it's been waiting for this moment longer than I have.

I slow down at the circular turnaround and turn off the engine. The silence that follows feels heavy, filling the air around me.

The front door is already open.

I hear the girls screaming in my head, "Don't do it, Maddie." Back then, I escaped through a door. Now, I'm walking in, facing my demons and welcoming the darkness.

No maid—no butler—no welcome.

Just that gaping threshold, like a mouth waiting to swallow me whole.

I step out, gun held low and steady. I scan the windows. No movement. No faces peek from behind the curtains.

I mount the steps one by one—each one feels like a countdown.

I step inside.

The air is stale and heavy. It feels still, as if the house is pretending not to breathe.

Marble covers everything—floors, walls, and even wide staircases. Every surface shines as if recently cleaned. But there's a smell hiding beneath the shine—something sour and old, like blood scrubbed from tile.

I call out, my voice breaking the silence, "Mr. Taylor?"

No answer—no footsteps—no sound at all.

I move deeper. I pass untouched furniture set like a showroom display. I go by a fireplace too grand to ever be lit. The portraits on the walls don't see me. They seem to look away.

Then I see him—standing between lights, half of his face in the dark, the other half still in shadow, even in the light of day.

Perfect suit—calm eyes—like this is a therapy session and I'm the one who is late.

He looks up at me—smiles like we're old friends.

He fits the bill: his age, his charm, and his connection. Now, seeing him alone, I notice a hint of darkness in his eyes. They're not green like in the video. Suddenly, Rush's theory makes much more sense.

My hand trembles, but I hold still. I glance sideways, not sure what I've gotten myself into—not sure where to start.

"There's no need for the gun," Taylor says, his tone clear and firm. It's different from before. This voice has no mask. It has faced darkness and even created it. This makes me believe him, or maybe it's my fractured mind playing tricks. "There are cameras everywhere," he adds. "If you get caught, that gun will only cement your place as the Comedian who killed all those girls."

I don't respond—I feel like he needs to spill everything before I ask anything.

"It's funny how technology can fake anything," he says, unmoving, calculating. "It can make you see whatever the man behind the camera wants you to see."

"Show me your scalp," I demand.

"That," he says with a smirk, "you should have asked Lorenzo, the guard."

Before I can process his words, I turn around—and there he is—Lorenzo.

I aim the gun at his forehead. I tiptoe, my hand trembling, wanting to pull the trigger. But I need to see his face first. I have to know it's really him.

Lorenzo plows his big forehead against mine with such hatred I can't understand—I fall back; I drop the gun.

A shiver hits my core and spreads. It feels like dying. I'm trapped by memories and pain. I try to tell myself this isn't real. I didn't just meet the Comedian. It can't be that simple or even mundane.

No fire. No screams. No finale. Just a man who does dark things in a darker world.

Something feels so off, but I can't put my finger on it.

It takes a few minutes on the floor before I realize neither Lorenzo nor Taylor intend to kill me.

I get up, one knee at a time, and grab the gun. Lorenzo stands next to Taylor. They both watch me, their eyes unreadable.

"You really want me to be the next Comedian, don't you?" I ask, unsure if I even believe the words coming out of my mouth. "Why?"

"You have it in you, Maddie," Taylor says, sounding almost sincere. "Do you know how many people have it in them? Let alone women?"

I'm unsure what this conversation is about. I see a devil drawn to an innocent soul. He wants to corrupt it, buy it, and drag it into the fire with him.

"You don't remember, do you?" Taylor leans slightly forward, hands now in pockets.

"I do remember—the girls—leaving them behind—I remember it all."

"That's not what I'm talking about," Taylor says. "Do you remember the first Comedian?"

"First?" I grimace. "Is this him?" I point at Lorenzo.

"Nah," Taylor waves a hand dismissively. "The first one—before Lorenzo—the one you hammered to death."

CHAPTER 76

"I don't remember," I whisper.

Taylor doesn't flinch. "That's all right. Most people wouldn't. It's not the kind of thing your brain wants to hold onto."

He leans on the marble banister. His hands are folded, like someone discussing the weather, not madness. His posture is so casual, it only serves to heighten the dark energy radiating from him.

"That's why I called you the Beautiful Cuckoo," he says. His voice is smooth, like poured glass. It feels like he's sharing something very ordinary.

"You mean Beautiful Cocoon," I correct automatically. "Like the metaphor—transformation."

He chuckles, soft, dry, and humorless. "No, I meant Cuckoo. Like Cuckoo1812, the password you used in the Ashwood Asylum. You know why this was the password? Before they used words like 'patient,' they used to call them Cuckoos. Back when they just called people what they thought they were."

He tilts his head and studies me. There's no warmth in his gaze— just cold calculation, like he's watching an insect ready for dissection.

"Cuckoos, Maddie—that's what they called them before they were sent to the freak show."

My skin crawls. I feel it in my neck, that quiet twitch that comes before memory, before fear. His words stir something deep within me, and the hairs on the back of my neck rise.

"You see, I didn't invent 'evil,'" he says, using air quotes. His fingers move gently, as if sharing a scientific finding. "I'm not the devil. I'm just another man doing what mankind did long ago."

Maybe it's him. Maybe it's just my broken mind.

"There are two kinds of people, Maddie," he says, almost philosophically. "Those who rule—and those who are ruled. The powerful. The weak. And the art? The beauty? The comedy?" He smiles faintly. "It's just the suffering of the weak that entertains the strong. The mask, the show, the layers beneath the layers of power. Do you not see?"

I swallow, trying to push the words back. No, this is not what I should be thinking about.

His smile widens, like he can see my struggle. His voice is calm, smooth, and each word flows like a lullaby laced with poison. "You always think you know what's happening, but you don't. I used to watch the faces of the women at the parties. They loved me. They thought I was sophisticated and wealthy. But all I ever wanted was to corrupt them. Every smile was an invitation to break them. That is the power—the ability to turn innocence into darkness—to make them love the very thing they fear."

A chill runs through me, deeper than anything I've felt since I first walked into this house.

His gaze never leaves me. He studies me like a scientist would his prized specimen.

"Come," he says, his voice like velvet wrapped around broken glass. "I want to show you something."

I follow him. Not because I want to. Because I'm curious—and stupid.

I don't want to—but I do.

Down past the great hall, past the silent piano and the walls that feel too tall, we move toward the back of the house. A narrow staircase lies behind a door. It clicks open with his thumbprint and spirals down.

The air changes immediately. It's colder here, older. I know this place before I see it.

My feet hesitate on the last step.

The basement.

The one—my basement.

I freeze.

The cage. The smell. The damp that lives in your lungs. I see the door—the one I escaped from on the other side. I never knew there was another one that led straight into the house. I didn't know I was in a house in the first place.

Taylor sees the question in my face. "When you got out, you collapsed just outside. Lorenzo brought you to the car. We drove you to Brooklyn and left you there. We needed you alive."

Alive, but lost.

"Is that how you made Lorenzo a Comedian?" I ask.

"Lorenzo is a natural—like me," Taylor's lack of sympathy or conscience makes me want to vomit. "Some are like you—they have it but need to tap into it."

"You left me for six years trying to tap into it?" I scoff, my voice filled with disbelief and anger.

"You were in an asylum, Beautiful Cuckoo." He pantomimes a bird's wings with his fingers, mocking my very existence. "And even if you weren't, who cares? You either found the darkness in you or you lived lost in a world of boredom."

"What... are you?" I ask, not sure if that is a question he understands. His oblivious look makes me change it and ask, "Why? Why do any of this?"

Taylor smiles again—not friendly—not cruel—just... hollow. It's the smile of a man who sees the world only as an experiment, as a vast stage for his personal theater.

"I'll tell you if you promise to listen," he says, narrowing his eyes as if I'm meant to grasp his twisted logic. "Most people don't believe me. They think it's just about power, lust, or some Freudian nonsense. But it's not that—at least, not at first.""

He steps closer to the bars—to the place I used to sleep. His voice takes on a contemplative tone, like he's unraveling a secret he's kept for too long. "I was rich—obscenely rich—at a young age. I didn't do much. Yes, I built the foundation for New York's top cloud storage system. But after that, I had nothing else to do."

He counts his wins on neat fingers, a dark gleam shining in his eyes.

"He takes a brief pause. It hints at his humanity, but it quickly fades away. I bought things just to say I did. I even gave to charities. I bought hospitals. I named wings after my mother."

His voice lowers, turns sharp. "But I was miserable."

He takes a brief pause. It hints at his humanity, but it quickly fades away.

"Then I ran into an old friend—Sam Willet. He said, 'What's the point of money if you can't do the things that no one else can do?'"

I can barely breathe. The basement is swallowing all the oxygen.

"I thought he meant power, politics. But no—Sam had moved beyond that. He introduced me to the Comedians—and by that I don't mean Lorenzo's job. We, whoever we are, call ourselves the Comedians, mostly because no one suspects who we are."

He closes his eyes for a second, like he's back there.

At first, it felt strange. Then, it was like finding a hidden door. I stepped into a secret world—dark and euphoric. It was suffering-as-art, and no one cared or dared to look. I was just the man who kept the data."

I grip the cold iron of the cage. "Who runs it? Who's the boss?"

Taylor smiles. "That's the beauty of it—no one knows. It's a web so tangled it defies names. Everyone's both a puppet and a puppeteer. No one gets caught. The world is made to keep us hidden. Almost everyone important knows this."

He looks at me dead in the eye.

"Until you, Maddie, broke the rules."

CHAPTER 77

I'm uninterested in what he says about me. Whatever he has in mind isn't me; that's his projection of me, which is simply his protection of his own sick world. His eyes might be looking at me, but that doesn't mean they actually see me for who I am. I'm not going to be an apprentice. I was never going to be. I never will be.

All I do is tuck my hands in my pockets and ask him to tell me more—about the corruption, the names. I'm not even pretending to be the next Comedian. He just brags, thinking he's inviting me into some dark Neverland.

Taylor eventually mentions the financial and political side. Important people mess up sometimes. They might play the basement game, watch a livestream, or even be the Comedian for a day. After that, they're slaves to the system forever. If those films get out, it's over for them.

I let him talk. I'm recording everything with the phone in my pocket. A livestream straight to Kat's computer. Who needs conspiracy theories when you have a full confession streaming online?

That being said, I'm not sure how much time I have left.

My hands are numb. My soul is dull. I'd rather face a lion lunging at me than sit through another second of this man. Darkness I can handle. It implies there might be light. But the abyss? There's no light there—and that's where I am now.

There's one thing left. Two things. Three.

First, I want to ask him how he could do this—or let other Comedians do this to Poppy? Who am I kidding? She isn't his daughter. I wouldn't be surprised if this network regularly adopted girls for sadistic games.

Second, the one I'm afraid to ask, but I have to.

"So, what happened to the girls?"

"Pardon me?"

"Amy, Annie, and Sadie?" I swallow hard. "Are they dead?"

"Who are Amy, Annie, and Sadie?" Taylor's sincere confusion makes me want to bury him alive—slowly, for eternity. He doesn't know who I'm talking about—why would he? I'm the only one he remembers—because I didn't break.

"The girls in the cage with me—six years ago—did they all die?"

"Most probably." Lorenzo shrugs, casual as if we're discussing bad weather.

Which brings me to the third thing.

No, it isn't about how I killed the Comedian before Lorenzo. I don't care anymore. I am who I am. Flawed. Fractured. But I'm not darkness. I'm a child of light, whether I want to be or not.

The third thing is the mask.

I interrupt Taylor mid-ramble. "So... where is the mask?"

His face lights up. "Are you sure?"

"You have girls I can torture?" The words drip out bitter and poisonous.

"I didn't think you were serious," Taylor says. "Lorenzo, go get the mask. Do you know what a woman Comedian would mean to the community?"

"And a hammer, Lorenzo," I add. "Will I be the first?"

Taylor's sick little grin answers for him.

Lorenzo returns with the hammer and the mask.

I put on the mask. I can feel it—a glimpse into the void. It's the strength of a coward, a false power that comes from hiding my face. It's seductive. It disconnects you from your actions. No wonder ancient cultures feared masks—they knew what they unleashed.

But enough games.

Johnson probably already has the confession out there.

As for me, I have something else to finish.

"Which one of you wants to die first?" I ask.

Lorenzo chuckles.

Not the laugh of someone who's seen me kill before.

That's when I realize.

Taylor was the Comedian all along.

He lied.

Let his henchman take the fall.

The devil made a fatal mistake—he took the offer he couldn't refuse.

Through the dark mask, I run into Lorenzo and hammer his knees. I don't know who I am anymore. I'm not me. I'm the mask. I'm digging deeper into my darker shadow.

Was I just fast enough that he didn't see me coming?

Or did he commit the ultimate sin—underestimating a woman?

His knee cracks, and it takes him a moment to process the pain. He's a big guy. He didn't expect it. Thought I was bluffing.

No, bastard. I've been saving this. All the times I held back. All the moments I swallowed my rage. The thugs in the neighborhood. The times Rush came to save me. I couldn't hit back, but that wasn't cowardice. That was waiting for this—waiting for the one big strike that matters.

And now, it all comes crashing down—a storm of pain, unstoppable, unforgiving.

I'm sorry for what's about to happen to you, Lorenzo. No, scratch that. I'm not sorry at all.

Lorenzo lunges—too slow.

I duck and kick him in the back. I jam his head between the bars of the cage behind me. His head is too big. He can't slide through, but I will make it.

With the hammer.

But first, crack his other knee. His head slides down against the bar, dripping blood. I pull his hair back and check for a wound on his scalp. There isn't one. I feel nothing. I don't know where this strength is coming from anymore.

Like thunder and lightning, his scream fills the room. It's not the pain, but the betrayal in his voice that gets me.

He falls. I lean in and turn his head around.

"Here's a cure for darkness," I whisper, and drive the hammer into his eye.

He isn't dead.

But he's blind.

And pain will be his only companion from now on.

Taylor moves for the stairs.

A camera watches from above.

I smile at it, waving like a maniac. How do y'all like the show now?

I chase Taylor, hammer raised.

He is fast—he scrambles upward.

I slam the hammer into his ankle from the back.

It shatters.

He crumples to the floor, like a marionette with severed strings.

I drag him down the stairs.

One step at a time.

His skull hits every stair on the way down.

"I'm sorry," I hiss, kneeling over him. "Should I've befriended you a whole month before I killed you?" I smash his fingers.

One hand.

Taylor screams.

"I guess I'm not into foreplay," I whisper in his ear. "I don't wait around. I fuck things up from the start."

Then the other.

His pain, like Lorenzo's, comes from denial more than anything. It's as if he never thought I would hurt him. But he wanted a Comedian, didn't he?

"Are you cured yet?" I ask.

He pleads for me to let him go. My answer is simple. "You can only plead about one thing, darling—mercy killing—and that I'll have to think about."

I pull him by his broken ankle, back to the cage.

The rest?

You don't need to know.

But someone, somewhere, is watching it on a livestream—if you want to watch, you'd better pay.

In the back of my mind, Madeline Stray's words burn bright.

"By the way," she said, her voice soft as silk and sharp as steel. "If anyone tries to break you again, just do what you do best. Bite them. Break their hands, skulls, or scalps—whatever works.'"

I guess the Comedian was right, thinking of me as an apprentice. Because I've never knew I have this darkness in me.

CHAPTER 78

Two hours later.

I sit on the front porch of the Hamilton Estate. The sun is setting, hiding behind the trees like it's shy. I stare ahead, lost in thought. Blood stains my shoes, and I haven't moved.

Voices swirl around me. Officers shout codes into radios. Reporters yell over each other. Cameras click a hundred times, hoping to make me flinch.

I don't.

Rush is here—he called Johnson and brought the cavalry.

Kat uploaded the entire video. It showed Taylor's confession, his twisted beliefs, the abuse, and the legacy of the masks. Gen Z picked it up and spread the message quickly. Now, it's everywhere. The world knows.

But I'm still here, feeling like something is missing.

Johnson steps onto the porch. She takes off her blazer. Her eyes are heavy, and her face looks too tired for victory.

"Are you okay?" she asks.

I shake my head. "No—I'm not."

She doesn't try to push it—just sits beside me, silent for a beat, then pulls me into a hug.

I let her.

I feel nothing.

But I appreciate it.

Her warmth means something, even if I can't feel it yet.

"The scandal's too big," she says after a moment. "We can't hide this anymore. The basement looks like a war zone. Taylor's servers, the cameras, the masks—it's all there. It's over."

I nod—no words come.

"Sam Willet's in custody," Rush says as he joins us, his voice quieter than usual. "The video forced the mayor's hand—I've never seen justice executed this fast."

That gets a small breath out of me—a fractured exhale—I'm grateful—I really am—if you call this justice.

But my chest is tight.

I turn to Johnson, blinking through a blurry haze. "I'm sorry."

She furrows her brow. "For what?"

"For Kelly—I should've saved her."

Johnson's jaw clenches, and for a moment, she's not the commissioner—she's just a grieving mother now.

We cry together.

No theatrics—no music swelling in the background.

Just two broken women on a porch that once guarded monsters.

"You really never had training?" Johnson asks, half a smile shining through the tears. "I mean the way you butchered those two men, girl."

"Who said I didn't have training?" I nudge her with my elbow. "It's a long-term camp called life."

Johnson smirks, ever so slightly. "Kat ditched the part about you killing those men, especially Taylor," she says.

"What did I do to him?" The memory is faint and unclear. I was wearing the mask then, lost in darkness for a few minutes. If I killed another Comedian before and forgot, it makes sense I can't remember it now.

"If I tell you, I'll vomit," Johnson rolls her eyes. "You've been through a lot, kiddo—we'll figure out a way to explain their deaths and keep you out of it."

"I'm okay with being jailed for killing them."

"I'm sure you are, but you don't need to be," she points to my pockets.

I tap my jeans, blood-spattered and all, but I know what she means. "You mean the certificate of insanity."

Johnson nods and glances at me, then to the side. This is our secret. It's how we outsmart the system that once outsmarted us.

"So you'll send me back to the asylum if they find a way to charge me?"

"On paper, yes," Johnson puts her hands in her pockets, acting casual. "Homer will help you escape. Kat will create a new identity for you. Rush will drive you to the airport. I will look the other way."

"No one cares for those in asylums, so no one will ever find out." I smile, appreciative. "That's quite the Avengers we have here—you, Homer, Rush, and Kat."

"More like Mission: Impossible if you ask me," she says. "Now, I think you need to breathe and experience some real life." Johnson stands. "Taylor had a large wound on his scalp, hidden with some plastic surgery—it was him."

"I know."

"Why are you so sure?"

"I could feel him when I was too close to him."

Johnson looks at me, hands on her hips. "Press is all over the place —do you want to talk to them this time?"

I chuckle—my jaw hurts—it must have happened when I was fighting Lorenzo or Taylor. "Nah—I'm kind of not good with people."

Johnson chuckles back.

Rush stands nearby, waiting for us to finish—when Johnson leaves, he lends me a hand in standing up.

"We should get you out of here," he says gently.

I nod.

We walk to the Camry.

Rush opens the passenger door and waits for me to get in. Once I'm seated, he slides in behind the wheel and starts the engine.

As we roll down the gravel path, past news vans and crime scene tape, he says, "Homer wishes to see you when you're ready."

I look out the window.

Homer can wait.

"I don't feel like seeing him today," I say. "Can I sleep at your place?"

"Of course. I'll sleep at my sister's to give you space. I'll bring Stray along, too."

"Thank you," I say, holding his hand. "And tomorrow I want to go see Poppy."

I really do, because with everything that's happened, I still feel that something big is missing. This case isn't solved yet.

CHAPTER 79

The next day, I visit Poppy in the hospital. It's not easy, especially with Victoria. I butchered her husband yesterday.

The hospital smells like sterile floors and distant grief. I walk down the quiet hallway to Poppy's room. Each step feels heavy with what I still don't understand.

Victoria Taylor sits in a chair just outside the door, hands folded tightly in her lap. When she sees me, she stands too quickly, like she's been rehearsing this moment.

"Detective," she says softly. "Thank you for coming—and... for saving her."

I nod. There's nothing to say to that—not yet.

She looks tired. No, exhausted in a way makeup can't hide. Her eyes have dark shadows that no concealer can hide. Her perfect posture has also faded.

"I'm sorry," her voice breaks on the words. "I'm sorry for what Alexander did—I swear I never knew—but..."

Her fingers twist the wedding ring she still wears.

"To be honest, I suspected something wasn't right. His behavior changed over the years. Became distant, secretive. He never wanted children—not ever." Her eyes drop to the floor. "I used to think he was just career-obsessed. But now? I wonder if he didn't want children because he feared they'd become targets."

I want to offer her some sympathy, but I can't bring myself to do it. I don't know. I'm not judging, but failing to unmask a man like Alexander Taylor for years seems questionable. Again, I'm not one to judge. I just think she should have done better.

"Can I see Poppy?" I ask instead.

Victoria nods and steps aside.

I push open the door.

Poppy lies in bed. She's surrounded by machines and wires. Her skin is pale like the hospital sheets. Her lips are cracked, resembling drought-stricken earth. She looks like she's been to hell and back. Because she has. Her eyes find mine, and something flickers behind them. Recognition. Relief.

She tries to speak, but only a broken stutter comes out.

"Don't push yourself," I say, moving to her bedside. "You're safe now."

Her fingers twitch on the blanket, not strong enough to lift. She gestures with her eyes toward her hand, and I understand immediately. I lean over and place my hand gently on hers. Her fingers barely move, but they wrap around mine as best they can.

"You're a brave girl," I whisper. "I'll visit you all the time—every day until you recover. I promise. Then we can go on some crazy trip to Cancun or something."

A weak smile forms on her face. Her lips tremble with the effort to speak.

"No older, charming men this time, okay?" I joke, unsure if it's an appropriate joke to make. But the reality is that it's not a joke. I have questions, and I can't bring myself to push her for answers. I wish it came out naturally.

Poppy chuckles—or tries to. Her cheeks give it away. And those exhausted eyes still know how to smile. I brush a strand of hair from her face. "Don't worry—same here—always had a thing for older men."

She shakes her head slightly, eyes intent, as if she wants to say something. "Not because... he was older—it was..."

"It was what?" I lean forward.

Poppy points at her phone. I guess she prefers writing to speaking at this point. She pulls out a note app and writes:

I liked him more because of his deformation.

What is she talking about? I let her write more:

He was beautiful inside—loving life—loving art—he didn't care about his face—or his limb.

"He limped?" I ask. "And an issue with his face?" That doesn't track. None of it fits the Comedian we hunted. None of it matches the man behind the mask. My throat tightens with sudden dread. "Poppy... do you have a photos of him?"

She writes: **Yes, sure, only for you—I hid the photos because he was embarrassed of his looks, not because he was older.**

Poppy unlocks a hidden folder on the cloud of the Comedian. I'm perplexed and extremely baffled. I thought it could be Alexander Taylor, but that felt dark and awkward. Lorenzo seemed like the better choice.

But that's not who the Comedian who kidnapped her is.

She opens the folder.

The man in the photo stares back at me from beneath a wide-brimmed hat and a scarf pulled high over his mouth. His face is partially twisted, like he'd been in a terrible accident—or born with something rare.

Poppy writes: **I thought that he was a fighter like me, but then he turned out to be...**

And suddenly, everything fractures as she starts to cry.

Who is this Comedian? I squint at the picture a little longer. I notice he has kind eyes. They look weathered and, unlike Alexander Taylor, more human.

And green.

CHAPTER 80

I text the photo to Kat and Johnson. I ask if they recognize the disfigured man.

They don't.

No hits. No names. No records.

Just an unfamiliar, badly scarred face, half-buried in shadows and erased by mystery.

Kat checks every database for his image, but finds nothing. It's as if he's a ghost. She promises to keep searching and will update me later.

Johnson comments that his eyes are the same as the man in the video—so Poppy isn't making this up.

Poppy said he never allowed her to take a picture. She only got one by accident. Her hands were shaky. He always wore a hat and scarf, even in warm weather. It was his permanent disguise.

She had seen him without it—still, her descriptions never helped —his features, she said, were hard to place.

Perhaps a natural disfigurement.

Perhaps it's an old accident.

Perhaps both.

The car he drove was stolen weeks before he met Poppy. It had no registration, no fingerprints, and was burned out. It sat abandoned near the Jersey line.

Kat went through all the basement footage again. There was no mention of a disfigured man as the Comedian. Not even a customer appeared in the livestream, not even in the shadows behind the camera. Whoever this was, he didn't belong to Taylor's circle. Not publicly and not on record.

The real Comedian—at least the most recent one who kidnapped Ivy and Poppy—is someone we haven't caught yet.

This reminds me of Alexander Taylor's last words: "And it all changed when you showed up, Maddie."

I thought he meant when he had kidnapped me.

Or did he mean something else?

If the recent Comedian isn't Taylor or Lorenzo... did Alexander Taylor not know him either?

Did he think it was me?

That night, I return to Professor Homer's apartment. I'm ready to ask my therapist a few final questions.

The Empire Institute is cold and dim. Weak lamps barely light the way. Nurses glide by like ghosts. Most people avoid me. I'm the crazy detective who broke through the basement after all.

But tonight, for once, it doesn't feel haunted to me—I feel quite at peace visiting Homer now.

He's in his office—paperwork stacked high, glasses perched low—but his eyes lift the moment I enter.

"You did it," he says simply. "You cracked the whole case."

"I didn't do it alone." I ease into the leather chair across from him. "You stayed with me—you didn't run when you should've—that means something."

He shrugs modestly—but something warm slips through his guarded eyes.

"Why do you still live here?" I ask. "You never really said."

Homer folds his hands. "Because my wife lives here."

I didn't expect that.

The mystery of Homer's wife is about to unfold—in the strangest way.

"When Johnson mentioned your alibi, did she mean you were with her? Here?"

He nods. "I guess she mentioned that her room has cameras—that's why it was an indisputable alibi."

"She is..." I'm reluctant to say it. "Is she your patient?"

"She has Korsakoff's syndrome. It began after our divorce. She drank a little, not what you'd expect. But it took her memory. Our life together is mostly lost to her, except for rare moments. We divorced before it worsened. Still, I stayed when it escalated."

I swallow hard. "Why?"

"Because I believe in possibilities." He looks away for a beat. "And because there's always a chance."

"Yes, you do." I smile at him. "And you believe in people."

"By the way," he says softly, "your papers are ready. The certificate of insanity is gone. You're officially free now."

"Thank you," I whisper.

"You showed me something," Homer says. "Healing isn't just about fixing what's broken. Sometimes, it's about surviving long enough to rejoin the world."

I stand to leave, but not before one last thought slips from my lips.

"You showed me the world through a different lens, Gabriel. I saw it from a patient's view—a mad person's view. I'll always remember that."

"You helped me too. I saw you do the impossible." He gives me the smallest of smiles. "And I'll be here—with her—until she remembers me."

I walk up to him, rise on my toes, and press a quick kiss to his cheek—it's spontaneous—he deserves it.

"I think you should change that line in your book," I whisper. "The one about wishing to be anyone you want when you don't know who you are."

Gabriel blinks, stunned—grateful—suddenly more human than a professor.

"You have an edit in mind?" he asks, his voice low.

I step back, arms flinging out as I walk away backward.

"Look at me," I grin. "I finally know who I am—and I don't want to be anyone else."

I blow him a kiss over my shoulder, then turn and disappear down the hallway.

When I leave the institute, the air feels sharper—like the world has edges sharp enough to cut.

My phone buzzes. It's Johnson. I wonder if she still thinks I'm a detective. It's just days until I apply to med school again.

"Sam Willet's daughter is missing," she says. "She vanished yesterday."

The news sinks in like a stone. "Does she fit the profile?"

"Yes," Johnson says. "But it's way crazier this time."

"How?"

"He sent you a letter—to my address," Johnson explains.

"What does it say?"

"He pinpointed his location exactly."

I close my eyes—this can't be good. "Where?"

"King's Hospital."

"One of the most infamous abandoned asylums in New York."

"Here's the kicker," Johnson says. "He wants you to come alone—or he'll kill her."

CHAPTER 81

King's Hospital looms like a forgotten curse over the northern edge of the Bronx. Its red brick façade has faded to brown, like dried blood weathered by decades of rain and rot. Many windows are broken or boarded up. A rusted sign hangs on the chain-link fence outside, flapping in the wind.

CLOSED BY ORDER OF THE CITY OF NEW YORK – 1996.

It was once a premier psychiatric facility until it wasn't. Stories vary. Some say a doctor poisoned his patients. Others say the city covered up unspeakable treatments in the lower levels. But everyone agrees on one thing:

King's Hospital was cursed long before it was abandoned.

I walk up the cracked steps alone.

My boots crunch over scattered glass and gravel. The front doors are off their hinges, leaning against the wall like they gave up long ago. I duck through the frame, and the smell hits me—mold, rot, and something metallic underneath. It's like the past has been festering here, waiting to be seen again.

Flashlight in hand, I move through the corridors.

Peeling paint hangs like curled skin. Wheelchairs rust in the corners. Graffiti covers the walls with crude faces and half-finished messages. I see reminders of the past. Beds are bolted to the floor. Straps hang down. Cabinets have cracked glass. Patient files lie scattered like bones.

The Comedian left no guards, no distractions—just an address. That alone makes me feel the weight of the trap.

I head toward the basement.

The stairs creak with every step. Something scurries in the shadows. I grip the flashlight tighter and descend. The air grows colder, wetter, and more alive with silence.

The basement door is open.

And I hear her.

A whimper. A muffled plea.

Zoey—Sam Willet's daughter.

I round the final corner, and there she is—caged, tied to an ancient, rusted surgical bench. The kind with leather restraints and wheels. A cloth is stuffed in her mouth. Her eyes are wide with terror, wild like she hasn't slept in days.

Next to her stands the Comedian—surgical gloves on, golden mask glowing in the faint light.

He only moves a few steps, just enough to notice the limp—like Poppy said. Then he stops. He doesn't speak. Just watches me.

I raise my hands, palms forward.

"You want me alone. I'm here. Let her go."

No answer.

Behind me, I know Johnson is somewhere—watching—waiting for the signal. I told her not to follow. She said she wouldn't.

But she will—she always does.

And part of me hopes she does—because I'm not sure how this ends otherwise.

Not yet.

Silence lingers too long. I feel deeply uncomfortable because I don't know what's going on.

I watch his eyes, his stance, and how he breathes. His breath is shallow and careful, as if he knows someone is watching—even though I can't see them. His eyes are green—two gleaming emeralds behind the mask.

"You have a choice," he says in that voice changer. "You or Zoey in the cage."

It's an exchange I thought about before coming here. It feels personal. I just don't know why—and that terrifies me.

"Before I decide anything," I say slowly, "I need to know who you are."

He still doesn't respond—green eyes gleaming in the dark.

"I'm not here to play games," I go on. "You want me in the cage? Fine—but I want to understand who I'm talking to."

The Comedian tilts his head again. The mask catches the flickering light—gold and grotesque—a monarch's crown twisted into a prison.

I step closer to the cage, to Zoey—just enough to see that she's breathing—still conscious, but terrified. She doesn't scream—he's probably shown her what happens *if* she does.

Still, as crazy as it sounds, I don't feel the darkness I felt with Alexander Taylor in this Comedian.

"I don't think you're evil," I say carefully, trying to win him over. "And I don't think you were working for Alexander Taylor—or the rich—or anyone."

Still no response.

"I think you wanted to expose them—all of them." At least that's what I'm hoping—but I could be dead wrong.

"You turned suffering into power. You made pain a business. You cracked their system, not mine."

The Comedian faces me squarely, then begins to clap.

Slow, hollow, mocking—but behind it, a tremor. Emotion. Or something like it.

His voice rises, still artificial and warped. "That's sweet."

"Not sweet," I say. "True—it's how I feel about you—it's how I've felt from the beginning—do we know each other? You always talk about the headache, about being my better half, and that I need you."

He stands there for a long moment, silent once again.

"Listen, I know there wasn't just one Comedian—that it was a job," I say. "You often acted like the old Comedians, or at least the idea of them. You became them, but for a different reason. Maybe to lure me or to find me—I'm not certain. All I want is to know you and to see you."

"Here I am," the Comedian says, removing the mask.

I didn't expect him to look worse without it.

But he does.

Somehow, the mask made him a monster.

Now, he's something else entirely—something broken. I see him now. And I wish I hadn't.

A patchwork of trauma shows in his scars. Burn marks and grafted skin mar his body. One side of his jaw is sharp, while the other is collapsed. One eye sits lower, framed by permanent purple. His nose is twisted, and his scalp is uneven. And yet, beneath it all, there's the unmistakable sadness of someone who once dreamed of being human. A part of me recoils. Another part aches.

"You're..." I can barely speak. "I'm sorry."

He laughs—a broken, awful sound.

"Liar," he spits.

I blink. "What?"

"You didn't say that when I was in the cage." He growls it, eyes glinting with something older than rage. "You didn't care then—you looked away—you always looked away."

"You weren't in the cage with me," I start, confused. "There were four of us—only girls."

"I was there, Maddie—I screamed—I bled too—I cried when you cried—but no one looked at me—not even you."

I feel it all start to fracture—the edges of my memory, already soft, already bruised.

Is he lying?

Is he deluded?

Or am I?

I'm pretty sure we were all girls.

My mind stutters.

No—that's not—

"I was a girl once," she says, softer now. "And I am a girl—now let me explain."

CHAPTER 82

The Comedian paces slowly, barefoot on the concrete. Her limp holds her back. The dim light makes scary shapes on the walls. But it's her voice—soft and childlike—that really chills me.

"Imagine you're me a few years ago—a young girl," she says. "Nineteen years old. You don't really know who you are yet. You think you're soft, but you're stronger than they think. Then one day, someone who called himself the Comedian kidnaps you and locks you in a cage underground."

My pulse stutters.

"You're drugged, tortured. You can't scream properly because your throat's raw. You cry with the other girls. You don't remember how long it's been. You stop counting days because the lights never change."

She looks toward Zoey's cage, but she's not seeing her—she's seeing something else, someone else.

"Then one day, the door was left unlocked. Maybe he forgets. Maybe it's a test. You don't care. You run."

I don't blink.

"And he finds you. He hits you in the head with a hammer. You drop to the floor like meat. He doesn't check if you're dead. Why would he? You're just another disposable thing. So he leaves you in the corner like trash and moves on to finish his little 'treatments.'"

My lungs tighten. I think I know what's coming.

"And then, there's Maddie—pretty, smart, unbreakable Maddie. He lets her go."

I take a step back, feeling nauseous.

"The first Comedian kills them, but you... you're not dead. You're still breathing. You can't scream. Can't move. But you feel everything."

Her voice hardens.

"And then, he drags your body with the others. Dumps you all in a river like garbage. They float. You sink. But somehow, some miracle, you drift to shore. You're found. You live."

She turns to me now, eyes gleaming, alive with rage, sadness, and something inhuman.

"But when you wake up, what's left of your face is unrecognizable. *Your jaw is twisted, your cheekbones crushed. You look in the mirror and don't recognize the thing staring back. You're a monster.*"

I want to speak, to stop her, but I can't. The words are lodged in my throat.

I know who she is now.

Oh God.

"So tell me, Maddie—if you were in my skin, what would you do? Crawl back home? Show your parents what's left of their daughter? Try to live a normal life, dragging around everything they did to you? A life you know you don't deserve?"

She shakes her head.

"No. You disappear. You hide. You hustle. You make money off your freak face on OnlyFans. Because there's always a market for monsters. You survive. And every single day, you ask yourself one question."

Her voice drops to a whisper.

"Was it because I was a woman? Is that why the Comedians

picked me? Why did all of this happen? Just because I had a uterus? A womb?"

The silence between us is louder than any scream.

"Then," she continues, "I began reading about old treatments. They used things like lobotomies, hysterectomies, and iron cages on women." They faced drip torture too, all for being labeled 'hysterical.' And suddenly, it made sense. None of it was personal. It was just because I actually was a woman."

She shrugs.

"So I stopped being a woman. I took a few razors, found some painkillers, carved at myself until I didn't have to wonder anymore. I became... this." She points at her body.

"And that's when I realized—if I couldn't undo the pain, I could redirect it. And maybe—just maybe—I could make the world look at what it's been trying to ignore."

I'm shivering. It's not the cold. It's everything else.

"And yes," she says, stepping closer, "I wanted revenge. Not just on the Comedians—on you. Because you got out. You never looked at me. You never came back for me!"

"I'm sorry. I made a terrible mistake. I know how it feels—"

"Shut the fuck up!" Her voice ricochets off the walls. Then, like something inside her softens, or remembers, her breathing steadies. A bitter smile flickers on her lips—or maybe it's not a smile at all. "You know how I seduced Ivy, Poppy, and Zoey?"

I shake my head, but everything about me says, "Tell me."

"One day, in the university library... I was reading about ancient treatments for mental illness. Most of my face was hidden—a scarf, a hat—but this girl looked at me." She pauses, eyes drifting to some place I can't follow. "She really looked, Maddie. And lo and behold, she didn't think I was ugly. I mean, she did. But she appreciated it. She saw it as something brave. Defiant. A kind of beauty that breaks the rules."

I don't know where this is going, but I'm starting to guess.

"I asked her, 'Do you see how hideous I am?' You know what she said?" She lets out a dry, humorless laugh. "She said I looked like her dad."

Even she hears the absurdity in it—but I believe her.

"And she loved her dad."

I swallow hard.

She was nineteen and studying physiology. She was brilliant, sharp, and vibrant. Full of dreams, hopes, and odd ideas, she was ready to challenge the status quo. But she was also hooked on antidepressants.

Her voice cracks, but her posture remains rigid.

"And then I realized—not only did she believe that I was a man, not a woman—she thought I was the type of man she wanted in her life. A mature one."

The words hang heavy, dripping with invisible tears. She doesn't know if it was a compliment... or cruelty.

"That's when I figured it out. Girls—rich girls, broken girls—had a soft spot for me. The ugly, older man is quiet and withdrawn. He loves art and photography. He reads books with big, twisted words." She lifts her hands and flutters them like a clown bowing after a performance. "And ta-da! I got to feel love. Appreciation. Like a real human being. I was the philosophical beast that the beauties wanted."

It's chilling—and tragic.

"So I became the Comedian." She lowers her head, then lifts her eyes—sharp, green, and gleaming. Her finger wags in the air like a warning. "The new one."

"Is that the reason why you kidnapped rich girls?" I ask softly. "I thought you wanted attention."

"Of course I wanted attention!" She flings her arms wide and tilts her head toward the ceiling, like she's about to summon thunder and lightning. "How fucking stupid are you, Maddie?"

Her hand glides to the table next to Zoey. It lightly touches scalpels and shiny tools, like a magician getting ready for her trick.

Her voice and stare steady, oozing with confidence and pride, all of a sudden. "What do you think a beast like me does—after six years studying the system, learning about the dark films? After lying on the floor, playing dead, and watching Alexander fucking Taylor do what he did to you?"

Did she see that?

"Tell me, Maddie," she grabs a scalpel as if it's a key from thin air. "What should a beast like me do when she knows these men have daughters?"

I close my eyes—full circle—I understand now.

"Girls with issues—like you—like me." She rolls the scalpel between her fingers—graceful, casual, deadly. "That's when the new Comedian was born. He's not a descendant of the system; he's an imitator. This groundbreaking comedian is set to craft his own masterpiece. She pauses to breathe, maybe even to reflect. "I can't say I had a calculated plan—but I started hurting their offspring so I could hurt them. Also searching for you—to punish you—maybe kill you—I didn't know. But I had to make my madness scream so loud they had to listen. Someone needed to expose them."

"So... Alexander didn't hurt his stepdaughter, Poppy?" I murmur. "He did everything else—but not that." I pause and say, "Listen—" I skip her name. That girl is gone. Now, she's the Comedian. As the Comedian, she feels strong and in control. "Let me help you—"

"Only I set the rules here, Maddie." She lifts the scalpel and turns it slowly, like it's dancing in her fingers. "Shhh." Then she frantically limps toward Zoey. "I'm giving you a choice now."

I stare at her.

"Get in the cage and suffer like I did. Or let her suffer. Let her bleed on that bench while you walk free. Either way, a girl dies tonight."

I look at Zoey—she's trembling, eyes wide, gagged and bound—she doesn't deserve this—neither do any of us.

The Comedian leans in. "Justice or guilt—mercy or survival—you decide."

And then she sings in the most distorted voice:

"I'm a mad, mad, mad girl in a mad, mad world—it's not a bad, bad thing if I'm crazy."

My breath shatters. No—it can't be—but then again, I have known it for the past few minutes. "Kelly?" I whisper.

She tilts her head and flails her hands sideways.

"Oh, sorry—I guess you didn't recognize me with my new makeup on?"

Commissioner Johnson's daughter. The girl I failed to save. The girl I thought was dead.

My knees hit the floor.

"Oh my God." My voice breaks. "Kelly—Kelly, I'm so sorry—I didn't know—I didn't see you—I should've—God, I should've—"

She watches me, unmoved—her face is rigid, but her eyes flicker with something like pain.

"You left me," she says. "You didn't even look."

Tears spill down my cheeks. I inch forward, hands outstretched.

"Please, don't do this to Zoey. You've already exposed them. We caught Taylor and took the system down. You did it. You helped me expose them. You don't need to keep this up."

Her hand hovers over the scalpel.

"Please," I whisper. "Forgive me."

For a moment—just a flicker of a moment—I see her waver.

And then—

A door crashes open behind me.

Footsteps thunder.

"NO!" I scream, whipping around.

But it's too late.

Johnson stands at the top of the stairs—gun raised—breath ragged.

And she sees her.

Kelly—her daughter.

But Johnson doesn't recognize her.

To the Commissioner, this isn't her child.

It's the Comedian—the latest version of him.

She doesn't even register that the person standing there is a woman.

And me?

I'm dressed in a black shroud from head to toe, one that's dipped in tar at the bottom of the abyss.

No amount of screams or reaching upward will fix anything.

"Don't shoot—!"

I scream from deep in my lungs—my arms fly forward, and my body twists as if it might tear itself apart to stop her.

But I'm too late.

Johnson shoots.

A single bullet.

No hesitation.

CHAPTER 83

The air outside King's Hospital stings like cold glass. Sirens wail, camera flashes pop, and whispers of disbelief fill the space. The building behind me towers like a corpse, with a rotting history and many ghosts.

Zoey is safe.

She's wrapped in a thermal blanket. An IV is in her arm, and an oxygen mask covers half her face. EMTs gently guide her into the ambulance. Her eyes stay on me. It's not fear—just a quiet understanding. We've both seen too much to ever be the same again.

She did nothing wrong. Her father is a scumbag, and that's it. It's not about being rich or poor; it's about being normal. That's the cruel joke. The irony comes from a mad girl.

Commissioner Johnson stands still on the pavement by another ambulance. Her gun is missing. Her badge dangles at her hip like a forgotten ornament. Her hands hang loosely at her sides.

She looks... lost.

And tonight, she's lost more than any soul should have to bear.

Sara lets out a laugh that sounds like it's made of splinters.

"I didn't recognize her," she whispers, like she's confessing a sin to the void. "I looked her in the face and I didn't know her. What kind of mother does that make me?"

I step closer. "You loved her. You never stopped."

"She was right there, Maddie," Johnson says, her voice cracking. "Singing that song as a kid. I wore a plastic badge. My blazer sleeves were too long for her. I should've known. I should've looked harder. I should've—"

"She was hurt and scared. A whole system kept her hidden, and we just found it. You didn't fail her."

She blinks, dazed. "But I shot her."

I reach for her shoulder. Thank God you shoot as poorly as I do."

Sara breaks into a laugh that breaks the heart.

"And you're going to stay with her now," I say. "The rest of your life, if she'll let you."

"I'm resigning today."

"It's a terrible job, anyway."

She lets that sit. Then she nods once—slowly, deliberately—like she just shrugged off the weight of the entire NYPD.

"Kat's working on the paperwork," I tell her. "Kelly was never the Comedian, and the police arrived long after the shot.. So, as far as anyone knows, we never caught the last Comedian."

"In Kat we trust," Johnson says, almost smiling.

"Funny how a system so corrupt can't even catch the good guys when they use the same corruption to beat it."

"And Zoey? What happens to her?"

"I talked to her. She despised her father enough to want the best for Kelly," I say. "I'd let her deal with her demons at this point. I wish her the best."

"And Ivy?" Tears well again in Johnson's eyes. "My daughter killed her."

"Yeah. It was wrong. And all we can do is pray for her. There's nothing you can do about it. Still, life goes on."

I don't know if that's the right thing to say, but it's a whole mess—all we can do is help the living live.

The EMT opens the ambulance door and motions for Johnson to join us. We convinced the paramedics she's a victim, and she is. Once she gets to the ER, we'll make her vanish. Homer will work his magic to get her out.

Funny, the little gang of misfits we've become.

"I don't think she recognizes me," Johnson says, nodding toward Kelly on the stretcher.

"She will." Free assurance and lies from the mad girl, Maddie, y'all.

"I hope she forgives me one day."

I smile back at Johnson. "I hope she forgives me too."

Johnson climbs in without a word, takes her daughter's wounded hand in hers, and doesn't let go.

The doors close.

The siren wails.

And they disappear into the night.

Then my favorite person in the world calls my name.

Stray comes yapping—I kneel down to catch him as he jumps halfway into the air.

Rush stands back, giving us privacy. I nod to thank him for looking after Stray. Then, I hug Stray tightly, trying to pull out all the humanity I miss in people.

Rush takes Stray away. I need a moment alone. I look around, filled with haunting memories. Still, I feel a sense of victory in the world around me.

I stand there, surrounded by people—and yet I am more alone than ever.

Not broken—not healed.

Just another mad girl in a mad world—who made it through one more day of madness.

And out of the cage.

EPILOGUE

Dear Comedian—*whoever you are these days,*

I still think about you. Isn't that funny?

You know why? Because I wish I'd run into you again and ask you: Who laughed in the end, motherfucker?

I live in Hawaii now—with Rush. Yeah, I know. Awkward, quiet Rush—he's not exactly a rom-com ending.

I can picture your smirk.

The Comedian's girl ends up with the nervous cop. There's no true love story here, but life's too short for that.

He's not a cop anymore.

He found his calling in AA meetings. He stays sober, keeps his mind busy, and helps others do the same. He also keeps me grounded.

He's out shopping now.

When he's back, he'll cook for me. We rotate the housework—split the tasks across the week.

Except Wednesdays—

Wednesdays are 'fucking days.'

I'm referring to the kind that needs soundproofing for our beach bungalow. My screams of pleasure sound oddly like my screams of terror. Who would have guessed?

I'm back in med school, too—private detective in my free time. I find things. People like me when I find things for them.

The door opens now.

Rush's keys clink. It's him. His footsteps pad across the floor. Stray still doesn't like him. I can't tell if there's a reason or if it's just jealousy.

"Hey, Beautiful Cuckoo," he calls from the hall. "I'll start cooking right away. I need to take a shower first."

Beautiful Cuckoo.

I'm a cuckoo, all right?

That's what he used to call me back in New York—a flirtatious, teasing name—he's been calling me that the whole year.

But today feels different.

I remember Alexander Taylor correcting me. I thought he said, "Beautiful cocoons."

Shit.

I just noticed I've never shared this.

Everyone believes he called us the Beautiful Cocoons, not Beautiful Cuckoos. In those asylums, they used to call patients "Cuckoos."

Rush is still showering—and I'm thinking.

Was he involved with the Comedians, but just played his cards right? Did he commit the perfect crime and convince me he was on my side? I mean, Rush has always been contradictory. And he was originally hired by the mayor of New York to keep an eye on me.

Is that possible—or am I just reaching now?

You know what? I'm not giving it any more thought.

Because if I've learned anything, it's this:

If someone loves me right, I'll love them back. But if they try to break me—I'll break them first.

—sThe butterfly who still keeps a hammer
under the bed — My own #1 fan,
XO, Maddie

THE END
Keep Reading Here

THE HOSPITAL

A.G. TWIST

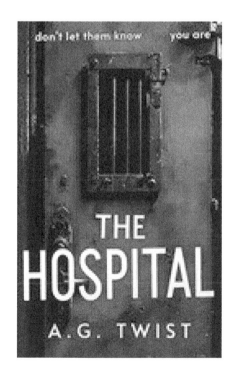

ORDER HERE

Waking up in a hospital without memories, Jane Doe remembers one thing though: don't you dare tell them who you are — not even yourself.

Read The Hospital Here

Or you Can Read **The Stalker** (next page)

THE STALKER

A.G. TWIST

ORDER HERE

She knocks. He opens the door. She is soaked in blood. Accident, she says. He let her in. Wipes blood off her lips. He doesn't know she crashed on purpose to meet him. Worse--he doesn't recognize her, but she does...

Read The Stalker Here

BOOKS BY A.G. TWIST

The Cage

The Hospital

The Stalker

ABOUT A.G. TWIST

A.G. Twist's debut thriller *The Hospital* was optioned for film before publication. *The Cage* came next, and *The Stalker*—the third book—is available in June 2025.

[f]

Made in the USA
Middletown, DE
10 June 2025